STRAIGHT UP

STRAIGHT UP

A Murder on the Rocks Mystery

Cathi Stoler

To Marci and Cindy Brenholz
with love and thanks always

Praise for STRAIGHT UP

"Stoler serves up another round of 110-proof suspense in this engaging serial killer thriller. Well worth bending your elbow for."—Richie Narvaez, author of *Noiryorican*

"*Straight Up*—the third round in Cathi Stoler's binge-worthy On the Rocks series—is a frothy mix of mystery and thriller that will leave readers chilled, shaken and thirsty for Stoler's next pub date!" — *New York Times* bestselling author Wendy Corsi Staub

"In her latest Murder on the Rocks mystery, *Straight Up*, Cathi Stoler invites readers in for a drink at The Corner Lounge, where everybody knows your name and murder is on the menu. Plucky bar owner Jude Dillane must sidestep the FBI as she hunts down a serial killer, all while trying to keep her business humming and her best friends out of trouble. If you're thirsty for a delicious read, then order this one: *Straight Up!*"— Alan Orloff, Two-time ITW Thriller Award-winning author of *I Play One On TV*

"If you're looking for fun with a 'twist,' you can't go wrong with Cathi Stoler's latest installment of the adventures of Corner Lounge owner Jude Dillane. While the fearless restauranteur helps hunt down a serial killer before she becomes his next victim, she still manages to attend to 'business,' which means we get to learn the ins and outs of running a popular New York City watering hole. Stoler is the perfect hostess who doesn't miss a beat as Dillane juggles business, pleasure and crime." — Charles Salzberg, twice nominated Shamus award author of *Second Story Man* and the Henry Swann series

"Murder on the rocks…with a twist! A dark and gritty look into the bar scene in New York's Lower East Side. Female protagonist Jude Dillane, tough chick from the Bronx and owner of The Corner Lounge, lives in the shadow of Art Bevins, the New Year's Eve serial killer. She grapples with night terrors and panic attacks after finding one of his victims in her apartment, and tries desperately to claw to her way back to 'normal' but it seems futile. When her friend and landlord is sucked into a sting, Jude decides to take matters into her own hands. A riveting, authentic portrayal of the intimate - but complicated - relationships forged around a neighborhood bar; an edgy murder mystery that rockets to a satisfying conclusion, and a savvy heroine to love. Grab this one!" — Kerry Peresta, author of the Olivia Callahan Suspense series

"Cathi Stoler's third entry in her Jude Dillane Series, *Straight Up*, provides taut suspense, breezy dialogue, a compelling mystery, and another round on the house with her appealing heroine. Check your coffee maker, because this one may keep you up all night!" — Richard Helms, Shamus Award-winning author of *Brittle Karma*

"You'll need a stiff drink to calm your nerves as a vortex of danger swirls around bar owner Jude Dillane, growing stronger with each page, in *Straight Up*, book three of Cathi Stoler's Murder of the Rocks series. Well-developed, intriguing characters and pulse-pounding suspense make this New York City mystery a must-read! I can't wait for the next book in the series!" — Lori Duffy Foster, author of *A Dead Man's Eyes*, a Lisa Jamison Mystery.

"I'm a little mad at Cathi Stoler for keeping me up so late at night with *Straight Up*. The novel is a terrific read with lovely characters, tightening suspense, and subplots that lurk beneath the surface like sharks. You're going to be tired the next day, and it's going to be worth it."— E.A. Aymar, author of *The Unrepentant* and *They're Gone*

Prologue

American Airlines Flight AA307

LAX to JFK

Having money makes everything better. The thought flowed through Dolores Castel's mind as she eased back into the supple leather seat and let it envelop her in its cocoon-like comfort. The first-class cabin on the top deck of the 747 aircraft was as good as it gets when it came to flying commercial. At the moment, booking on a private jet was out of the question.

Although, this was roomy, quiet, and luxurious enough. Dolores had always understood the value of traveling well and accepted the twenty-five-hundred-dollar one-way fare as part of doing business.

She smiled to herself in anticipation of the journey ahead and what it might bring. A small, satisfied sigh escaped her lips as the young flight attendant assigned to the cabin approached holding a silver tray filled with beverages in crystal glasses.

"Would you like a glass of Champagne or orange juice before takeoff?" the woman asked in sweet, honeyed tones.

Dolores reached for a glass from the tray and nodded her thanks. She glanced over her shoulder toward the left side of the plane where Diego was seated one row behind and opposite her. He noticed her looking and moved his hand from the Champagne he'd been reaching for to the orange juice instead. He offered the flight attendant an open, inviting smile. "Maybe some Champagne later, with lunch." She beamed back, then moved on to the next passenger, her eyes tracking behind, fixed on Diego.

Dolores knew she needed to watch him carefully. He was just a little too handsome for his own good with deep chocolate brown eyes women found hard to resist and chiseled movie star features. She hoped his good looks and easy, laid-back California style would serve him, and her, well in New York.

He didn't always obey her rules, rules that were instituted for a purpose. Such as no flirting with women like the pretty, young flight attendant, which could derail his focus from the plan she'd formed.

Dolores hadn't booked seats together for this flight. She made sure that the seat opposite each of them held someone else. You never knew what opportunities would arise from a conversation with a stranger. She watched as a tall, slim woman in a black Armani suit took the seat next to Diego. A little young, and much too preoccupied with her cell phone to be of any use to them. In any event, Diego seemed less than interested.

A few moments later, a well-dressed man who appeared to be in his early sixties slipped into the seat across from her and nodded a hello. She nodded back, then turned to face the window and sipped her Champagne. She knew he'd be stealing glances at her. Men always did. She'd give it a little while before exchanging pleasantries. Then she'd see.

In the meantime, she had plans to firm up for New York. The first, and most important, was to secure an apartment for Diego and herself. She had thought about renting something on the Upper East Side, but quickly put that aside. Things never changed in that part of town. People were ensconced there for generations and someone might recognize her from when she'd been a resident in her younger days. That hadn't ended well and she couldn't take the chance.

She needed something different until she could find the right situation. Perhaps downtown, where the people were more diverse and she could stay under the radar. She reached into her Hermès handbag and removed a small leather notebook and Montblanc pen. She jotted down a reminder about contacting a realtor who'd been recommended by the one person in New York she'd remained in contact with for all these years. An old friend she'd trusted and who had never let her down.

She watched from the porthole as the plane lifted off and banked over the city. Would this be her last view of the sprawling metropolis and would she miss it? Probably not, especially if things in New York went well.

A little while later she let her eyes wander to the left and the man sitting opposite.

He didn't miss a beat. "Hi, I'm Stan. Pleasant flight so far, isn't it?"

"Why, yes it is," Dolores replied, extending her hand. "My name is Dolores and it's lovely to meet you." As she chatted with Stan, she realized things were already looking up. Taking on New York would be a piece of cake.

Stan's chauffeured town car was waiting outside the terminal when they exited. He was on his way home to Greenwich but had insisted on giving her a ride to her hotel, the Monclare, an elegant private establishment on Mercer Street.

Stan had taken the seat next to her in the back of the limousine. Now he exited and opened the passenger door, hovering as she stepped out. "Dolores, I hope we'll see each other again very soon." He handed her his card.

"I'd like that very, very much," she replied, tapping his arm with her hand and casting a seductive look his way. The doorman took their luggage into the lobby and Dolores smiled and waved as the car pulled away into traffic.

Greenwich meant a house, most likely a wife and children. That was not part of the plan. She tossed his card into the waste bin inside the front door. Once Stan's car was out of sight, she asked the doorman to call her a taxi. "We won't be staying after all." She smiled sweetly.

Dolores directed the taxi to Twenty-eighth Street just off Second Avenue. She'd done research online and had found a small, modern Airbnb apartment that was adequate and relatively inexpensive. She entered and looked around. *This would do nicely. For a few days anyway,* she thought. *We'll be settled somewhere better by then.*

A woman walks into a bar...

Chapter One

If I had known that renting the empty apartment on the seventh floor would have caused such heartache, I would have told Sully to lock the door and throw away the key.

I can't say what happened was my fault. It wasn't. Or that I could have prevented it. I couldn't. But still, I wished I had seen it coming. But that's hindsight for you. You don't always have the foresight to see what seems so obvious later.

Sully was sitting in his usual seat at the corner of the bar and staring into his Jameson. *Sulking,* I thought as I glanced his way. *He's got to get out of this funk. It's just not good for him. Or me.*

I understood the problem. Having had the New Year's Eve Serial Killer living in his apartment complex was not a resounding endorsement for the property or the landlord. Still, none of it was his fault and it had been over three months since the murder. It was spring, a time for new beginnings, right?

I'd tried to persuade him to get past it. He knew I was as devastated as everyone else in the neighborhood, especially since we were together when we discovered the body of Michael Bevins in The Corner Lounge's dumpster on New Year's Day. The whole episode last January, including Dean's abduction and torture, had taken a toll on all of us. Dean was my friend and my head bartender, and I couldn't help but feel responsible.

Sully hadn't been able to bounce back. As a former Marine Lieutenant, he was used to being in charge of his men, and himself. I knew he was feeling anything but 'in charge' at the moment. He'd gone back to his volunteer job at the Big City Food Bank where he was responsible for shipping out food deliveries to distribution centers and food pantries all over the city. The job kept him busy, but something was still missing. He looked drained, his silver-grey brush-cut hair seemed dull, and his usually brilliant blue eyes held an undercurrent of sadness. He needed a distraction to get him back to his old self. I walked over to his corner, plopped my elbows on the bar, and leaned in close. "Hey, you. Whatcha thinking about?"

Sully shrugged. "The usual. Who's going to rent that empty apartment when they find out what happened there?" He looked me in the eyes and answered his own question. "No one. That's who."

The apartment he was talking about was the one directly over mine, only he'd added the adjacent studio and turned it into a two-bedroom, two-bathroom gem. "I think you're wrong. Nothing happened in that apartment," I replied. *Well, almost nothing.* "You're not responsible for a crazy killer."

For years, the F.B.I. had been searching for the serial murderer they'd dubbed The New Year's Eve Killer. He'd started his vicious rampage on New Year's Eve in nineteen-ninety-nine with the murder of a Danish tourist—at least that was the first one attributed to him until the F.B.I. discovered he'd been killing long before.

Since then, he'd gone on to kill several more men, always on the last day of the year, three that they knew about, and maybe more deaths that were never reported. The most shocking aspect of the case was that there were actually two killers working together. In a weird twist of fate, the second killer murdered the brother of the first and left his body in my dumpster.

"Art Bevins was murdering people long before you bought the buildings," I continued and shuddered at how close Dean had been to becoming one of his victims. "And you know Jim Deems was the perfect acolyte, easy to manipulate and bend to his will."

"I know you're right, Jude. I gotta get on with things, but—"

His cell rang just then, cutting him off from finishing his thought. "Speak!" he demanded in his usual greeting. *Well, at least one thing is normal,* I thought as I hid a small smile.

"Really?" Sully's tone had moved up a few notches from flat to warily interested. "When? What time? Okay great." He clicked off and I could see a glimmer of something hopeful in his face. "That was Buster Dunlap," he explained, "the realtor."

I nodded. I knew Buster. He was the one who brokered the deal that allowed my partner, Pete Angel, and myself to lease The Corner Lounge on the bottom floor of Sully's corner building. It was a primo location on Tenth Street and Avenue B on the Lower East Side, and we'd been extremely grateful to Buster for finding it, and for introducing us to Sully, who turned out to be more friend than landlord.

"So, what's going on with Buster?" I asked, praying silently he'd found a tenant for the empty apartment.

"He's got some woman, a Dolores Castel, and her personal assistant, Diego Lowell, from California, who are looking to rent in this neighborhood. "Buster is bringing them over tomorrow afternoon at two to take a look." He turned his empty glass over on the coaster and rapped on the bar, his usual signal that he was done. "I'm going to go check out the premises, make sure the space looks good. Probably be in for dinner." With that, he left.

I watched him as he exited The Lounge. It was more animation than I'd seen in him since the murder. Was he walking a little taller? Or, was it my imagination? Maybe the news had propped him up and he'd finally turned a corner. I hoped this woman liked the apartment. I couldn't bear to see Sully disappointed again.

Chapter Two

I finished setting up the bar, admiring the gleam of its hundred-year-old burnished wood I buffed almost every day. Then I waited for the deluge of the after-work crowd to come pouring in like the wind and rain from a superstorm saturating my chic and elegant restaurant with raised voices and raucous laughter. The murder and the publicity had brought the looky-loos out in force and business was still booming. Not the way I'd ever imagined, or wanted, to increase my business. Did these people actually expect another serial killer to take up residence in the neighborhood?

I figured it would all die down in another month or two and things would go back to the way they'd been—people dropping by for Pete's great food and my delicious drinks, rather than gossip and seeing all my regular customers happy and satisfied.

The Lounge had suffered some hard times in the last few years and nothing would make me happier than having a little more normal in my life.

At seven, Dean joined me behind the bar. He was tall, blond and, beautiful. The customers, especially the women, adored him. His kidnapping and rescue from the clutches of the serial killer Jim Deems added a certain thrill to his appeal. My heart nearly stopped each time I thought about what could have been. He was the one that got away. And now, the ladies, who'd all heard the story, were after him like hounds on the scent. They tossed sultry looks his way from under over-mascaraed lashes. Good luck with Dean getting away from one of them. Dean Mason was a hot, romantic—if almost tragic—hero and they wanted a piece of him.

I looked over at him as he worked. It seemed like he'd bounced back pretty quickly, but it was hard to know what was going through his mind. I'd seen him start at the odd noise once or twice and he looked up every time the door opened. He still had a ways to go, I thought. It didn't help that Art Bevins, the other serial killer, was still at large and might strike at any moment. It wasn't easy to walk around thinking there was a target on your back.

Dean always talked about becoming a movie star and thought working at the bar was the perfect preparation—acting the role of the consummate bartender and playing to a captive audience every night. After everything that happened, I wouldn't be surprised if a talent agent approached him with an offer of representation. I'd miss him like crazy, but would be happy for him to have his shot at stardom.

Dean worked the main part of the bar while I took charge of the service area where I could look over the dining room. Nearly every table was filled and the diners were enjoying themselves.

I glanced at the front door every once in a while, expecting to see Sully come in. I guess he'd decided to have dinner elsewhere.

Of course, the apartment looked perfect. Sully had had it gutted and renovated from the hardwood floors up. New crown moldings, a more open plan, new kitchen, new bath, high-end appliances, plus the addition of the studio apartment, transformed the space. The perfect updates for a classic Renaissance Revival building with graceful archways framing beveled glass front doors.

Sully was thinking of redoing all of the apartments in both buildings. I begged him to start with mine but hadn't gotten very far.

"Your place?" He'd sneered. "First we'd have to find the floor under all your sh..stuff." At least some of the snark was still there.

He still couldn't be checking that *House Beautiful*-worthy apartment. He'd erased every last sign of Art.

As a former Marine Lieutenant with twenty-five years of discipline under his belt, Sully had the muscle memory to keep everything in perfect order. Unlike mine, I knew that apartment was spotless.

I lived in the building, number 310, on the sixth floor. The Lounge was located below. The empty apartment that had belonged to Art Bevins, was right above mine, Against my better judgment, I hoped the Castel woman would take it, if only for Sully's sake. I was still leery of having someone live right over me, even though I knew there was no way it could be another killer moving in.

The evening moved along and before I knew it, it was closing time. I said goodnight to Dean and had a quick word with Pete. He was taking the day off tomorrow to deal with some personal business. Alain, our sous chef, would run the kitchen. I counted out, shut off the lights, locked up and, went upstairs to bed.

Maybe tonight I'd get to sleep through. No tortured dreams of bodies with knives jammed through their hearts, or young men bound and gagged startling me awake in the middle of the night. Maybe I'd turn a corner as well, and wake to a brighter day.

Chapter Three

I awoke to the sun streaming in through my bedroom window and automatically reached over to cuddle with Eric before my hand reached the cold, empty spot on his side of the bed. The term 'sensory memory' came to mind. It had fascinated me when we studied it in psychology class. Even after something you've seen is no longer there, you remember it. For one minute I'd forgotten we were taking a 'break', a separation I wasn't sure we could ever overcome.

It was my fault really. I'd lied to him, or at least bent the truth, so many times as I became involved in the search for the New Year's Eve Serial Killer, that I wasn't sure he'd ever be able to get past it. People said love hurts. But not as much as doing without it. Trust me. I knew.

New day, Jude, I told myself as I headed for the shower. I looked over my shoulder imagining Eric was standing in the kitchen brewing up a pot of that strong, El Pico espresso coffee that he loved. I shook my head, made it to the shower and, turned on the water as hot as I could stand it. Self-flagellation? Or just a holdover of being named for St. Jude, the patron of helpless causes, which I was beginning to think my relationship with Eric was.

My pity party was done. I had things to do, people to see and places to go. Our liquor representative was stopping by later. I needed to visit my tiny basement office where the paperwork for The Lounge awaited me. Another reason for me to miss Eric. He also did all the bookkeeping for my business, a task that made him a god in my eyes—and one that I really sucked at.

Chapter Four

I entered The Lounge and grabbed a cup of coffee from the pot the busboy had brewed, As I sipped the dark, steaming drink, I ran my hand over my beautiful wooden bar. It was a find from a hundred-year-old tear-down that I'd had to have and I lavished it with special attention to keep it gleaming.

I looked around The Lounge. I loved it as much as I did when we first opened.

The pearl grey walls with their streaks of silver and subdued lighting gave off a chic yet comfortable and welcoming vibe. The Lounge had been my sanctuary.

Art Bevins had almost destroyed the meaning it had for me. Almost. There was no way I'd let that happen.

I scooped up the mail and brought it downstairs to the office. I started to separate it into different piles: supplier bills, restaurant supply catalogs, junk, and personal mail.

My hand hovered over a plain white envelope with my name hand-printed on the front. There was no stamp and no return address. Someone had obviously pushed it through the mail slot and left it for me to find. It was innocuous enough. Just an envelope. But that didn't stop my mind from making an unbidden, giant leap to Art Bevins.

I couldn't catch my breath. I felt as though someone had punched me hard in my stomach and knocked the wind out of me. *Calm down and breathe,* I told myself. *You don't know if it's from him.* But I did know from the other white envelopes I'd received over the last few months. Art Bevins had reached out from whatever rock he'd been hiding under and was coming for me.

His partner in crime, Jim Deems, had written me several letters since he'd been in jail on Riker's Island, awaiting trial. Those were easy to spot, marked with the jail's return address and its postmark. Of course, each time one arrived in my mailbox, it freaked me out, and I picked it up by the corner of the envelope and tossed it in the trash.

This was different. If an envelope could emanate pure evil, this was it.

I don't know how long I stared at the envelope, afraid that if I touched it, some vile presence would take over my body. I left it where it was and eyed it warily as I picked up my phone and called Sully.

"Please come down to my office," I said in a shaky voice I hardly recognized as my own. "Art Bevins is back and he's looking for me."

It didn't take Sully long to arrive, striding into the space in full command mode. He eyeballed the envelope, sitting like a white beacon in the middle of my desk. I told him what I feared, that it was from Art Bevins.

"Did you touch it? "Did you open it? How did it get here? When did it come?" He shot questions at me rapid fire.

"No. No. I don't know. I don't know." I shook my head, my responses rocketing at him as I tried to keep it together.

"We're going to call Lanie, and get her it to examine it. If this is from Bevins, she'll need to know."

"Okay. Okay." I nodded my assent. Special Agent in Charge of the New York F.B.I.'s Behavioral Analysis Unit, Elaine Garlinger, was the agent who'd worked the New Year's Eve Serial Killer case and captured Jim Deems while Art Bevins, the mastermind of their horrid operation, managed to escape and disappear. The BAU's mandate was to capture and imprison serial killers and mass murderers. Easier said than done. I knew Agent Garlinger would do anything to apprehend Bevins and put him away for life.

Fifteen minutes later, Elaine Garlinger's Bureau SUV pulled up in front of the building, red light flashing on the dashboard, siren blaring. A minute later she joined us in my office.

She gloved up and picked up the envelope. Where did you find it?" she asked. "When?"

My breath was raspy and my hands shaking. as I replied. "It was mixed in with the mail that came through the slot this morning."

Garlinger turned the envelope over. I gasped when I saw what was there. On the back flap, there was a drawing of a small knife with drops of red ink drawn to resemble blood. It was a reminder of Art's preferred method of killing that I knew well.

Garlinger studied it for a moment, then put it in an evidence bag.

"How did he…where is…?" I asked.

Sully put a hand on my shoulder, trying to keep me calm. It wasn't working. "We'll take a look at it down at the lab and go through the forensics," Garlinger said.

"I need to know what it says." I tried to sound calm. "You have to tell me."

She nodded trying to reassure me. "Of course, I will." Tucking the evidence bag into her briefcase, she turned to leave.

"I'll walk you out," Sully said and followed her up the stairs. "Stay put, Jude. I'll be right back," he commanded.

I knew what Sully was up to. He wanted to have a private conversation with her, most likely about my safety, or maybe my sanity. He might have seemed like he was rock steady about what had just happened, but I knew how worried he really was.

He and Elaine Garlinger, the lovely dark-haired F.B.I. agent who'd come to The Lounge at a moment's notice, had discovered they knew each other when she showed up to investigate The New Year's Eve Serial Killer case. They'd dated for a while and it hadn't worked out, although they'd remained friends. This new twist had brought them back in contact and I wasn't sure how good, or bad, that would be.

Every time I thought of Art Bevins, which believe me, I tried not to do, I imagined him in shackles, shuffling along a cement floor in the deep, dark recess of a supermax prison. Sometimes, my vision extended to a dungeon, where he would be chained to the wall, lacerated and dripping blood. Too bad we didn't do that kind of thing anymore.

I knew Art had a much better imagination than mine. He'd written hundreds of thrillers, murder, and scary TV and movie scripts, and I'd bet he'd learned all the ins and outs of crime along the way. If he was imagining anything, it was probably me covered with stab wounds, dead at his feet.

A few minutes later, Sully clomped back down the stairs. "Lanie will get back to us as soon as her team goes over the envelope and what's inside." He paused. "She's also sending over agents to canvas the neighborhood for any sightings of Bevins." He shook his head. "Lot of people around here knew him and know what he's done. If anyone has seen him, I'm sure they'll let the F.B.I. know."

Those people, neighbors, and friends had been just as horrified as I was to learn about Art's long-term killing spree. I was sure they would turn him in on sight if they could recognize him. I was certain by now, he must have changed his appearance drastically and no one would be able to spot him. I shuddered, thinking about how he could wander around the Lower East Side like he didn't have a care in the world, plotting how to kill me.

Sully was staring at me. "What?" I asked.

He glanced at his watch. "I...I have to go. Buster is bringing that Castel woman over to look at the apartment..." he threw up his hands in frustration. "I don't want to be late."

I was sure Sully wanted to give the premises a final run-through before the potential renter saw them. "Go," I said. "I'm fine. Really. I have to meet with our liquor supplier in about ten minutes. I'll go upstairs and wait for him there. The busboys are working and Alain will be in soon. I'll be okay," I added, lying to him and myself as I shooed him up the stairs and followed.

Chapter Five

I stopped by the kitchen to check in with Alain about the day's specials. He was preparing the menu items he and Pete had gone over last night. I know it was selfish, but for once I was grateful my partner and chef wasn't there. Pete had gone through a lot with me over the last few years. Between my involvement with both the murder at the Big City Food Bank last year, and the murder this New Year's Eve, he'd expressed his doubts and concerns about staying in the business. He had the right to know about Art Bevins's letter and the potential threat it posed to us and our business, even if it meant he'd leave. I was relieved I could postpone sharing the news until tomorrow. There was no way he would take it well, but by then, Agent Garlinger should have more information from Bevins's letter. I hoped it would hold a clue to where he was hiding, but I knew how clever he was and he wouldn't make it easy to find him.

I was about to go up to my apartment to get ready for my shift when Sully walked in. His head was hanging down and I couldn't see his eyes. My stomach clenched as he sat down on his usual stool in the corner. *Oh, no. He didn't rent the apartment,* I thought.

When he looked up, a smile lit his face. "She took it, Jude!" he said in amazement. "I can't believe it."

"Hey, why not?" I asked. "You made it so beautiful she couldn't resist, right?" I grabbed a bottle of Jameson, poured him a shot, and placed it on a coaster in front of him. "Congratulations." I tipped the glass of seltzer I'd been sipping toward him. "When is she moving in?"

"They," he said. Her personal assistant, Diego Lowell, will be living here, as well."

"Her assistant is going to live with her?" My voice went up a notch in disbelief. It seemed strange to me. "Doesn't she pay him enough to rent his own place?"

"I didn't ask," he replied. She wants to move in over the weekend. Dolores said she'd find some furniture, at least the bare minimum for now, and have it delivered by Saturday."

"Wow, that's fast. Did you offer to help?" I asked with a tiny bit of sarcasm in my voice. Sully was a sucker for a pretty face. I'd bet this Dolores was attractive and knew how to use it to her advantage.

"I told her I'd get a few of the guys I know to pitch in. I could see she appreciated that. She just wants to get settled as soon as possible after leaving California." He shrugged. "Her husband passed away recently and she said she needed a change. She also mentioned she has a new business opportunity and wants to get it up and running right away."

"So, what does she look like?" I asked sweetly.

Sully's face got a little ruddy. "Oh, she's…nice looking. You know, reddish hair, smart clothes…a good figure. In fact, you'll meet her and the assistant tomorrow night. I invited them for dinner at The Lounge." He gave me a crooked smile. "It will be nice for you to get to know your new neighbors."

"I can't wait," I replied, trying to keep the snark from seeping through. I'd become mistrustful over the last year. It seemed to me this Dolores was in a big hurry and I wondered why. I hoped Buster Dunlap had vetted her and her finances thoroughly. I'd call him and make sure. If he hadn't, I would. Sully would have leapt at any chance to get a tenant and might have glossed over any potential problems, like suspicious finances. I didn't want to see Sully get screwed over in any way.

Sully knocked back the rest of his Jameson, turned the glass over, and rapped on the bar. "Got to get going. I'm meeting my buddy for dinner and a Knick's game, although with their record it seems like a waste of time."

"Me, too." I looked at my watch. "Need to get ready for my shift and open the bar to paying customers." I paused for a moment, hesitant to change the mood and the subject. "Any word from Agent Garlinger?" I asked.

"Not yet. Don't worry. She's on it. She'll let you know as soon as she has anything." With that, he stood and left.

Even when I was a kid, I'd never liked waiting for things. My turn for the jungle gym, a why-aren't-we-there-yet car trip, lines for a movie. It drove me crazy. But right now, I had no choice. Justice didn't run on anyone's schedule, especially mine.

I stepped out from behind the bar, let Alain know I'd be back in half an hour, and went up to my apartment to get ready. Somehow, I always expected Eric to be there and it felt empty without him. I headed to the shower where I hoped I could wash away my disappointment. It didn't help.

I decided I wouldn't wait to call Buster Dunlap. How could it hurt to do a little poking around?

"Dunlap Realty," he answered on the first ring. "Buster speaking. How may I help you?"

Buster was a short chubby man with bright blue eyes and a small bald spot on top of his light brown hair. He was professional and pleasant.

"Hey, Buster. It's Jude Dillane."

"Good to hear from you. What's going on?"

I thought about how to frame what I wanted to ask. "I need a favor," I began. This was harder than I thought. "You know Sully's new tenant, Dolores Castel?" I stammered.

"Sure," Buster replied, unable to keep the puzzled tone from his voice. "Why are you asking?"

"Well," I cleared my throat, were you able to confirm all her financial information?"

I continued before he could respond. "I know it's irregular for me to ask about a client…but…after what happened…I don't want Sully to get burned."

"Jude, you know I shouldn't be telling you this, but I'm trusting you here. There's a discrepancy relating to the value of her property in California. She told me she's sorting it out and would have the updated paperwork by next week. Her other financials checked out, but I did mention the problem with the property to Sully." Buster paused. "He was satisfied with everything else."

Of course, he was. He would have rented it to almost anyone who was breathing.

"Thank you, Buster. I won't say a word to anyone. Promise."

We said our goodbyes and I clicked off my phone and started pacing around my living room.

I knew there was something fishy about her wanting to move in so quickly. This Dolores Castel was up to something and I was going to find out what.

Chapter Six

Dolores entered the small apartment she and Diego were using for the moment and kicked off her black pumps. The whole transaction had gone smoothly and she and Diego would be in a good position to move forward.

The apartment on East Tenth Street was actually very nice, as was the landlord, Thomas Sullivan. It hadn't taken him long to ask her to 'Call me Sully. Everybody does.'

She'd dressed on the conservative side for the meeting. A simple black wool Calvin Klein suit, a strand of pearls, and small gold earrings. Just right for a woman with some means who wanted to make an impression. It had worked and she could see he was already a little smitten.

Dolores knew she had to be very careful. She'd left California at just the right time, before anyone could look into Olivier's death too carefully. She'd thought about how he died and felt a surprising twinge of sadness She had loved him after all. She'd just encouraged him to join her in the physically taxing hiking, rock climbing, and running he'd enjoyed when he was younger and his heart was healthier. It had finally stopped beating on the summit of a small peak near their home outside Los Angeles. He'd taken a break to drink some water and they'd walked a little more. Then, suddenly he collapsed. She sat holding his head in her lap reassuring him that the ambulance she hadn't yet called was on the way.

It had been, she realized, a good marriage, at least by her standards. And the massive insurance policy, property, and investments added up to a considerable sum.

More than enough for her to move back east and start over. She was still young, just fifty-three, and there was potential she couldn't pass up. Like Thomas "Sully" Sullivan.

She took her notebook from her purse and started jotting down her thoughts and impression of her new landlord. *Former Marine. Late fifties. Owner of valuable real estate. Other investments? Lives alone. Relatives?* It was early days and she'd add to her notes as things moved along.

Her information was sketchy and she needed to do a little research, but it seemed like he might be a good prospect at least for the short term. There was no need to rush into bigger plans just yet.

Dolores sighed and rose from the couch. She looked around for a place to secret her notebook—no reason for anyone else to see it, including Diego—and settled on a narrow spot behind the refrigerator. A moment later, she cast her eyes to the street below. It was a lovely sunny day in New York. A bit chilly for spring, but clear and filled with promise. She scooped up her coat and purse and left the apartment. She needed to go to one of those inexpensive furniture stores that would deliver in a few days. She wanted a nice, big bed for starters. She had an idea that very soon, she might be using it for more than sleeping.

Dolores smiled to herself as she locked the door. This little detour could be good. Even better than she'd imagined.

Chapter Seven

While I worked some mousse into my short black hair to make it spikey, I thought about my conversation with Buster Dunlap. I was balancing on a wire here, tottering between my loyalty to Sully and casting aspersions on his new tenant.

My decision would have to wait. I was due at the bar. I added eyeliner, mascara, and lipstick. Then I slipped into my work clothes—black jeans, black sweater, and black boots. I loved clothes and dressing up in vintage pieces, but for tending bar, this was my uniform. Easy peasy and no competition to my female customers who rather I faded into the background. Sometimes, I'd hear them whispering about my looks. I couldn't help it, my long, lean body was genetic. *She's so thin, Do you think she ever eats? No, She probably starves herself.* Then, they'd throw me a sideways look or two to top off their comments. It used to bother me, but now I let it slide. I loved to eat, just not in front of my customers.

I checked for messages on my cell to see if Eric had called while I was getting ready. He hadn't. I slipped it and my keys into my back pocket and left the apartment, as empty again now as when I'd arrived.

Downstairs, the bar was ready, ice bins filled, glasses polished and stacked, and gleaming bottles of wines and spirits waiting to be poured. It didn't take long until people started coming in. I smiled to myself. My regulars seemed to be programmed to enter at the same time every day, take the same seats, and order the same drinks. I wondered what would happen if when they went to plop down one evening, someone else was already occupying their space. Thankfully, that hadn't occurred yet.

About an hour later, Dean joined me and took over the main bar. I concentrated on the service area and the dining room, which was just starting to fill up.

I was in the zone, shaking up a few cocktails for one of the waitresses to deliver to a table, when Tony Napoli and Oscar Lupe came in and sat down near my station.

"Hey, Jude…" Oscar began to sing the Beatles song, winking at me. "We'll have a few beers."

"Hi guys," I replied. I hadn't seen them in a few weeks and they'd been pretty much no-shows since New Year's.

Along with Sully, both Oscar and Tony had been members of what I referred to as The Tenth Street Irregulars, kind of what the neighborhood kids would call a squad. Sully, former Marine Commander, leading the troops. The two men who'd turned out to be serial killers were also part of the group. Before the killings, Oscar, who was a cable company repairman, and Tony, known to everyone but a few of us as a manager for a small tech company, had stopped in nearly every night. It was good to see them tonight.

I placed two draft beers in front of them, their early-bird drinks of choice, and planted my elbows on the bar. "What's up?" I asked, pretty much guessing why they were here and what they were going to say.

"A couple of F.B.I. agents came around today," Oscar started, "and asked if I'd seen Art Bevins in the neighborhood." His pale blue eyes were filled with worry. "I…we thought you might know what was going on," he added, nodding his head toward Tony, who dipped his handsome face toward the bar.

My easy mood from a few minutes ago evaporated like wisps of a cloud in the wind, replaced instead by this morning's letter hanging above me like a guillotine.

"Unfortunately, I do." I filled them in on my visit from Agent Garlinger and her take on the situation. Usually, I wouldn't give Oscar, who loved to gossip, any information. But I wouldn't mind if he spread the word that Bevins might be back in the neighborhood.

Tony had remained silent throughout my explanation. He shot me a quick glance as I went through the details. It had been mostly through his efforts that we'd rescued Dean and captured Jim Deems. Tony was an undercover narcotics cop and had caught onto what was happening. He was still maintaining his cover as an IT guy and I wasn't going to blow it. Only Sully, Eric, Agent Garlinger, and I knew his true occupation.

Both men were quiet when I finished, somber and subdued. "So," I said brightly, changing the subject, "Sully rented 7B today to some woman. She's moving in with her personal assistant. A guy," I added, giving Oscar more grist for the gossip mill.

"Her assistant's going to live with her?" Oscar asked, a confused look furrowing his brow.

"They're from California." I shrugged as if that explained it.

"Well, good for Sully." Tony finally spoke. "I hope it works out."

"Me, too," I said as a little curl of my newfound mistrust worked its way down my spine. I knew people scooped up Manhattan apartments as soon as they found them. Even so, Dolores Castel had moved pretty fast. I knew I was being overly suspicious, but after what I'd learned from Buster, I couldn't help feeling bad vibes about this. Maybe it was my Bronx girl upbringing: in our close-knit community strangers were suspect. Eric would have told me I was looking for trouble where none existed. *Well,* I told myself, *I'll see how I feel tomorrow night when I make her acquaintance. I could be wrong.*

Chapter Eight

The next morning, Agent Garlinger called to say she'd like to stop by. She arrived at my apartment about half an hour later. This was service above and beyond the usual F.B.I. treatment, especially from the Special Agent in Charge, or SAC, of the New York office, and I appreciated it.

"Should I ask Sully to join us so you won't have to repeat everything when he corners you?" I'd said it lightly, so she'd know I'd hadn't been entirely serious.

"That's okay. Let's keep this between us," she replied, a smile touching her blue eyes.

I gestured for her to take a seat at the kitchen counter and poured her coffee, which I knew she took black. I was sure she could see how apprehensive I was and I tried to remain composed as she removed a sheet of paper from her briefcase.

"I'm sorry to have to confirm this, Jude. It's exactly as we thought." She placed the letter in front of me so I could see it clearly. "It's from Art Bevins."

My hand started shaking as I reached for it. I took a deep breath and began to read. The words, although they might appear innocuous at first glance, grew more chilling as I read, and a cold dread spread over me.

My Dearest Jude,

It appears that you are well, if maybe just a bit haunted-looking around the eyes. You probably should get more sleep but I understand why you might not. I know that Eric is no longer your live-in partner and it's hard to rest easy when someone you care about is missing. Well, c'est la vie! I'm not sure he was long for the relationship anyway.

But, I digress. I wanted you to know how much I miss you. I've been thinking about you every day and the pain and hardship you've caused me. All the subterfuge I have to go through just to remain anonymous. The disguises I have to adorn to walk outside. This living in the shadows. It's very wearing and quite frankly, boring. I long to show myself, my true self. Turn my face to the sun as it were and satisfy my innate nature. Ah well, don't feel too sorry for me. Patience has always been one of my virtues. I'll get there soon enough and you'll be the first to notice when I do.

AB

The coffee I'd just drank came bubbling up and I excused myself and ran to the bathroom where I retched until there was nothing left inside. When I walked back to the kitchen, Agent Garlinger handed me a glass of water.

"I'm so sorry, Jude," she said again. "This has got to be incredibly hard on you. Believe me, we've got agents everywhere looking for him. We think, because of some of the contents of this letter," she gestured to the piece of paper I'd left on the counter, "that he's in the area."

"Really?" I knew I sounded sarcastic. "You mean because he's been stalking me and wants to kill me?" I asked. "And, there's his threat against Eric?" This was the first moment since Eric had left that I was glad he wasn't here. At least, at home in the Bronx, away from me and The Lounge, he'd be safe.

"We'll keep a team on Eric until we catch Bevins." She put her hand on my arm. "Nothing will happen to him."

Her coffee long gone cold, Elaine Garlinger reached for my hand. "He can't hide forever. Someone will recognize him or he'll make a mistake. We will find him before he can hurt you. I promise."

I knew she meant what she said, but I couldn't just leave it to the F.B.I. It was my life that was on the line, and I was the one who was going to fight for it.

Chapter Nine

The day only got worse from there. After Agent Garlinger left, I dressed and went down to The Lounge. I decided not to call Sully and fill him in. Not yet, anyway. I knew he'd go into overprotective, rant mode and I wasn't ready to deal with it.

My priorities were more pressing than that—I had to let Pete know what was going on. He had a stake in all of this.

We were scheduled to meet at two o'clock to discuss upcoming business plans, including our first-time participation in New York Restaurant Week. Pete was so excited about this opportunity for the restaurant and I didn't want to squash his enthusiasm before we even got started.

But I knew it was only right to tell him about Art Bevins's letter. I hoped he'd understand this was out of my control. I took a deep breath and headed to a table in the back of the dining room where Pete was sitting and looking over the menu.

"Hey, how'd it go yesterday with the guy from Allied?"

Of course, I didn't come out with my Art Bevins news right away. I answered Pete's question as I stalled.

"Good," I said in the most even voice I could muster. "He's sending us a new Vodka from Uppsala, Sweden he swears our customers are going to love."

Pete shook his head. "Probably tastes like reindeer." Give him a shot of Stoli and he was happy.

"Pete, there's something I have to tell you." My hands were sweating and my voice cracked.

Pete leaned forward and put his hands on the table. "What is it? Are you okay?" His eyes searched mine and I could barely meet them.

Just then, Alain, Pete's sous chef brought out sandwiches for lunch. We usually took this time to sample new items that Pete was thinking of adding to the menu, but today we planned to discuss staffing and our upcoming Restaurant Week promotion, a twice-yearly event that took place at restaurants all over New York City.

All of that was forgotten as Pete's eyes bored into mine. "C'mon, Jude. What's going on?" His eyes searched my face while he wanted for me to answer.

"I got a letter yesterday morning mixed in with the mail for the restaurant," I began, then paused.

"From who?" Pete's voice was wary. He'd had bad news delivered by me several times before. "The bank? The insurance company?"

I looked down at the table before answering. "From Art Bevins," I replied quietly.

Pete pushed back his chair so hard, it almost toppled over. He stood up and was shaking with anger, his hands balled into fists and his voice a hiss. "And you're just telling me about this now?"

"I...you weren't here...I called Elaine Garlinger and she's investigating. The F.B.I. is looking everywhere for him. She's positive they'll find him." My excuses sounded lame even to me.

He moved away from the table and started pacing. "I am your partner. How is it possible you wouldn't tell me right away?"

He was still simmering but stopped behind his chair and faced me. "We... this." He swept his arm to include the whole restaurant. "It's all in danger."

I expected him to add, "and it's all your fault." But he didn't.

"I've got work to do in the kitchen. We'll talk about Restaurant Week another time," he added and turned his back on me.

Chapter Ten

Dolores was humming to herself as she checked her reflection in the apartment's tiny bathroom mirror. She tilted her chin up and surveyed the results of the high-end Charlene Cressida makeup she'd had applied at Saks. It was subtle and skillful and just right for her dinner engagement with her new landlord. She'd tipped the cosmetologist well and purchased an eyeshadow and lipstick.

She practiced her smile. Just a hint of flirtation would do. Maybe a slight touch on his arm once or twice during dinner to show she appreciated something witty he'd said.

Dolores had been an acting student when she lived in New York many years ago and took classes on the Lower East Side. She loved playing a role, taking on a new personality, and pretending to be someone else, even for a short time. She'd met so many interesting people; other actors, playwrights, costume designers, producers, and directors. They'd often get together after a class or audition and talk film and plays over drinks at some local bar. She dated a few of the men.

One scriptwriter, in particular, stood out. Turo Bevacqua was from Ohio, although he took to the city as though he were a native New Yorker. He was an amazing talent and she loved acting in the playlets he wrote. Turo was handsome and great in bed, but he had no money at the time, so eventually, she'd left him. She imagined he'd done well, but hadn't followed his career.

Dolores had known her path lay elsewhere, to the wealthy Upper East Side and the monied men she'd find there. It hadn't been hard. She'd gotten a job as a sales associate in one of the upscale Madison Avenue designer men's boutiques and it wasn't long before her fortunes changed for the better.

Mark Lowell fell hard. Dolores had been helping him choose a spring wardrobe, bringing out various items for him to try on when she realized he'd stopped talking and was just staring at her.

"Will you have dinner with me tonight, and every other night?" he asked as he took her hand in his.

Of course, she said yes and the relationship began.

He'd been wonderful to her. Buying her a lovely apartment on East Eight-First Street, splurging on designer clothes and jewels, and taking her to the theater and fabulous restaurants. When his divorce from his wife was finalized, he asked Dolores to marry him immediately.

Since he was older than her, he wanted to make sure she'd be taken care of if something happened to him and he set up a trust in her name. It was incredibly generous and Dolores was thrilled.

The marriage was never to be. Mark passed away from a heart attack just days before the wedding. The first Mrs. Lowell was certain Dolores was responsible, but there was nothing she could prove or do.

Of course, Dolores had felt sad, but consoled herself with the sale of her apartment and the income from the trust.

That was all in the past, she reminded herself, the long-ago past. Before Olivier and California. It was time to move on to new adventures.

But the need to be with Turo had been hard to break. She'd seen him on and off even when she was living with Mark. He was like a burr in her brain, sometimes causing her pleasure, other times pain. She'd seen him one more time, then said good-bye for good.

No sense dwelling on the past. Better to focus on the future. After one last look in the mirror, she checked her watch and smoothed down the fitted black Chloe sheath she was wearing. *Yes,* she thought. *I am definitely ready.*

Chapter Eleven

"Do I look okay?" Sully patted the front of his shirt and looked in the mirror on the back bar.

This was the second time he'd asked me about his appearance and I had to stop myself from rolling my eyes. "You look fine," I replied.

In fact, he looked very handsome. He'd obviously taken time getting ready. A light blue dress shirt with an open collar and black tailored pants suited his trim physique. Even his brush-cut silvery grey hair looked perfect.

He noticed me giving him the once-over. "Well, I wanted to make a good impression," he said with some bluster.

"Remind me again. Who's the landlord and who's the tenant? And which one should be trying to create the right impression?"

"Yeah, yeah. I know. I want her to like the apartment and stay, and not get the idea we're a bunch of thugs and try to break the lease." He took me in from head to toe.

I tossed a bar mop at him. "Who are you calling a thug?"

He was saved from answering my question as Dolores Castel and her assistant, Diego, made their entrance. She paused just inside the doorway and looked around for a few seconds before spotting Sully. It gave the patrons at the bar just enough time to turn as one to see who had just walked in.

Sully had downplayed Dolores's looks as I could tell by appreciative glances being tossed her way. "Down boys," I wanted to say to the regulars nearly drooling in their beers. "I think she might be taken."

She was a knockout. Tall and slender with shoulder-length auburn hair and wide green eyes the color of sea glass. She looked elegant and sophisticated and dressed for the part with a simple black dress that looked like it had been designed just for her...*unless she borrowed it or stole it.* I chided myself mentally for thinking mean thoughts. I hadn't even met the woman yet and here I was giving her the stink eye. But something about her blipped on my radar, although I didn't know why. Maybe it was the way she focused those eyes on Sully like super-hot laser beams.

He'd caught her entrance and walked over to greet her. "Welcome. I'm so glad you could join me for dinner."

Laying it on a little thick I thought, but kept that to myself.

"Dolores Castel. Diego Lowell. I like you to meet Jude." He turned toward me. "She is one of the owners of The Corner Lounge."

"Hi," I said, smiling and extending my hand to each of them in turn. "Welcome to The Lounge and the neighborhood. It's nice to meet you. Would you like a cocktail before dinner, or would you rather be seated at your table?" I could do pleasant when I had to.

"I'd love a glass of Champagne." Dolores smiled at me. "If you have it." There it was again. I might not have heard any snark in her voice, but I could feel it vibrating between us. *What was she doing* here? *A woman who looked like* her, *on the Lower East Side? Park Avenue seemed like it would be more of a fit.* Blip. Blip. Blip.

"Of course. Coming right up." Did she think we were some sort of scummy dive bar like the ones on the Bowery? All she had to do was look at the soft lighting and contemporary design to know The Lounge was classy.

I looked over at Diego. "And, for you?"

"I'll have the same," he replied and tossed me a mega-watt smile that could light up a room. He was handsome. Very, very handsome with deep brown eyes, a wide mouth that turned up slightly at the corners when he smiled, and teeth so white, they rivaled George Clooney's. His looks were almost as captivating as Dean's. Almost. Again, I felt like something was missing. Like a bowl of yellow straw pretending to be tasty, extra virgin olive oil-slicked spaghetti.

I poured their Champagne and a Jameson for Sully and moved on down the bar to wait on my other customers who'd stopped gawping and gone back to drinking. Every once in a while I snuck a glance at the threesome. Sully was talking a mile a minute. Dolores looked as if his every word was fascinating.

Diego turned from Sully and Dolores and struck up a conversation with the young woman sitting next to him, beaming at her with his gorgeous smile. She picked up her cell from the bar and handed it to him. He tapped on the keypad, then handed it back.

Dolores turned and shot him a look. Maybe her personal assistant took care of very personal tasks.

Soon after, they moved to their table for dinner and it looked as though they were enjoying their meal. I got too busy to keep up my spying and when I finally looked up, they were getting ready to leave.

Sully took Dolores's arm and was leaning in close, talking as they passed by the bar. He didn't even glance my way to say goodbye. That was a first. And I didn't like it. Not one bit. I supposed he'd stop in tomorrow and tell me how he'd impressed her with his charm and wit. But from where I stood, it appeared Dolores Castel might have turned the tables and had her new landlord right where she wanted him.

Chapter Twelve

The next day, there was still no word from Eric. I picked up my phone, put it down, picked it up again. I struggled with the idea of texting him. Finally, I gave in.

Can you ever forgive me? I typed and hit send. The words were the title of a movie we'd watched together and enjoyed. I checked the phone every few minutes and after an hour, I finally gave up. His not replying was a clearer message than any words could be.

It had been almost three months. Spring was here, a time for love and romance. Yet, I felt in every inch of my body Eric and I were over. I hoped no one would ask me about him. I couldn't bear to discuss my broken heart, or *'coeur brisé'* as the French would say. French had been my favorite subject in high school. It had allowed me to wallow in my teenage misery in a beautiful language my parents didn't understand. They just called it being moody.

There was also still no word from Elaine Garlinger. I knew I had to make a choice: worry about Art Bevins stalking me every minute of every day, or try and live a normal life, whatever that was.

Normal sounded better. I got dressed quickly and decided to go out for breakfast. I bypassed by the Dive Diner, the regular breakfast spot I'd shared with Eric, and wandered into Coffee Couture, a new place on Tenth Street, just off First Avenue. There was no doubt the neighborhood was gentrifying even more if this cafe with its carefully curated mid-century decor was any indication.

As I tucked into my waffles, bacon, and home fries, a crowd began to gather across the street in front of the old Blackthorne Collier building. The waiter came by to refill my coffee. I nodded toward the melee. "What's going on?"

"The preservationists are protesting. City wants to tear it down." He filled my cup and started to leave.

As he was walking away, I heard a voice call my name. "Jude! I can't believe it's you." My old friend, Shivani Patel, flew over to my table, gave me quick air kisses on both my cheeks, tossed her lustrous, long black hair over her shoulder, and told the waiter to bring her a coffee. He nodded meekly and continued on his way.

Shivani was a force of nature. Taller than me, with curves I'd never have, she was a tawny-skinned beauty, both talented and impetuous. We'd met at yoga class and become fast friends, although we hadn't seen each other in a few months.

"How are you?" she asked, concern flooding her face. Of course, she knew what happened on New Year's Day and what followed. Everyone in the neighborhood did. "I couldn't believe it when I heard about Art Bevins. He was a friend, right?"

"No. Just a customer," I stammered out.

Shivani shook her head. "He seemed so normal."

Most serial killers do, I wanted to tell her, *at least that's what I'd read.*

"Did you. . . know. . . him?" I asked, afraid to hear her answer.

"Not really. I met him once or twice through a friend who's a producer. They were working on a project together."

She shuddered and changed the topic. "And how is Eric? Have you two moved in together permanently yet?" she teased, as she settled more comfortably into the seat across from me.

"He's gone," I replied and stared into my coffee.

"Well, when will he be back?" she demanded. "I'm having a party on Saturday and you both have to come."

I shook my head. "Gone, as in gone for good. We broke up." I couldn't bring myself to tell her he'd broken up with me. That it was my fault.

Shivani gave me a long look, sized up the situation. "Then you definitely must come. There will be some smokin' hot guys from home, just your type. Tall, well-built, and very, very sexy." She raised one perfectly manicured eyebrow, and I couldn't help but laugh. Shivani liked pretty things. A lot.

Home was, or had been, Mumbai, which she'd left to attend New York University. Four years later, she'd earned a degree in communications, and decided to make New York City hers. She founded a successful public relations company and was a walking billboard for her high-end clients, from the Gucci blouse, Chanel jacket, Tom Ford trousers, and Prada pumps she was wearing today. It wasn't unusual for people to stop and stare at her as she strode by.

Shivani was also famous for her lavish parties, which were always filled with interesting people and great conversation, not to mention lots of booze and amazing food. Her apartment was huge, the top floor of a new building on Eleventh Street, roomy enough for the fifty or so guests that would wander in and out throughout the evening.

"You are coming, right?" She gave me a stern look. "Good. That's settled."

Before I could respond, shouting and jeers from the protesters provided a distraction. "What do you know about the plans for the Blackthorne Collier building?" I wondered if she'd heard anything through her PR contacts.

"Not a whole lot." She twisted her hand back and forth. "I understand it used to be quite elegant and the rumor is the city stands to make a bundle by selling it."

"Yeah, I'm not surprised." If you looked hard enough, you could still see its "good bones" under the mess it had become. It was probably too beat up to qualify for landmark status.

I'd read about the building a while ago. It had been a prestigious girls school in the early Nineteen hundreds. After a while, enrollment fell off and the school closed. As far as I knew, it hadn't been used for anything since.

It was a beautiful limestone Beaux-Arts building then, with a low curved stoop, a mansard roof, and stone carvings. Now it was a wreck, damaged and broken-down, often filled with garbage, squatters, and druggies.

"I think the city's planning to sell it to a developer who'll gut it and build a sixty-story high rise on the lot, right?" I asked.

"I did hear that." Shivani nodded. "The Lower East Side Preservation Initiative went ballistic. They rallied the neighborhood people and declared war." She gestured toward the street outside. "I think they want to restore the building and turn it into a community cultural center. I imagine that's what today's protest is all about. That, and riling up the mayor."

I turned in my chair to get a better view of the action. If the crowd gathered today was any indication, the city and the developer were in for a huge battle. As I watched the people across the street, I noticed someone at the edge of the crowd who looked familiar. It was a guy in a bomber jacket and scarf pulled up high around his face with aviator sunglasses covering his eyes. While everyone else was facing the speaker on the steps, he was turned in my direction and was staring straight at me.

I could feel sweat beading on my face. I started shaking and nearly dropped the coffee cup I was holding. *Oh my God! Was it Art Bevins? Had he tracked me from home?*

"Jude? Jude, what's the matter? Are you alright?" I hadn't realized Shivani had still been speaking to me.

I shook my head. "Nothing. I'm fine." Lifting the coffee cup to my mouth, I peered over the rim and took another look. The guy was still ignoring the speakers and staring straight at me. Although the sunglasses masked his eyes, I could tell I was his target.

As I watched him, I realized his posture and stance were all wrong for Art, who was shorter and stockier. His hair was different, too. Light brown with blond streaks that were glistening in the sun. It could have been a wig, but it wasn't. It was Diego Lowell.

"Do you know that guy who's looking at us?" Shivani frowned. She'd noticed him, too. Subtlety wasn't his strong suit.

"I do. It's Sully's new tenant's personal assistant and my new neighbor."

"How is Sully?" she asked, my stalker all but forgotten. That was so Shivani. Jumping from one thing to the next like quicksilver. "He is so sweet. Please make sure to tell him I said hello."

Shivani prattled on and I nodded every once in a while. Honestly, realizing it was Diego didn't make me feel all that much better than if it had been Art.

I'd been followed and I wondered why. What interest could Diego have in me? We'd just met. But, it was no coincidence that he turned up here.

It struck me then that Dolores had sent him to tail me. Once more, I wondered why?

My internal radar started blipping again like an urgent warning of two planes about to collide in a mid-air disaster. She was up to something and I was going to find out just exactly what that was. I hoped it didn't have anything to do with Sully.

I turned my attention back to my friend, who was giving me a peculiar look. "I will come to the party," I surprised myself by saying, and found that I was looking forward to it. I glanced at my watch. "Gotta go. I've got some things to do before I head back to The Lounge."

I got up and air-kissed Shivani. "See you on Saturday." I paid my bill and wandered off for some good karma shopping at my favorite thrift shops in the neighborhood. We'd see how long Diego could keep up with me before reporting back to Dolores.

A few hours later, I was loaded down with packages, including a Mondrian-style black mod mini shift dress from the sixties, with an off-center white stripe from the neckline to hem and one across the waist, and a pair of low-heeled Ferragamo pumps with white trim. I'd pair these finds with fingerless racing gloves and a small clutch handbag. I was all set for Shivani's party. I'd also found a beautiful Halston asymmetric draped maxi dress in off-white crepe. With a long slit up the side, it was Seventies super sexy.

While I was shopping, I kept glancing in the store windows I passed. Diego was still on my tail. Dolores must have told him to stick close by.

I reviewed what I knew about him. It wasn't much. He hadn't made a great first impression. The looks were there, and that incredible smile, but not much else came through. I'd bet he was a fraud. No close friends. No connections. No real interests. Except pleasing his employer, or whatever she was to him.

Well, I'd given him a run for his money but now it was time to head home. Thankfully, Diego was nowhere to be seen as I retraced my route past the Blackthorne Collier building. With the protesters gone, it looked more forlorn, downtrodden, and decrepit than ever. I stared at the building for a moment and realized someone was peeking out through a small opening in a boarded-up window. I felt like whoever was there was staring straight at me. *Jude, now you're being paranoid,* I told myself. Still, it creeped me out for the second time today, and I hurried on by, feeling like that lone eye was boring into my skull.

Shivani and my retail therapy had helped lift my mood for the moment, but it was sinking fast. I had no doubt I'd find trouble waiting when I returned to The Lounge. It was just that kind of day.

Chapter Thirteen

I usually love being right. But not this time.

The minute I entered The Lounge, Pete came out from the kitchen. "Jude, we need to talk," he said and I knew it was serious. I nodded yes, afraid if I spoke my voice would betray my fear.

I gulped and followed him to the back of the dining room and took a seat at our usual table, facing him.

He got right to what was on his mind. "I've made a decision." He was staring down at the table as he spoke, unable to meet my eyes.

This was not good.

"I'm leaving the restaurant." All the air seemed to leave my body in a single whoosh. Deep inside I'd feared this was coming. And, I'd been right. Pete finally raised his eyes to mine. There was sadness there and a play of emotions from sorrow to pity flitted across his dark eyes. In the end, his expression settled on resolve.

"No. Pete, please—"

He held up his hand. "Let me finish. Too many bad things have been happening here." His eyes traveled across the restaurant, the beautiful space we'd created together. "It's not good for me. . . or for you." He reached over and put both his hands on mine which were resting on the table.

"We've always been a good fit and I love working with you, but I need a simpler life.

"Marlee and I are going to leave the city. Move someplace upstate. Maybe open a small cafe and keep it low-key."

"But you love the city," I protested. Pete had often told me how living here in the center of things fed his energy, inspired ideas for new foods, pushed him to be the best. To me, he was the best of the best.

He was shaking his head from side to side. "Not anymore. Jude, I won't leave you high and dry." He paused and I wondered if he could see my heart racing as fast as a runaway train. "I'll give you six months to find another partner, or to buy me out.

"You shouldn't have any trouble attracting someone to partner with. You're amazing and the business is good and should keep growing." He removed his hands from mine and drummed his fingers on the table. "My lawyer will be in touch. We need to set a value for the business and see where we stand."

I was thunderstruck. *Lawyer? Value the business. What did this all mean?*

"Pete, I…can't believe you're doing this. How could you?"

"I have to. This just isn't working anymore." He stood and turned toward the kitchen. "I'm sure we can figure it out."

I shook my head as I watched him walk away from me…from everything we'd built here. We'd started The Lounge on a handshake and an equal investment. Now, we were reduced to dealing with lawyers. How could my heart be broken twice in one day by yet another person I'd trusted?

I'm not what you'd call a big crier but, I put my head in my hands and wept. What would I do without Pete? Would I lose The Lounge into which I'd poured my heart and soul?

I was gulping for air like a drowning swimmer when I felt a hand placed gently on my shoulder. It was Sully.

"Jude! What is it? What happened?" He was poised over me, concern and fear intermingling on his face.

I burst into another round of wet, sloppy crying, barely able to get the words out. "Pete is leaving the business. Leaving me."

Would Sully eventually do the same? What was inside me that made everyone I loved disappear from my life?

Sully gently helped me from my chair and guided me upstairs to his apartment. He treated me as though I were in shock, which I guess I was, sat me down on his sofa, and went to make me a cup of tea with heaps of sugar and a shot of Jameson.

I wrapped my hands around the cup, drawing its warmth into my body and inhaling the fragrant steam as if it had life-giving properties.

When I finally stopped sobbing and hiccupping, Sully spoke. "Start from the beginning and tell me everything." For once, it was a request, not a command.

I did. "I knew Pete was getting fed up with all the drama of the past few years. In a way, I can't blame him. Having people question his integrity, being hauled off and harassed by the police for no good reason, it would get to anybody." I let out a big sigh. "Look at Eric. He left, too. Nobody wants to be around this kind of chaos."

"You don't seem to mind," Sully replied.

"That's not true," I spat out, startled by his words. "I want things to be even and peaceful. I am not looking for trouble." I crossed my hands defiantly across my middle and glared at him.

Sully stood up and started pacing with military precision. Compassion time was over. "Then prove it," he shot back. "Forget about Art Bevins. Let the F.B.I. and Lanie do their jobs." He stopped moving and stood in front of me. "That's the best way." He gave me a chance to absorb his advice and took a sip of his own spiked tea.

"You'll figure out something for The Lounge. I know some people would kill to have a piece of such a successful business. You'll see. There'll be someone out there just waiting to buy in."

I know he was trying to boost my confidence but I wasn't sure about his theory. He seemed confident I'd find someone.

Suddenly, a thought grabbed me. *He couldn't mean Dolores, could he? I'd rather abandon The Lounge and set it on fire than have* her *as a partner.* I tried to keep my expression as neutral as possible and hoped my horrified thoughts didn't give me away. Sully did have his own superpowers, but mind-reading wasn't one of them.

He knew Dolores was looking for a business opportunity. But it was never going to be The Lounge. Never. Ever. Over my dead body.

There it was again. An instant, visceral recoiling at just the thought of her. Other than a few crappy boyfriends, I usually had good instincts about people. I attributed it to my time at the bar, figuring out who was real and who was a fake. When it came to Dolores, I didn't like her, or more importantly, trust her. I needed to figure out why.

I wanted to tell him about Diego following me but I resisted the impulse. Sully would give me "the look." The one that said, see, this is the problem, Jude. You're fantasizing and making stuff up.

Bullshit. I knew what I'd seen. Problem was, no one could back me up. I never told Shivani it was Diego Lowell outside the Blackthorne Collier building, just that it was my new neighbor. I let it slide for now.

"I gotta get going," I said, "and open the bar in a few." I rose to leave and planted a kiss on his forehead. "Thanks for coming to my rescue, old man."

I closed his door, took a deep breath, and marched downstairs, leaving the order and serenity of his neat and tidy apartment behind me.

Chapter Fourteen

I opened the bar but Sully didn't make his usual appearance to chat while I set up. Maybe it was better that way. A little distance from my resident voice of reason could be just what I needed, kind of like one of Pete's between-courses palate cleansers that were complimentary with dinner. The idea had been a big hit with our customers. Now, it seemed like just another inspiration that would leave a bad taste in my mouth when Pete was gone. Quit it, Jude, I told myself. Stop brooding and start working.

Our bus girl brought up ice and loaded it in the cooler where I placed bottles of wine to chill. Then, I polished my beautiful bar. It was the one chore I never tired of doing. Keeping it gleaming usually gave me a sense of accomplishment.

But today, every time I glanced up, I caught one of the wait staff, eyeballing me, then looking away. I knew Pete well enough to know he hadn't discussed his decision with anyone on the staff. But somehow, they knew something—something bad—was going on. There was no place more rife with speculation than a restaurant, especially rumors that could affect someone's job. The staff seemed to sniff them out of thin air. Often it was about our customers, but today it was definitely about The Lounge. Maybe it was that way in every business, but restaurant people had it down to a science.

I ignored the looks and kept working. I served my early bird bar patrons and mixed drinks for our cocktail lounge. When Dean joined me for the night's shift, he kept sliding his eyes my way while he chatted with the customers.

He'd come in early for family dinner and had heard that something was going on.

After one more sideways look, I turned and faced him. "What?" I demanded. "What did you hear?"

He stared at me, his mouth open and closing like a fish out of water. Finally, he spoke. "Are you . . . closing the restaurant?" Of course, that's what the staff was worried about.

"No," I snapped back. Then I softened my voice. "No. It's not…it's more complicated." I paused. "I can't explain right now. But I will soon, Dean. Okay?"

Dean nodded and went to his end of the bar and his waiting customers. Thirty seconds later, he was smiling and laughing as usual as he mixed their drinks.

He trusted me, I realized, and believed I'd do the right thing. I wouldn't let him down. I couldn't.

Chapter Fifteen

Dolores was a little confused and she didn't like the feeling. Sully had called earlier and invited her to stop by his apartment for drinks. He said there was something he needed to tell her.

She hoped he wasn't changing his mind about the lease. She'd put her plan in place and wanted to implement it.

When she arrived at his apartment, he appeared nervous as he opened the door.

"Dolores. Come in. Come in. So good to see you." He gestured for her to take a seat on the sofa. "Would you like a glass of Montepulciano?"

She smiled up at him. "That would be lovely."

"So," he said, as he handed her a glass of the dark red wine. "There's something you and I have to talk about."

She managed to keep her expression neutral as she wondered what the hell was going on. From what she'd observed, Sully didn't appear to be the secretive type. Just the opposite.

"After I tell you, I'd understand if you decide not to move in."

Now she was even more confused. "Why would I do that?"

Sully cleared his throat. "You may have heard of the New Year's Eve Serial Killer."

"Yes, I read about what happened. It was big news even in California. He killed quite a few people, as I recall."

"Mostly here in my neighborhood."

She could literally feel the anger in his voice coming toward her. "But they haven't caught him yet, have they?" She gave him a questioning look.

"You're right. They're still searching for him. He's managed to elude the F.B.I. for months."

She'd been twirling the stem of the wine glass while he spoke. The conversation was making her nervous, something she thought she'd mastered.

Sully leaned over and took the glass of wine from her hand and set it on the coffee table.

"Dolores, he lived here. In the apartment you're taking." He let the words sink in. "He was also a pal, one of The Tenth Street Irregulars, as we called our small group who hung out at various bars in the neighborhood, including The Lounge. We were so freakin' conned by him." The emotions that he'd been taken in for all those years came to the surface. "So, if you want to change your mind, I understand."

"Oh, Thomas, I'm so sorry for you." Dolores called him by his given name. It was more sympathetic and seemed to have a positive effect. She leaned over and took his hand. "None of what happened is your fault. I'm ready to sign the lease right now." She looked up into his eyes. "It's perfect for me here."

He met her glance with his own. "It's been pretty hard on everyone. We all thought Art Bevins was a great guy. Funny, smart, lived here before I bought the building. He was a successful TV and movie screenwriter. And, a serial killer." Sully hung his head at his last words.

Dolores almost let out a gasp, but stopped herself just in time and Sully hadn't noticed. It hadn't clicked when she read the stories in Los Angeles. The name, Art Bevins, had sounded vaguely familiar, but she was too preoccupied with her own plans to dwell on it. Sully could never find out she'd lived in New York before and had been connected with Bevins, known to her as Turo Bevacqua from the acting studio they'd attended. Or that he'd been her lover.

Sully continued, not having noticed her reaction. "He also had a protege, Jim Deems, who was caught and will be serving a life sentence. The worst thing about Art not being arrested and behind bars is that now he's after Jude. He blames her for getting caught and swears he'll get his revenge."

"That's terrible." Dolores grasped his hand and let a tear slip from her eye, all the while thinking, *That might be best for everyone.*

"Oh, Sully. They'll find him. I'm sure they will and then you can get back to normal."

She rose and picked up her wine and then snuggled closer to him on the couch. "Why don't we finish our wine, and we'll talk some more until you feel better."

Chapter Sixteen

The last few days had been hard to deal with on so many levels. I'd finally let myself accept the fact that Eric was gone for good and that wasn't going to change. It wasn't easy and I still found myself thinking about him at odd moments. As if that wasn't enough, every time I stepped into The Lounge, I felt eyes on me—sad, confused, angry, questioning—from my employees who were still speculating on what was going to happen.

Not that I could blame them. While they were wondering what, I was wondering why? When I thought about it logically, I could understand Pete's reasons for wanting out. But logic wasn't my strong suit. Emotion was and I was an emotional wreck.

I'd called a lawyer, Carol Batista, and had an appointment to meet with her next week. Even though she came highly recommended by Sully, the idea of retaining an attorney was about as appealing as having a root canal. Still, I had to do it. I needed to understand all the options that might make the difference between keeping The Lounge and losing it. Sully said he'd come with me and I was grateful, even though I knew he'd probably butt in every chance he got.

I sighed and stepped into the shower in hopes it would help wash away my churning thoughts. It was Saturday, my day off, and the night of Shivani's party. I was looking forward to it and to wearing my new sexy, 60's mini dress. I remembered the hotties she had mentioned and paid a little more attention than usual to my makeup.

I had planned to do my makeup exactly like Twiggy, the quintessential cultural icon for the Swinging Sixties look. She was the first supermodel. Tall and rail-thin with short sleek hair, big eyes, and long eyelashes, with extras painted under her bottom ones.

My short, curvy mom, who was a few years younger than the model, had loved her and of course, wanted to be her. Mom would look at the teenage me and tell me, I reminded her of Twiggy. I couldn't see it at all.

I stared in the mirror and thought of mom. I missed her and Aiden, and dad. Like Eric, they were gone for good.

Sighing, I decided to switch my mod look for my new Halston. Shivani's parties were usually elegant affairs. With gold sandals and a beaded evening bag, it would be fabulous.

When I was finally ready, I left my apartment and slipped into The Lounge by the back door. I wanted to grab a bottle of Cristal to bring to the party, although Shivani would probably have plenty to drink. When I peeked into the dining room and bar, the waitstaff all looked happier than I'd seen them this week. Guess my absence hadn't gone unnoticed. I left without speaking to anyone and headed to the party.

Chapter Seventeen

Shivani greeted me with triple kisses. "You look great," she said as eyed me up and down. Then she whisked me inside and brought me over to a group of extremely good-looking people. "Jude, this is everyone. Everyone, this is Jude. These are my friends from home I was telling you about." She gave me a long, slow wink. "Have a good time."

Having made the introductions, and her snarky remark, she took the bottle of Champagne from me and sashayed off in her silky Tom Ford dress, leaving me surrounded by a group of strangers.

"Would you like a drink?" one of the men asked. "I'm Mital. This is Deo and Karan," he added as he introduced the men in the group. "And, this is Bhavini and Indira." He nodded to the women. The men wore elegant custom suits and the women, stunning cocktail dresses. I was glad I'd decided to wear the more glamourous Halston.

"Nice to meet you all." I smiled at each one. "And yes, I'd love a glass of red wine."

As Mital moved off to get my drink, I gazed around the room. Shivani had outdone herself. Candles shimmered everywhere casting a flickering glow over the guests. Lamps were draped with sheer colorful silk fabrics, and chairs and sofas were piled high with beautiful pillows. The atmosphere was so captivating and inviting, I instantly felt surrounded by its warmth.

My eyes were taking it all in and had moved past a different group of people on the other side of the room. My head swiveled back in surprise. Right there in the middle of them was Tony Napoli.

He must have felt someone staring at him because he turned and looked right at me.

Just then, Mital returned with a goblet of dark, ruby wine. I thanked him and excused myself. I'd decided to go out on the terrace that ran the length of the living room to sip my wine.

A moment later, the door opened and Tony joined me.

"Tony, I'm surprised to see *you* here." As usual, my filter abandoned me and I knew I sounded more than a little snide.

Tony raised one eyebrow in a look that put me in my place.

"That didn't come out right," I said looking chastised. "I didn't mean you shouldn't be…." I could feel my face getting hot. I was probably scarlet.

"Oh, what did you mean?" he asked, tucking a little snide of his own into his question.

"Just…I."

I had overstepped. He'd rescued me, and we were friends, sort of, and I'd been incredibly rude.

I changed the subject quickly "How do you know Shivani?" I asked.

Just then Shivani popped out onto the terrace. "Oh, do you two know each other? I had no idea." She tilted her head to the side, setting off a tinkle of long, dangling earrings. "It makes sense. You both live in the neighborhood."

"Tony and I know each other from The Lounge," I replied.

Shivani put her hand on his arm. "He's a gem. He's saved my bacon more than once."

I looked over at him a question forming in my eyes. Did it, I wondered, have anything to do with his undercover work?

"I've been helping Shivani with her IT programs," he replied evenly, ignoring my implied look.

"Well, he's a whiz," Shivani added. "Now you two come inside. We're about to have dinner."

We followed Shivani back into the apartment where guests were helping themselves from enormous platters of aromatic and delicious-looking food arranged on long, teak tables. As I moved along the buffet, an odd feeling came over me. As unsettling as it had been to see Tony at the party, it wasn't as if he didn't belong here…well, not exactly. He was here as Shivani's friend and co-worker, I reminded myself, even though this didn't seem like his kind of crowd. I remembered the people he was speaking with when I'd spotted him earlier. A couple of guys who looked pretty slick and a little out of place. Maybe they were Shivani's clients and she had told them about Tony and his IT business.

I wondered if she knew he was an undercover cop? Or, if she'd care?

All this was flying through my brain as I began to fill up a plate. I was so distracted I didn't hear Mital calling my name at first.

"Jude." He tapped me on the arm and finally got my attention. "Would you like to sit with us for dinner?"

I smiled at him and nodded. "That would be lovely." As we walked toward the couches where his friends were seated, I glanced over my shoulder at Tony. He was seated next to Shivani and they were deep in conversation.

Several hours later, I said my goodbyes to Mital and his friends, then found Shivani on my way out. "Thank you. It was a lovely party." I hugged her close.

"Well, I'm delighted you enjoyed yourself." She glanced over at Mital. "You seem to have made quite an impression." Then her mood changed and her voice became serious. "Be safe going home," she added and squeezed my shoulder before turning to other guests who were about to depart.

Was she thinking of the person who'd been staring at me through the diner window, or had Tony mentioned something about my brush with Art Bevins? I looked around the room but didn't see him. He'd probably left, as well.

As I walked the few blocks home, Shivani's words echoed in my head and I paid more attention than usual to my surroundings. It wasn't fear, I told myself. It was caution. I wondered if this was my new normal. If it was, it sucked.

Chapter Eighteen

Dolores was shaking her head in disgust at Diego. "What were you thinking?" She sighed aloud and looked up at the ceiling. "Do you think she recognized you?"

She walked across the room and stared out the window, trying to get herself under control. Yelling at Diego wouldn't do any good. The damage was already done. That's if Jude had recognized him.

Diego hung his head and stared at the floor. "I didn't realize she'd see me." He shrugged in a how-could-I- know way. "I'm…not even sure she did." His voice took on a defiant tone. "She was in a coffee shop and then… she looked out the window. I was across the street in front of the building where the protestors were…" his voice trailed off.

It's a good thing he's handsome, Dolores thought, because smart, he wasn't.

Diego picked up his tale of woe. "She just kept on staring right at me and even though I had on glasses and my scarf pulled up, I…think she knew it was me. Maybe her friend, too. But, I'm not sure."

"A friend?" Dolores asked, even more appalled.

Diego nodded. "A tall, beautiful Indian woman. They looked like they knew each other pretty well."

Better and better. Well, she couldn't do anything about the friend, now. Maybe Jude hadn't said anything to her. "Where did she go after the coffee shop?"

"Shopping," he replied. "To a bunch of those vintage stores on Seventh Street. It got late and I figured she'd be heading home soon. You know, to The Lounge, to work."

He was probably right. Jude worked every night except Saturday. Dolores had learned that from Sully, who mentioned he usually dropped in when she was setting up the bar. She'd added that to her notebook, as well.

Those two were close. Too close for her purposes. She'd have to see what she could do to change that. Dolores had instantly sensed Jude's distrust. After all, she'd honed her instincts for danger over many years. She didn't believe she could sway the young woman towards liking her or even accepting her, and she'd have to act accordingly.

But first things, first. "Diego, from now on, you have to be more careful." She made her voice stern but not hard. "We don't want anything to disrupt our plans, do we?" she asked a little more sweetly.

He nodded. "No, Dolores."

"Good," she added and walked over to hug him. "Let's forget this ever happened."

Chapter Nineteen

onday morning, Sully knocked on my door at exactly ten a.m. We were going uptown to our appointment with Carol Batista, the attorney who hopefully would help me figure out a way to keep The Corner Lounge.

"Ready? Let's go." Sully was all business. Dressed in pressed navy pants, a button-down white shirt, and a check sports jacket, he looked the consummate business owner.

I'd made an effort, as well, and was decked out in a long, slim black skirt and a slightly oversize lavender Michael Kors sweater. Sully gave me an appraising look, then grunted his approval.

The Uber he'd called pulled up just as we left the building. I looked up the street to see if Diego Lowell was hanging around. Fortunately, he wasn't.

Once we were settled in the back seat, and on our way to East Seventy-fourth and Lexington Avenue, Sully turned to me looking like he wanted to speak. He cleared his throat several times but no words came out.

"What is it?" I asked. "Is there something I should know before we arrive?"

"Look, Jude," he began, "try to keep an open mind about The Lounge. I'm sure they'll be some way to work things out between you and Pete."

"I really hope so. If I lose The Lounge…I don't know what I'll do." I hadn't meant to say that, but it was true. The business was so much a part of my life I knew I'd be adrift without it.

"Not gonna happen," Sully replied and patted my hand.

We spent the rest of the trip in silence with me gazing out at the traffic passing by. It wasn't too bad for a Monday morning and we arrived at the attorney's office a few minutes early.

"Are you okay?" Sully asked as we stepped out of the car.

I nodded yes, but inside my stomach was roiling and I prayed I'd make it through the meeting.

Carol Batista's office was on the parlor floor of an older brownstone on Seventy-fourth Street. It was pleasant and low-key, for which I was grateful. The few lawyers' offices I'd been in before had felt stuffy and uptight. Looking around, I began to relax just a little.

A young receptionist greeted us from behind a modern glass desk that held a laptop and a vase of cheery sunflowers. She showed us to the conference room, a warm space filled with sunshine from the high windows that faced the street, and told us Carol would be right in.

She arrived a minute later with a smile on her face. She turned to Sully and pecked him on the cheek. Then she moved toward me. "You must be Jude. It's a pleasure to meet you," she said holding out her hand to shake.

"Likewise, Ms. Batista," I replied.

"Please call me Carol," she said as she sat across from us and placed a laptop, notebook, and pen on the conference room table. "So, why don't you tell me what's going on and we'll figure out how I can help you."

I filled her in as concisely as I could about what had happened at The Lounge; my partnership arrangement with Pete based on a handshake and an equal investment, the incidents over the last few years that led up to Pete's decision to leave, including my recent brush with a serial killer, Art Bevins, who was still out there somewhere. She nodded as I spoke and shot Sully a look at the mention of Bevins's name.

"Carol, The Corner Lounge is my life. I don't want to lose it." It was practically what I'd said to Sully in the cab.

"Jude," her voice was gentle as she spoke. "I know Sully is your landlord, as well as your good friend." She turned her megawatt smile in his direction again. "And, he also would like to keep you as both a friend and a tenant."

I glanced over at Sully and he was actually blushing. Was something going on between these two? Were there actually depths to the man that I hadn't known existed?

"I'd like nothing better," I replied, wondering again how we'd keep the tenant part going.

"First we need to place a fair value on the business."

I must have looked perplexed. Pete and I had never done this. Sure, we kept track of sales, expenses, and profits, but that was about it. Eric had helped with the books and they were up to date.

"You'll need an inventory of all the physical assets, including things like kitchen equipment, furniture, supplies, and other items you use every day," the attorney continued. "I know an independent broker who can do that for you." She made a note in the book on the table. "Once that's done, we'll have to look into the owners' benefits such as salary and profits." After I have all the information, I'll be in contact with Pete's attorney and we'll see where things stand.

By now, my head was spinning. How would I get through all of this?

"I know, Jude, it sounds complicated, but it doesn't have to be. Honestly, I promise. When we have that information, we can proceed to the best option for you."

"Do you think I might be able to keep The Lounge?" I asked, the hope in my voice obvious even to me.

"That's one way to go, if you can cover the buyout expenses. Another is to look for a new partner to join you, perhaps a working partner, a chef, like Pete. And, one other idea you might consider is to sell out to a restaurant group looking to increase its holdings. There are a few excellent choices who would like to have a viable restaurant on the Lower East Side."

I sat back in my chair, realizing I'd been leaning over the table as Carol spoke. I thought about what she'd said. I couldn't see The Lounge as part of a chain, but I couldn't see losing it either.

"Part of a chain," I asked, "like an Olive Garden?" I couldn't hide the dismay from my voice. That'd really go over big on Tenth Street.

"Not at all. There are some very good high-end groups who are always on the lookout for a good location. It's a very smart option and both you and Pete could come out of this with a profit.

"Let me give you a few companies to explore. You can Google them and see what you think." She was writing as she spoke, then tore out a page from her notebook and handed it to me.

"Thank you, Carol. I'll do that."

Sully had been suspiciously quiet as Carol discussed the plan. Had he already known what she was going to suggest? As my landlord, he did have a right to be aware of what was happening with his property.

I cleared my throat. "I do have one other question for you. Can you give me an estimate of your fee for this?" I didn't know how I was going to pay her, never mind negotiate a buy-out for Pete.

"Don't worry about that now, Jude. I owe Sully big time and it's covered."

I started to protest, but she shook her head at me. "Honestly, I don't want you to worry about it. We'll work it out."

An attorney that was kind and generous. Had I landed in an alternative universe?

A few minutes later we shook hands again, and said our goodbyes, with Carol promising to have the broker contact me as soon as possible.

Outside while we waited for the Uber to take us home, I turned to Sully and asked, "That was very generous of Carol, don't you think? What exactly did you do for her?" I knew I was prying.

He shrugged. "She needed a little help a few years ago, and I was able to provide it." His tone left no doubt that's all he was prepared to say on the matter.

For once, I dropped it and we rode home in silence.

Chapter Twenty

The next morning, I knocked on Sully's door and thanked him for coming with me to Carol's office. I said goodbye and told him I'd see him later.

I was still thinking about my meeting with Carol Batista as I went back to my apartment to get ready for the day. I decided to take a long walk along the East River and clear my head. It was chilly, but not too windy and the river was calm with soft waves rippling along its surface. I walked for a long time, checking every few minutes to see if Diego was following me. He was probably still at home, tucked up in his bed with a cappuccino from Dolores waiting at his side.

I thought about the two of them as I sat staring out across the water. What was Dolores's end game? Was she a smart opportunist? A nagging voice made me think about her motives. If it was money she was after, Sully had some but he wasn't *that* rich. It was hard to believe she'd grown to care for him in the short time she knew him.

I suddenly had an idea about how I could find out. Searching on the internet would be a good place to start. I'd also call my friend, Lena Larsson, a private investigator, who'd helped me out in the past. She knew Sully and liked him. Maybe she'd do me a solid again. I'd owe her free food and drink at The Lounge forever. That is if it was still mine. Or, maybe she'd take me on as an assistant investigator. I'd probably enjoy that.

On the way home, I stopped into a coffee shop for breakfast. All this thinking had stimulated my appetite. As I started on my bacon and eggs, a lump formed in my stomach. Prying into Sully's love life was none of my business. Although he never minded butting into mine. I also realized Sully would probably never speak to me again if he got wind of what I had in mind.

By the time I got home, it was too late to start my internet search into Dolores. I had a food order to call in and inventory to complete. I changed into my black jeans, black sweater, and black boots. Today, the color matched my mood perfectly.

Despite my new plan to save Sully from himself, a feeling of defeat washed over me. Even with the optimism Carol had offered yesterday, I knew I had to face the fact that The Corner Lounge could be gone, and worst of all my friendship with Pete, as well.

Today, I could have used one of those novenas my great aunts, Carmela and Fannie, made on a regular basis. They prayed for everything from good weather for a family picnic so the lasagna wouldn't get rained on, to happiness and good fortune for a new bride and groom. Along with my Grandma Ree, they were a force to be reckoned with, and I missed them.

When I went back down to the lounge, Eltee, our bouncer, was already in. He was at the coffee station making sure I'd have the fuel I needed to get me through the day.

Eltee had been at The Lounge since we opened. Sully had known him from the Big City Food Bank where Eltee provided security for the trucks that came and went all day long. By the time I did my undercover stint there, he was already working for me.

Eltee had literally been a lifesaver one or two times in the past. I remembered how he'd protected me from being attacked by my psycho ex-boyfriend, Roger, and how he stared down the swarms of reporters outside The Lounge looking for a story about the body we found in the dumpster out back.

At six-four, and two hundred fifty pounds, Eltee cut an imposing figure. No one ever tried to mess with him. Well, I did sometimes, but fortunately, he liked me.

"So, Jude, girl, how's it going?" he asked as he handed me a steaming cup of coffee. His tone and his face gave away the fact that he knew something was happening at The Lounge.

"Shouldn't that be Jude 'woman'?" I asked teasingly, trying to deflect his question.

All I got was a long stare for my trouble.

"Not great," I finally replied. I looked around the dining room at the servers setting up. "I suppose you heard the rumors," I added.

He nodded slowly. "A few. Nothing I think we should talk about now." He shifted his gaze to the dining room and the wait staff who were pretending they weren't trying to eavesdrop on our conversation. "You'll get around to telling me what you need to when you're ready.

"I hate to add more bad news to your plate," he continued, "but I had to run off a wacky-looking character when I got in today." His dark brown eyes narrowed to slits as he recalled the incident. "He was pacing up and down and muttering, stopping every few seconds to stare at the front door."

My mouth had gone dry and when I tried to speak, nothing came out. Finally, I croaked out a few words. "What did he look like? Did he seem familiar?" I could feel myself growing anxious as Eltee replied.

"Crazy, matted hair, long beard, dirty, ragged clothes, and a bunch of shopping bags. He was about average size, but a little stooped over." He took the coffee cup from my hands, which had started to tremble. His voice became deeper and more intense as he spoke. "Have you seen him before? Has he been bothering you?"

"No. I…haven't," I stammered.

"I'm calling the cops," Eltee said taking out his cell phone. "Shoulda done it right away."

I reached out toward the phone. "Stop. It's okay. I just got a little spooked." Eltee knew Art Bevins was still out there and I could see from his expression how worried he was. "I'm sure it was just some guy off his meds wandering around." I forced my mouth into a small smile. "Just keep an eye out, okay? And, let's keep this between us."

I retrieved my coffee cup from where Eltee had set it down and took a long sip giving myself time to calm down. Changing the subject, I asked, "Have you seen Pete yet?" trying to keep my voice unemotional.

"Yeah. He got here a little while ago. He's in the kitchen."

"Thanks. I'll check in with him in a few."

Back behind the bar, I turned away from Eltee and moved into the corner farthest from the door. I picked up my cell and stared at it. Was my imagination running double time? Maybe a crazy guy was just a crazy guy. Then I thought about the sensation I'd had of someone watching me through the boarded-up Blackthorne Collier building. And, the fact that Art Bevins, with his movie and TV background, could easily be a man of many disguises, as the failure to capture him proved

Why, I wondered? Why would he take the risk of someone recognizing him as he paced in front of The Lounge? It was foolhardy. I shuddered, understanding hitting me like a tsunami barreling towards the shore. For him, revenge was a stronger impulse than caution. Maybe, only my death could satisfy his bloodlust.

Great, Jude, I told myself, *make yourself even crazier.* I was shivering from fear. I knew couldn't ignore this. I punched in a number and started speaking the moment Agent Garlinger picked up.

Chapter Twenty-One

gent Garlinger calmed me down, telling me it probably was just some weird guy, not Bevins. I could hear the strain in her voice, and I wasn't sure I believed her.

She also said she'd send someone over to keep an eye on The Lounge and made me promise to call her instantly if I saw anyone suspicious hanging around.

I asked her not to mention anything to Sully. I didn't need him worrying about me any more than he already was.

I felt better when we ended our conversation, but only marginally so. Every day seemed to bring something new to be troubled about, and I wanted that to end.

Steeling myself for the next trauma, I moved through the dining room and headed for Pete's domain. I wouldn't mention the weird guy Eltee had seen, which would probably send Pete over the edge and running out the door. I'd just stick to the meeting I'd had with Carol Batista.

Pete was speaking with Alain. Their voices were low and respectful, as if they were in awe of the beautifully marbled slab of beef they were examining. I imagined they were discussing how to cut it and prep it for tonight's special. I waited until Alain walked away, then headed toward Pete.

"Hey," I said, putting on my game face. "Got a minute to talk?"

"Sure." Pete led me into his office and closed the door. It was cramped, but private, although I was sure glances were flying around the kitchen like bats in a cave looking for a place to land.

"So," I started, "I went to see a lawyer today, as you suggested."

Pete pulled back a little, thinking I was being snarky.

"No. It was a good idea…the right idea," I added. "She had some positive suggestions for how we could work this out." I gestured to the restaurant. "It may take some time and there are a few things we need to do together."

By now my emotions were beginning to spill out for about the tenth time that day. If I didn't control them, tears wouldn't be far behind, and I didn't want that to happen. "So, we need to—"

Pete cut me off. "Jude, I'm not leaving here tomorrow. We will figure this out." He sighed. "I just need a change. I can't take…" He lifted his hands toward the ceiling as his words petered out and I was glad I hadn't mentioned the crazy guy pacing out front.

"Okay." I nodded and told him what Carol had said about valuing the restaurant and the independent broker she recommended. "If your lawyer has something else in mind, please let me know."

"No. That sounds like it should be okay. I'm sure we can work with that."

I turned to leave but Pete put a hand on my arm to stop me. "You know I think you're the best, Jude."

I nodded as I opened the swinging door into the dining room. Right. If that were true, leaving me on my own was sure a strange way of showing it.

Chapter Twenty-Two

I got the bar ready for business and Eltee unlocked the front door. I could see him through our floor-to-ceiling windows as he nonchalantly—for him—walked outside and glanced up and down the sidewalk. He came back in and went toward the kitchen, giving me a high sign as he passed the bar. I winked letting him know I got that he was on the case.

As usual, the first customer through the door was Sully. He was dressed as nicely as he had been yesterday and had even added a tie. "Going somewhere?" I asked.

"Uh, yeah." He seemed reluctant to tell me.

"Care to elaborate?" I raised one eyebrow at him.

"Well, I'm meeting Dolores for dinner. We're going to some new place she heard about in Soho."

If I wasn't so suspicious of her, this would have been funny. "Gee, she's only been here a few days," I said, as I placed a coaster in front of him followed by his usual tumbler of Jameson, "and she already knows all the hot spots." I filled my voice with wonder. "How does she do it?"

"Don't be snide, Jude. It's unbecoming."

This time, I couldn't help it. I snorted out loud. "You like her, don't you?" I asked while thinking she was getting her hooks in deeper and deeper.

Sully gave me an appraising look. "I do. She's a nice woman. Smart and fun." He paused and looked down into his Jameson. "You should give her a chance."

What was that expression? Oh yeah. I remembered, *When hell freezes over.'*

"Well, I can try," is what I said instead. "Is she meeting you here?"

Sully nodded and looked at his watch. "In about an hour. We're going to stop in a gallery on Spring Street after dinner. Dolores is thinking of getting some art for the apartment."

Gallery? Sully? Instead of snorting again, I bit my lip and nodded politely. "How about if I put a bottle of Champagne on ice? She'll like that, won't she?" There I was, being pleasant again.

"Great idea, Jude."

While I found a good bottle and set it in the cooler to chill, Sully began talking with some of the other regulars who wandered in. The Champagne would be icy cold when Dolores arrived. Now, if I could only find some arsenic to go with it.

While I was thinking about Sully's new playmate, Tony walked in and took his usual seat at the bar. We both nodded and said "Hey," at the same time. I poured a Johnnie Walker Black and placed the glass in front of him. He hunched over a bit, circling the tumbler with his arms as if to protect his drink from being snatched away. Time for a little fact-finding mission.

"So," I said in my perkiest voice, tilting my head to the side, "did you have fun at Shivani's party?"

"Shiv's parties are always great."

Shiv? I'd never heard anyone but me call her that before. And, he'd been to her house before. How close were these two?

I leaned in closer. "Does she know what your *real* job is?" I asked. "That you're not exactly an IT guy?"

"Let me ask *you* something, Jude. If you were going undercover as a bartender, wouldn't it be helpful if you knew how to make a cocktail, or two?" He sat back and crossed his arms over his middle.

Ouch. He put me in my place, but he hadn't answered my question. I dropped it for now.

"How'd you like her friends from home," he asked.

"They were lovely," I replied. "Why?"

"I thought I saw you leaving with one of them, that Mital guy."

Now it was my turn to look surprised. I wasn't sure if I should answer. It wasn't any of his business. After a moment, I said, "I left by myself. I would have said goodnight, but I didn't see you anywhere. Figured you might be doing your *real* job."

"Listen to me, Jude." His voice was low and urgent. "No one can know what I do. Lives may depend on it."

I was sure he was going to add, "as yours did," but he stopped short of reminding me of that horrible night. I nodded dumbly. "Let me get you another shot," I said and turned away to reach into the cooler for ice.

"We good?" he said to my back.

"Yeah," I replied, turning back and handing over his drink with a smile.

"Ok, then." Tony lifted the tumbler toward me and nodded.

Just then, the front door opened and all heads swiveled in that direction as if they were skewered on an upright rotisserie. The lovely Dolores had arrived.

Chapter Twenty-Three

Dolores had given herself one final check in the mirror. She had to admit it, she looked good. Her makeup was soft and subtle And the bottle green sheath she'd slipped on made the most of her figure.

She was going to make sure Sully got the full effect of her personality, and that he appreciated it. There was no doubt he was interested. It was just a matter of pushing that interest further.

If anyone could do it, she could. She'd even decided to make nice to Jude. She'd rethought her position. Maybe, just maybe, she could win her over. If she could accomplish that, Sully would be putty in her hands. If not, well there were other ways of achieving her objectives.

She checked her Cartier diamond-studded watch and decided she'd be fashionably late. Anticipation was also part of the thrill and leaving Sully dangling for a few minutes would probably increase his.

All this plotting and maneuvering took so much energy. It was draining. So was keeping Diego focused on the plan. She hadn't expected things to fall into place so quickly. If it worked out the way she'd intended with Sully, she might be able to breathe and enjoy life. Stay here in New York, where she really belonged, and eventually revel in her days as a rich widow for the third and final time.

In the role of her personal assistant, it would be odd for Diego to take another job. But she had encouraged his effort to make friends, which he had, and do things in the neighborhood. She hoped he wouldn't fall for some pretty young woman, which could be a disaster.

Dolores let out a long sigh. So much to think about and accomplish. She glanced at her watch again and decided enough time had passed. Sully would be chomping at the bit, but she'd make the wait worthwhile.

Chapter Twenty-Four

I was facing the back bar reaching for a bottle of vodka and I just happened to glance in the mirror as Sully stood to greet Dolores. With his back toward the bar, he leaned in and gave her a brief hug. I caught her reaction in the mirror, as well. A look of self-satisfaction flashed across her face. It was gone in an instant and by the time Sully released her and I turned around, she was all smiles.

"Hi, Jude," she said as she took a seat at the bar. "How are you?" Just as friendly as could be.

For a second, I wondered again if Sully had told her about my troubles with The Lounge but dismissed the thought as fast as it had appeared. He wouldn't, plain and simple.

"I'm good," I added in my cheeriest voice. "You? And your assistant?" I gazed at the door as if I expected her boy toy to appear.

"We're both fine," she replied, but I could tell I caught her off guard, asking about Diego. "He does have a personal life and is out with some friends this evening." She couldn't mask the annoyance in her voice. "Maybe they'll stop by on the way home."

"That would be great. We always like to see new customers at The Lounge. It's nice that he's made friends already to share his free time with." Let her wonder if I'd caught on to her little ploy of having him follow me.

"And you, Dolores, how are you enjoying the neighborhood? Had a chance to look round yet?" I tilted my head toward the outside.

"I've always loved this part of the city," she responded.

"So, you lived in New York before?"

"No. I've…just visited." The slight catch in her voice told me my question surprised her but she recovered quickly and gave me a cold cobra smile. "I'm from California." She was as on to me as I was to her.

Sully interrupted this scintillating conversation. Didn't he think it was odd that a hot, young guy was living with her? He was clueless.

"Jude, why don't you get that bottle of Champagne you put on ice for us."

"Coming right up," I replied, and swung around and dipped my hand into the cooler, emerging with the icy bottle.

Sully turned toward Dolores. "Jude thought it would be nice to treat us to champagne this evening."

I did? That wasn't exactly what I'd said, but he was all smiles and I couldn't very well tell him that. Besides, I owed him for today. Dolores seemed equally surprised by my unaccountable act of generosity.

I put two flutes in front of them, popped the cork, and poured the bubbly. "Cheers," I said, leaving them and walking to the other end of the bar where some of my regulars were waiting to be served.

Pete stuck his head out of the kitchen to speak with one of the waitstaff and waved at me. Just looking at him made me sad, but I wasn't going to go there. I waved back and went on with my bartending.

Dean came in a little while later and took over the front of the bar. He was his usual, gorgeous, happy self, and I could see from his customers that it was contagious. Maybe he was finally getting over what had happened to him.

Sully and Dolores got up to leave, Sully giving me a thumbs-up as he headed for the door. Ugh. I didn't want to know what that was about.

That nasty woman was "up to no good," as my grandma Ree used to say. But, all I had were suspicions. I'd have to dig a little deeper to turn them into facts.

The Lounge was really busy and I lost track of time. At about ten o'clock, one of the waitresses, Mariana, came to the bar and handed me a note.

"The gentleman at table twenty-four asked me to give you a message." She started to relay what he'd told her. "He said he loved your margaritas and the chef's steak frites." She turned around and looked in his direction, then frowned. "That's strange. He was there a minute ago and now he's gone. Well, maybe he's just in the restroom."

I gazed at the empty table, then back at Mariana. A lump formed in my throat as I spoke. "What did he look like?"

She tilted her head to one side, her expression serious as she considered her response. "He was about your height with curly salt and pepper hair and gray eyes."

"What was he wearing?" I continued, trying to keep my voice calm.

She closed her eyes in an effort to remember his outfit. "Hmm. Just regular clothes. A black sweater I think, and a tweedy jacket."

She turned to head back to the dining room, then paused. "Oh, he also had a red baseball cap with some kind of logo on it, that he placed opposite himself on the table where a second place setting would be. He said he knew you didn't allow hats to be worn in The Lounge." She gave me a serious look, as if something had just occurred to her, then hurried back to her station, glancing over her shoulder every few steps. When she got there, she whispered something to one of the waiters and they both stared at me.

I just stood there. I could feel the blood draining from my face as though I were the victim in a horror movie with a chainsaw roaring toward my head.

The red baseball cap had been another way to taunt me. It had belonged to the killer's protégé, Jim Deems, who'd kidnapped Dean. I didn't know how he got hold of it—it should have been in the F.B.I. evidence room, not in my dining room.

I shook my head and called to Dean to watch the bar, and slipped under the opening at the service station.

Once I was downstairs, inside my office, I leaned hard against the door, the urge to barricade myself in taking over. Finally, my breathing calmed, and I slowly got myself under control, trying to sidestep the horror I was feeling. There was only one person I could think of who always ordered that particular combination of food and drink, and who would make a point of letting me know he was well and truly back, Art Bevins.

Chapter Twenty-Five

A few minutes later, my hands were steady enough to call Agent Garlinger.

Fortunately for me, she was at home, enjoying a rare night off, which I disturbed. She assured me this was much more important than the old movie she'd been watching and said she'd be at The Lounge in twenty minutes. She was also sending two agents I already knew, Ari Maguire and Rita Samuelson, to join Agent Bojack, who'd she'd deployed earlier to secure the area.

"Please ask them to keep it low-key. The restaurant is pretty full and I don't want to alarm anyone else." *I'm sure they'd love to know a serial killer was having dinner in their midst*, I added to myself.

While that was true, I was also terrified that Pete would find out Bevins had been dining with us. I'd tell him soon. I had to. But first I'd have to compose myself.

Agent Garlinger and I spoke for another few minutes and she gave me a list of things to do: keep Mariana on the premises so the agents could interview her. Ask her to search her memory for a better description of what her customer looked like, and anything else he may have said. Ask the people who were sitting nearby to remain in the restaurant.

"Jude, first thing, go to the dining room and grab the margarita glass and the cutlery Bevins used. Let's check the DNA against what we have and make sure it was him," Agent Garlinger directed. "Wrap it in a napkin and set it aside until Agent Samuelson gets there."

"Okay," I replied but I knew in my heart there was no reason to check. It was Bevins. It was just a waste of time. Time I could be using to find him.

I clicked off and headed upstairs. Instead of heading to the dining room, I slipped outside and started walking up and down Tenth Street, looking into every doorway. *He had to be somewhere close,* I thought, *but where?* I needed help, and the F.B.I. wasn't cutting it.

But by the time I got back inside, his table had been bussed and everything was in the dishwasher.

I found Mariana and pulled her aside. "Can you please stay behind after your shift?" I paused, thinking about how much to tell her. "That customer? The one who gave you the message for me? The police have been looking for him."

I could see I'd frightened her; she'd known something was wrong. "You're safe and not in any trouble. They may want you to describe him, that's all. You okay with this?" I didn't want to make things worse and kept my tone as light as possible.

She nodded her agreement.

After I finished speaking with Mariana, I called over Eltee and told him what was going on.

"I let you down, Jude. I should have spotted him and got you out of here." He glared at the dining room as if he could bring Bevins back and pulverize him.

I shook my head. "No, you didn't. He fooled everyone." I gestured down the bar at several men sitting there who'd known Art Bevins for years. None had recognized him either. "He was obviously in disguise. You couldn't have known."

"But I should have." He hung his head in disgust.

I reached over and squeezed his hand. "Do me a favor, find Mariana, and ask her if the people on tables twenty-three and twenty-five are still here. If they are, tell her to buy them an after-dinner drink to keep them happy until I can talk to them.

"After that, please pull Dean aside and fill him in. Try to keep him calm." I thought about how he almost died at Bevins's hand. "And don't mention this to anyone else."

He gave me a funny look at the last, like he never would, but nodded that he understood.

While I waited for the Fibbies, I realized I couldn't let Art's reign of terror keep reducing me to the quivering mass I'd become just a few minutes ago. He'd managed to ruin my life on every level. No more being scared. I was as mad as I'd ever been, and even though I didn't know how, I was going to get even.

After Eltee had spoken to Dean, I slipped back behind the bar and called to him to join me at the service end.

"Are you okay?" I asked, realizing how stupid the question sounded as soon as the words left my mouth. Dean looked terrible, ashen, and spent. A shell of the man who'd come to work happy and smiling.

"What do you think?" He snapped back, glaring at me. "The person who tried to kill me strolled into the restaurant and had a nice drink and dinner. And, not one of us noticed. No, I'm not okay."

He placed his hands on the bar, gripping the edge until his fingers looked like they might snap. Then he sighed and his body relaxed. He managed to soften his tone a little. "Garlinger's got to get him, Jude, and soon."

"You're right. I'm so sorry this is still happening." I took his hand. "She will." *Or I will.*

"I'd better get back to my end before the natives get restless." He gestured to the customers he'd been serving, who were so engrossed in their conversations they hadn't noticed a thing.

I nodded and turned back to the drink orders waiting for me. A few minutes later, Samuelson arrived. "What do you have for me?" asked the tall, attractive agent with long, wavy brown hair.

I told her we were too late to retrieve the glass and cutlery, but Mariana had tossed the napkin Bevins had used onto a pile behind the service counter. It had slipped to the floor. She had been too busy to pick it up then, but remembered where it was and retrieved it, holding it by its edge with two fingers, as if it were a viper who might strike at any second. It was now in a plastic bag in Samuelson's custody.

"I'll wait for Agent Garlinger out front, see what she wants to do next."

"Okay. I'll be right here," I said and turned my attention back to my bar. Every few minutes I glanced at the front door, hoping that Sully would walk in, finished with his fancy dinner and gallery opening. I wouldn't even mind if Dolores was with him. Well, not really. I would. I just needed him to be here.

In the meantime, I knew I had to let Pete know what was going on—if he walked, he walked.

I downed a shot of Bourbon and started for the kitchen, calling for Dean to watch the service end of the bar, too.

One look at my face and Pete knew something really terrible had happened.

"Jude? What's—"

I cut him off and told him everything in one long gush, staring down at the floor. When I finally finished and did look up, I couldn't read his expression. The worst was going to happen. I could feel it.

He just stared at me for a moment, then reached over surprising me with a hug. Sometimes, it's hard not to underestimate the people you love. When Pete stepped back, I could see anger flare across his face. I knew it wasn't directed at me, rather at Art Bevins.

Chapter Twenty-Six

When Agent Garlinger arrived, she checked in with Samuelson and had her take the bagged napkin to the F.B.I. crime lab at Federal Plaza. As soon as that was done, we marched down to my office.

I'd asked Mariana to join us and relate again exactly what she'd told me right after Bevins left The Lounge.

"Did the customer say anything else, anything that you can remember?"

Mariana's brow wrinkled in concentration. "I do. He said to tell Pete he hasn't lost his touch and that he'd be back soon to see you." Then her eyes filled with suspicion. "Why didn't he just stop at the bar and tell you himself?"

I knew she'd heard the rumors and was trying to put it all together. It took all of my willpower and energy to keep my voice steady and even as I replied. "He knows the F.B.I. is looking for him," I said, leaving out the part about him being the New Year's Eve Serial Killer. I didn't need a staff member freaking out.

Stay strong. Be brave. I told myself, fighting the numbness creeping over me. *Elaine and her team will find him and put him in a cage where he belongs.*

Bevins was stepping up his game. Instead of just leaving a note, he'd come to see me in person. Even though I'd determined to toss fear on the garbage heap, I was sure I was wearing it like a second skin.

"Jude?" Agent Garlinger called to me. "It's going to be okay. I promise."

"Sure." I nodded as if unconvinced. I'd heard that before.

"We've already pulled up CCTV footage from surrounding businesses and traffic cams in the neighborhood. I'll be going through it with the team as soon as I get back to the lab.

"I've also got patrolmen from the Ninth precinct doing a door-to-door canvas. If anyone noticed anything suspicious—anything—we'll find out." She nodded at me. "Six of my guys will be on duty around the clock. Bevins is not going to get near you again." Her tone changed and became more authoritative. "His days are numbered."

"How can you say that?" I asked. "He had no trouble walking in here." I swept my arm upward toward the restaurant. "And sitting down to dinner."

"It was brazen—"

"Brazen? You think?" I could feel my face flushing and my anger rising like a helium balloon about to explode. "He's not only trying to kill me, he also wants to keep ruining my life over and over. And, you know what? It's working." I gulped to suppress the emotions bubbling up in my throat.

Garlinger leaned toward me and put her hand on my arm. "We. Will. Put. Him. Away."

At that point, all I could do was nod and pray that she was right.

I remained in my office after she left to speak with her agents and coordinate the search. I don't know how long I sat that way, staring off into space. I was just about to go back up to the bar when there was a soft knock on the office door.

I bit back a surge of panic as I called out, "Who's there?"

"Who do you think?" shot back a voice I knew well. "What are you doing down here sulking? You've got a bar full of people up there." Sully didn't wait for me to invite him in. He walked through the door his words filling the space and raised his eyes to the ceiling. "Let's go," he commanded.

Sir. Yes, sir. I almost saluted as I followed him back to the bar.

I nodded at Dean and took my spot at the service end of the bar as I listened to Sully rant.

"Lanie filled me in, so I know what happened. That bastard was lucky I wasn't here." His eyes glinted like bright, newly forged blue steel, and his whole body tensed.

"No one knew it was him. Bevins is like a chameleon, blending in as he needs to." I shuddered. "He's been using that trait his whole life, hasn't he?"

Sully snorted with derision. "Can you imagine the sources he had from his career for information on disguises, weapons, and murderers? All he had to do was write something, see how it played out, and he was golden." He slammed a fist into his palm. "Bevins fooled us all, over and over again."

My cell phone chirped just as I was about to reply.

It was Agent Garlinger. "The CCTV footage paid off. We've got a lead on where he was heading."

For one second, it felt as though my heart had stopped. "You know where he is?" I demanded. Anxiety bubbled up from my stomach and out through my mouth.

"Not yet," she replied, "but we will soon. We're still combing through the images. I'll let you know when we have it put together."

"Can't you tell me now?" I yelled into the phone, then added a soft "please." I was crawling out of my skin waiting for the Fibbies to figure out where Bevins was hiding and capture him in his lair. I knew I was getting ahead of myself, but I couldn't help it. I wanted this to be over.

Sully had been listening to my end of the conversation and held out his hand for my phone. He had a brief conversation with Elaine Garlinger, then clicked off.

"Given the circumstances, Elaine invited us to join the team at the crime lab." He checked his watch. "She needs a few more hours to review the footage, then we'll head downtown. You okay with that?"

I gave him a slow nod. A few hours might not seem like much, but right now it felt like a lifetime.

Chapter Twenty-Seven

Two hours later, dinner service was over and the bar had quieted down. I tossed Dean the keys and asked him to close up. I could tell he was anxious to know what was going on, but I couldn't get into it right then. Who could blame him? He was the one who suffered most at Bevins's hand.

Two agents from my F.B.I. protection team peeled off and escorted Sully and me to a black SUV Agent Garlinger had sent for us. They made sure we were secure in the backseat and in seconds we were on our way downtown to the F.B.I. crime lab at Twenty-six Federal Plaza.

Agent Samuelson was waiting at the front door of the field office and led us into the building.

Elaine Garlinger met us just inside the lab on the tenth floor. A satellite of the main lab in Quantico, Virginia, it was smaller than I expected. A bank of cabinets along three walls held all kinds of equipment. I cut my eyes toward the rows of many unfamiliar-looking machines and nudged Sully in the ribs. *What the hell was all this?*

I did recognize some of it—microscopes, scanners, computers, and monitors, but I had no idea what the other stuff was. Banks of lights above softly illuminated the work stations below.

An agent was standing at one. The evidence bag from The Lounge was on the counter and the napkin was on a plate under a large microscope attached to a monitor which magnified it. Gloved, and wearing a mask, the agent peered through the eyepiece and focused on what looked to me like a small area, which was blown up many times on the screen. To his right was a tray with small vials and droppers. On his other side was a large machine I couldn't identify. It had spaces for several tubes and I imagined that it spun them at warp speed to tease out DNA. Well, I'd seen that on *CSI*. Everyone had. I wanted to tell the agent not to waste his time. They probably already had what they needed. Like a dog marking his territory, Bevins liked to leave his taint wherever he went.

Elaine was motioning us toward the back wall of the lab where there were two back-to-back high-top tables with four massive monitors attached to cables snaking out in every direction. A group of stools was clustered together in front of two of them. *The better to see you with,* I thought. The overhead lights were off and the computer screens emitted an eerie glow.

The lab was busy for this time of night. During the day, I was sure it was even more hectic, with F.B.I. forensic scientists examining critical evidence on everything from DNA samples to explosives residue. Evidence that could make a case.

Elaine began to explain about the monitors. "New York City has one of the most advanced surveillance systems in the world, and of course the F.B.I. has access to it."

She started walking us toward the monitors. "It's known as the Domain Awareness System and includes everything from low-tech CCTV to high-tech facial recognition." She was proud of the system, and the tools it offered law enforcement.

At the high-tops, she introduced us to Agent Tomas Arundo, from the Operational Division who'd been going through the various footage that tracked Bevins's progress from the restaurant. He motioned for us to take the seats on each side of him and made sure we could see the images clearly.

"They may seem random to you," said Agent Arundo as he manipulated the mouse, "like jump cuts in an old home movie because of all the cameras we're accessing. And there will be some blind spots that aren't covered. Eventually, the images will be merged into a continuous stream."

These thousands of cameras watching NYC citizens hadn't always been popular. People had protested about losing their civil rights, but now, no one even noticed their little red lights winking on and off. Big Brother was always watching.

"That's him there, leaving the restaurant." Arundo slowed the machine, then stopped it and pointed to Bevins. "The CCTV camera from the bodega across the street picked up this first image."

I could see Bevins in perfect focus. He turned his face up toward the camera, took off the red baseball cap, which I recognized as Jim Deems's, and smiled. He was exactly as Mariana had described him; the man who'd given her the message. The bastard was using the surveillance camera to goad us even more.

The agent resumed. "He walked out, then turned right onto Tenth Street, and continued west." His words echoed the images we were seeing on the screen.

"At First Avenue, he crossed the street and walked uptown toward Thirteenth." Arunda paused the images again and zoomed in on Bevins. "We lost him for a minute then—one of the blind spots I mentioned. It appears he ducked into an alleyway just out of range of the camera, removed the jacket he was wearing, and pulled on a hoodie. Probably had it stashed there earlier. We'll check nearby footage from the last few days."

"If he was planning this, he could have done it anytime," Sully added.

Agent Garlinger motioned to Samuelson. "Send a forensic team to scrub that alley. Get that jacket and see if there's anything else he left behind."

Arunda waited until Garlinger had finished with her orders, then turned his attention back to the screen. "See right here." He pointed to a man coming back out onto Thirteenth street less than a minute after Bevins had entered the alley. He moved in close. The camera had captured Bevins from behind. Arunda nodded. "It's him. The height, his posture. It matches the other video we've seen." He did something with the mouse and the screen split in half with two images of Bevins, side by side. "I'm positive. Looks like he's holding a small package in his right hand. Maybe had it stashed in the alleyway."

Sully, who had been staring intently at the monitor, leaned in closer. I heard the word "shit" come out in a low hiss.

"Where'd he go after that?" Sully asked, waving his hand toward the computer impatiently.

"He changed direction and started moving west, then cut over into Union Square Park."

Arunda sped up the machine and a series of images flashed by us, the steadier pace making them feel slightly more connected as each of the various CCTV and traffic cam cameras he passed tracked Bevins.

"The last image we have so far, is him ducking into the subway station at the southeast corner of the park." Arunda turned from the monitor and looked at all of us.

"What? No. That can't be." My words came out strangled. I wanted to tackle the monitor and shake it until Bevins fell out into the lab.

"We're not done yet," said Elaine. "Right Agent Arunda?" She gave the agent a pointed look.

"No, not at all," he replied. "Were checking every one of the subway routes that pass through Fourteenth Street. There are cameras covering every line from all angles. It's going to take a while longer, but we'll find him again."

"So, once you see what train he got on, you'll have to look at each stop on the line to see if he got off, or switched trains?" Sully sounded incredulous and shook his head from side to side. "And, what if he's hiding in one of those blind spots, and never took a train? He's lived here forever and is more than smart enough to have figured out where they are," he added with disdain.

I watched him calculating the possibilities in his head. "And if he did hop on the subway, there must be seven or eight lines that run through there. All over, to the Bronx, Queens, Brooklyn, Manhattan. Not to mention the PATH train to New Jersey. That's hundreds of stations to check." Frustration was pouring out of him. "Is this the best you've got?" he added, as his gaze bore down on Elaine.

"I said we're not done," she snapped back. Her composure was starting to show tiny cracks like earth scorched from the sun.

We...I needed her to hold it together. I shot Sully a look, which he ignored.

"We'll check every station, see where he got off, or if he transferred, and pick him up from there," Elaine continued.

"And how long is that going to take?" Sully fired back, shaking his head. "You got to do better than that. "

While Agent Garlinger and Sully had been arguing, I watched the monitors that continued to show the footage from the Fourteenth Street station's embedded cameras. It was a mob scene with hundreds of people flowing through the pathways at this busy transit hub.

I was concentrating so hard when a little bell went off in my head. There he was. I was sure it was Bevins. I turned around to get Garlinger's and Sully's attention, but they were too busy arguing.

I'd spotted a bald man carrying a hoodie, who'd managed to blend in with the crowd as he tossed a small paper bag into a trash can, whistling as he continued on his way up a staircase that led to the street.

"Sully. Let's go. Right now." It was my turn to do the commanding. Garlinger and her agents stared at me as if I'd lost it, but I was already halfway out the door. "Are you coming, or not?"

Sully nodded and followed me. "What the...?" he asked, hands raised to the sky.

"I know where Bevins went, and we're going to get him."

Chapter Twenty-Eight

Dolores dropped her keys in a small dish on the hall table just inside the front door. Her evening out with Sully had gone well. Actually, better than expected.

The real start of the evening had begun after they left The Lounge. She knew that witch, Jude, had suspected she was up to something. Dolores had almost slipped up with the woman's questions about New York, but she thought she'd handled it well.

Jude had put on a show of making nice for Sully. The Champagne, the smiles, the attentive service. Only a man would be taken in by that. Dolores would get around to her in time. Right now, Thomas "Sully" Sullivan was her main objective.

She slipped off her Prada pumps and gazed into the mirror over the console table. Dinner at Pourquoi on Prince Street had been exactly right for the mood she wanted to create. The new, upscale French bistro was all gleaming silverware, starched tablecloths, and soft lighting.

Sully had been impressed. "How did you find this place?" he'd whispered as the maître'd led them to their secluded table in the back.

"That's my secret," she'd said suggestively.

Delicious wine, excellent cuisine, and wonderful conversation made dinner even more romantic.

Sully was more well-read than she'd expected, and they'd wound up discussing F. Scott Fitzgerald's work and his friendship with Ernest Hemmingway. She'd thought Sully would be more of a pulp fiction kind of guy, and it was a pleasant surprise that he wasn't.

Their time after dinner at the gallery opening had been equally entertaining. They'd arrived late and the space was filled with artist types and well-heeled New Yorkers sipping wine and discussing art.

Dolores had implied that she knew someone connected to the show. In reality, she'd merely seen a notice in the *New York Times* about the opening of the solo show. She'd nodded and smiled at several people, moving Sully along from one painting to the next, praising the artist whose work she actually thought was dreadful. A few of the art patrons looked familiar, but Dolores managed to keep her face turned away from them. There was one man who'd glanced at her several times. It was possible he might have recognized her from years ago, which would have brought the evening to a crashing disaster. Using Sully as a shield, she had managed to stay out of his line of sight. Dolores did not need to run into anyone from her previous life in New York.

Thankfully, that hadn't happened. She shook off the near-miss and tossed her auburn hair. It caught the glow from the entryway light and she gazed back into the mirror reassured her that she was indeed still very attractive and appealing. Evidently, Sully thought so as well and hinted several times that he'd like to be invited in for a nightcap.

Instead, she'd let him kiss her good night outside the front door, before slipping inside. He was on the hook. She'd let him run the line, and reel him in when she was ready. Her lipstick was slightly smudged from the kiss. The memory made the edges of her mouth turn up in a slight smile. His kiss and his embrace suggested he wanted her. That was not on the agenda for tonight. She had gazed up at him and pulled back slightly. Of course, he was disappointed, but she knew it was better to leave a man wanting more.

As Dolores moved toward the living room and the drinks cabinet to pour herself a well-earned Bourbon, she heard a slight noise from her bedroom.

Diego must be in there. She frowned. He had his bedroom and should be using it. If she'd allowed Sully to stay, how would she have explained her assistant sleeping in her bed?

He had made some friends, and she thought he'd still be out with them. He'd said they were going clubbing and he wouldn't be home until very late.

She'd have to find something else for him to do, other than watching Jude. She certainly didn't want her to notice Diego every time she turned around.

She sighed and finished her Bourbon, placing the glass on top of the cabinet with a determination that wouldn't be denied.

She gently pushed open the door to her bedroom. Diego was on top of the bed, staring at the ceiling.

He gave her one of his dazzling smiles. "I know I shouldn't be in here, but I missed you..."

She sighed and moved toward the bed, shaking her head as she walked. "I understand Diego, but..."

A moment later, Dolores sat on the edge of the bed, leaned over, and kissed him.

Chapter Twenty-Nine

Sully hailed a taxi and we took it to the Union Square subway station. As we rode uptown, I told him what I'd seen: Bevins, now bald, dropping a package in the trash can, and walking toward the stairs at the Sixteenth-street exit.

"Why didn't you tell Lanie?" he asked.

When I didn't respond, he asked again.

"Why do you think?" I finally replied. "Bevins is threatening me, and I'm going to find him.

By then we were at our destination. I hopped out of the taxi and turned toward Sully. "Are you coming?" I asked.

I flew down the subway entrance, swiped my MetroCard, and made for the trash can where I'd seen Bevins ditch his package. I hoped no street person had gone through the contents yet.

Sully caught up as I was about to stick my hand down into the can. "Wait," he said. "There could be anything in there." He looked around, made sure no one was coming our way and dumped the contents out onto the station floor.

I spotted the package Bevins had tossed right away and picked it up quickly. Sully righted the can and we got out of there as fast as possible. We didn't need trouble with the transit police on top of everything else.

Outside, my adrenaline rush subsiding, I sat on a bench and slowly opened the package. Sully was peering over my shoulder as I unwrapped it.

Inside was Jim Deems's red baseball cap, and tucked into it was a knife with a wicked-looking blade.

I stifled a scream. He'd had the knife with him at dinner, and if he'd had the opportunity, he would have used it to kill me.

Sully came to the same realization. He hugged me tight and said, "Let's go home, Jude."

It was well into the morning hours and Sully was right. Home was where I needed to be. Tomorrow I'd face Garlinger, give her the knife, and let her rebuke me for my actions. Then, I'd start looking for Bevins again.

Chapter Thirty

I was in my apartment, doors and windows locked tight, and was still trying not to jump at every sound. John Lennon's song about instant karma kept repeating over and over in my head.

Did I have bad karma? I'd never hurt anyone so what was that all about? I'd have to shake off this awful feeling. My sleep had been fitful and now it was time to get ready for work.

That afternoon, Pete and I were sitting down to plan the menu for Restaurant Week, the twice-yearly event during which many upscale restaurants offered a weekday two-course lunch and a three-course dinner for a reasonable set price, along with a few wine selections and a specialty cocktail, also at discounted prices. Pete's food had been garnering praise from foodies and food critics and he'd been so excited at the opportunity to showcase The Lounge for the first time. I hoped he still was.

For our first time hosting Restaurant Week, we'd be concentrating on a Monday through Friday dinner menu.

Pete was waiting for me when I arrived, our menu and notepad on the table.

He got right to it. Not a word about Bevins.

"I was thinking I'd pull a few of the best sellers from here." He pointed to our regular menu. Pete, ran his eyes down the list of appetizers and entrees we served daily. "Then add one or two special items. We have to think about costs, but still give the diners a reason to come back," he added, tapping his pen on the notepad in front of him.

I nodded, wondering if his comment about cost had anything to do with the restaurant broker who was due to show up on Monday.

"Okay." I moved closer and looked at the menu with him. "How about our Pan-seared salmon?" Quick seared in butter and surrounded by red lentils and fingerling roasted potatoes, it was one of our most popular dishes. Just talking about it, I could practically taste how delicious it was.

"Perfect," Pete said, then ran his finger further down the menu. "Let's also do the roast chicken breast with rosemary, sautéed broccoli rabe, and sliced almonds, and our famous house burger with cheddar cheese and crispy onion tower."

Discussing our menu seemed so normal, just like things used to be between us.

"Jude?" Pete called my name. "Are you with me?"

"Practically in a food coma," I said, gliding over the fact that I'd been thinking about our past.

"Well, we need to include a pasta and a vegetarian option, as well," Pete added. "Alain could do his homemade linguine carbonara and I'll make that cauliflower and eggplant ragout with couscous and harissa that you liked."

I nodded eagerly. Going over the menu made me realize how hungry I was. We hadn't had lunch as we usually did when we met to discuss business at The Lounge, another change I'd have to get used to.

We'd saved the appetizers and dessert for last. I pointed to two of my favorites. First the appetizers. "I'd choose the field greens with cherry tomatoes and walnuts in a mustard dressing, and carrot, ginger, and turmeric soup." I licked my lips.

"Sounds good." Pete nodded. "We can add oysters on the half shell and figs stuffed with Manchego and wrapped in prosciutto for an extra charge."

Many restaurants did that for Restaurant Week, as well, so I was sure it would be fine. "And now for dessert," I said, looking over the menu.

"I think I've got that covered." Pete smiled at me, the first genuine one I'd seen from him in a while.

"I think two should be good, your favorite, mixed-up ice cream, and mini apple and pear tarts with caramel and chocolate sauces." He sat back, satisfied that we'd nailed the menu.

Mixed-up ice cream was my creation. Whenever I felt the need for that delicious treat, I'd go in the kitchen for a scoop or two of vanilla ice cream and raid the cupboard for chunks of dark chocolate, raisins, and a swirl of peanut butter, which I mixed with abandon. As a matter of fact, I could have used some right then.

"Okay, for the wine special, how about a Vermentino and a Malbec?" I made a note on my pad to call our wine supplier and place an order for several cases of each. "Let me think about a cocktail."

"Good." Pete gathered up his notes and the menu and stood up. "I'll be in my office, working on the produce and meat order for the weekend. I'll email it to you as soon as it's done."

I nodded and waited until he'd left for his tiny office at the back of the kitchen. Then I headed to my office downstairs and sat at my desk. I put my head in my hands and sighed aloud. Even though our meeting had gone better than expected, I was still sad at the idea of Pete leaving the business.

I don't know how long I sat there until an email on my computer alerted me to Pete's order. I placed it with our vendor, made sure we'd have it on time, then went back upstairs to get the bar ready for the day. No matter what I was feeling inside, outside, it was business as usual.

Chapter Thirty-One

The Lounge had been crazy busy, even for a Friday night. Dean and I were slammed from the start and I thought about the chaos that happened at the opening bell at the Stock Exchange. I was done in by closing time and happy that tomorrow was my day off. Tony had stopped in, took one look around, and left in a hurry. Sully also had come and gone, thankfully on his own this time. I didn't think I would have been able to take another dose of Dolores. I shuddered just thinking about her.

Eltee didn't let me out of his sight. Every time the phone rang, he'd raise his eyebrows at me. I knew he was hoping it was Agent Garlinger with good news. Each time, I'd shake my head, no.

Like one of Sully's marines focused on a target, he waited while I locked up. Eltee was determined to protect me and still blaming himself for not spotting Bevins at dinner the other night.

"Here you go," he said, after walking me out the back, testing the handle on the door to make sure it was locked, and nodding at the two F.B.I agents who were stationed in the alley. He deposited me in front of the entrance to my building and said goodnight.

"Thanks." I smiled. "See you tomorrow."

When I got off the elevator, I noticed there was a light spilling out from under the door of my neighbors. Tom and Marie O'Day were voracious mystery readers and were probably still up, each engrossed in one of the many books they purchased on a regular basis. It was nice to have neighbors you liked living next door, as opposed to nasty ones like on the floor above.

As I put my key in the lock, I froze. I thought I heard a noise from inside the apartment. Was someone there, or was it just the building giving out one of its random creaks?

Heart pounding, I turned the key as slowly as possible trying not to make a sound. When the lock finally gave way, I held my breath and inched the door open millimeter by millimeter until I could see my living room through a small crack. It was exactly as when I left it, my clothes strewn on the couch, coffee table holding my computer, phone charger, and coffee mug.

I eased the door open just a bit more and all looked fine. I was torn. Tom and Marie were still awake. Should I knock on their door and ask for help? Or, would I be alarming them for no reason?

Over the past year, since I became involved with Jim Deems and Art Bevins, I'd taken self-defense classes. It was all fine in practice, but if it came down to it, would I be able to protect myself from an attacker…someone who really and truly was determined to see me dead?

I took my cell phone out and punched in 911, ready to hit send if I had to. I took a deep breath and slid into the room. It was then that I noticed the door to my bedroom was closed.

I started to back out slowly, deciding I'd go to the O'Day's, rather than confront my intruder. Just then, the bedroom door opened.

I let out a startled cry and dropped my phone, bringing my hands to my mouth.

"Jude," was all Eric said before I propelled myself into his arms and kissed him like I was resuscitating a drowning man.

The kiss was long and passionate. About halfway through, my mind caught up with my body, and I pushed Eric away from me as hard as I could, then slapped him across the face.

"What the hell are you doing here?" I flung the words at him. "Get out. Now." I was ashamed I'd run into his arms, and I could feel my face burning red.

"Jude, wait." He held up his hands in front of him. "Please, let me explain."

"Just go. There's nothing to explain." I could feel the pulse in my throat beating thunderously loud. I pointed to the door.

"Please," he said again, "I'm sorry I just showed up. I was worried about you." He tried to take one of my hands in both of his, but I pulled away.

"I left because I was hurt. All the lies, the going behind my back…I couldn't take it."

"So, you just walked out, without a word? I practically begged you to come back and you—"

"I'm so sorry." He hung his head.

"Well, that's too little, too late. Sorry's not enough." I looked him in the eye. "You need to leave." I stood back giving him a clear path to my front door.

"I'm not leaving." He stood in front of me, hands crossed over his chest.

"Well, I am. You'd better be gone in the next five minutes," I said as I walked into the bedroom and slammed the door behind me.

It took me a while to calm down, the adrenaline rush from my fight with Eric taking time to subside. I sat on my bed and was so tired before I knew it, I was asleep.

When I woke up still tired, the knotted mess that was my bedding, confirmed my sleep hadn't been restful.

I got up and tossed on some jeans and a t-shirt, and quietly opened the bedroom door.

Eric was under a pile of blankets on the couch, snoring up a storm. He smiled in his sleep and snuggled down further into the cocoon. Against my will, a small grin of my own crept across my face.

Men, I thought, as I moved into the kitchen to make a pot of coffee.

Sleeping beauty boy woke up when I waved the strong Latino coffee he loved under his nose. He sat up and I handed him the mug. We had a lot to talk about.

I poured myself a mug of coffee and sat down next to him. "So," I asked, looking him in the eye, "why exactly are you here?"

He gazed back, giving me as good as he'd got. "I love you, Jude. And I miss you."

He paused for a moment and put his mug down on the coffee table. Eric went quiet and looked down at the floor.

My stomach clenched and I was sure I wasn't going to like what he was about to tell me.

He lifted his deep brown eyes to mine. "I heard about what happened with Art Bevins, the letter, coming in for dinner, and Pete planning to leave The Lounge. I didn't want you to face all that alone."

"How?"

"How what?" I could tell my question surprised him.

"How did you hear about Bevins?" I lifted my hand as if to encompass the whole mess that was behind, and in front, of me. "It was Sully, wasn't it? Mister Marine couldn't help himself. He had to tell you, so you could come back and protect me." A fit of new anger was making my voice shake. "I don't need your protection."

Eric was shaking his head the whole time I was speaking. "That's not what I'm offering. I do love you, and I want us to be together." He moved toward me and put his arms around me. I didn't resist. I realized I loved him, too. Even still, I hated to admit that what happened between us was mostly my fault.

We sat together for a long time discussing everything that had taken place since he left. We both made promises to each other about commitment and honesty. I knew Eric would keep his. I just hoped I could do the same.

Chapter Thirty-Two

Eric was driving back to his apartment in the Bronx to pick up some of his things and bring them here. He was moving back in, and I was happy about it.

He was going to stop to see his parents, Cecelia and Roberto, and let them know we were back together. I wasn't sure how they'd feel about that.

Before he left, I told him about Dolores Castel and her assistant, Diego. "There's something wrong there." I shook my head. "Her taking an apartment downtown and him living with her. A little kinky. It doesn't make sense. She's definitely more uptown."

I could see from his doubtful expression he was seriously trying to decide how to tell me I was probably overthinking things as usual.

Instead, he said: "Is that what's bothering you? That she doesn't fit in? Maybe she's looking for a change." He shrugged.

"No. It's more than that. It's her interest in Sully. I think it's phony, and she's out for something." I sighed. "I wish I had more to go on."

"You sound a little bit jealous." His voice was teasing but his eyes were serious.

"Of course, I'm not. Sully's like…a dad to me. I don't want him to get hurt." *Or worse,* I thought. That was true.

"I'm going to Google her."

"Do you think that's a good idea?" He made a face as he asked the question.

"We just promised to be totally honest with each other, so I'm not going to lie to you. My instinct is screaming at me that something's off. I want to find out what it is. I'll be discreet."

Eric had the good sense not to tell me that my instinct had gotten me into trouble before and that I hardly knew the meaning of the word discreet.

We said we'd see each other for dinner. I told him I'd find somewhere nice and romantic. I could always take him to Pourquoi on Prince Street and mention Dolores's name. Explain she'd recommended the restaurant. I expect I'd get a blank stare for my trouble.

Don't be a brat, I told myself. Besides, that would be stupid.

After Eric left, I flipped open my laptop and typed in Dolores Castel. I didn't find much about her. There was a photo of her with her husband, Olivier, in front of their home in California, the couple looking golden in the sunlight, surrounded by beautiful blue flowers. Nothing about a decorating business, or business of any kind.

There was also a link to an obituary for Olivier Georges Castel in the *Los Angeles Times.* A successful businessman from Southern California, he'd died a few months ago. The short piece listed some of his accomplishments and noted cause of death had been a heart attack he'd suffered while hiking in the hills near Santa Monica. It was brief and to the point. Nor was there any other information about the family.

I wondered if Dolores had been with him when he became ill.

I found it strange that Olivier Castel's obituary was the only other link that came up for Dolores Castel. If I searched my name, I knew a ton of links would pop up, most of which I could do without. Maybe Dolores led a charmed life. Or maybe it was something else.

The only way to find out everything was to do the kind of background search on her that I couldn't do on my own. That meant using my friend and private investigator, Lena Larsson.

I checked my watch and decided I'd make the next class at the Spin City Gym over on First Avenue. Lena usually took the Saturday afternoon class. I would tell her the truth—that I was worried about Sully and his relationship with Dolores Castel. That she seemed a little shady. That if she could do just a cursory background check, it would help a lot. I hoped Lena'd go for my idea to barter food and drink, since paying for her services was not in my meager budget, especially now.

As I left the apartment, Marie O'Day opened the door and came out into the hallway. "Are you okay?" she asked. "I thought I heard some shouting from your apartment late last night." She paused. "I made Tom get up and we listened for a while in case you needed us." She had the good grace to look sheepish. "Then, we heard Eric's voice and we figured everything was alright. Is it?"

I smiled and nodded. "It's fine. Eric surprised me, that's all." I shrugged. "With everything that's been going on, I didn't take it very well." I knew the O'Days were aware Eric had been gone for a while but I didn't feel like explaining.

Marie patted me on the arm. "Glad to hear you're okay. I'll let Tom know. Say hello to Eric for us."

I promised that I would, and hit the button for the elevator. I'd have to hustle if I wanted to get to spin class on time. When I got back, I'd go find Sully and let him know exactly how much I appreciated him calling Eric.

I made it to class with barely three minutes to spare. This spin class was very intense and competitive, even though there was a big sign at the front of the studio that stated 'No Judgements.' I usually liked to have more time to warm up my legs and get in the groove. I chose a bike near Lena, sat down, and started pedaling. "Buy you a coffee after class?" I asked.

Lena nodded yes, giving me a look that said she knew I was up to something. Then everything else melted away as I tried to keep up with the instructions our over-caffeinated teacher screamed out for the next sixty minutes.

After I showered and changed into street clothes, I met Lena in the studio's lounge. "Instead of a coffee, how about a shake?" She nodded toward the juice bar tucked in the corner of the room.

"Okay," I agreed and we walked over. Lena ordered something very green and very healthy. I opted for something fruitier. Then we seated ourselves on the cushions in the bay window that faced Twelfth Street.

"How can I help you, Jude?" She knew I wanted something. Lena was a private investigator, after all, as well as a blonde-haired, blue-eyed Swedish goddess.

I spilled out all my misgivings about Dolores Castel and her assistant. How she'd moved so fast. How I believed she was trying to manipulate Sully. And the reason I thought she was lying about not living here before.

"What do you think her motives are?" Lena asked.

"I'm not sure. Nothing good." I gestured with my shake. "It could be money. Although Sully's not rich."

"Are you sure it was her assistant who was following you?"

"Positively. He's wasn't very good at it, either. I spotted him right away."

"Well…" Lena slurped up the rest of her green glop. "I can do a basic search but it's going to take a few days. We're swamped right now."

I raised my eyebrow questioningly.

"A big insurance thing," was all she would say.

I thanked her and promised her dinner for a year for being such a good pal. She knew I meant it, especially the pal part. It was her findings that had helped me save Sully from a deranged killer last year.

We said goodbye outside the gym and I headed home feeling lighter than I had in a while. Eric was back. Lena was on the case. I had helpers I could call on. Now, all I needed was for the Feds to catch Art Bevins and bury him forever like the piece of garbage he was.

Chapter Thirty-Three

When I got home, I put together some information to send Lena. I described Dolores as best as I could. She said she was from Southern California. Probably LA if Olivier's obituary was anything to go by.

I thought she might be fifty or a bit older. I reminded Lena I thought that Dolores might have lived in New York City at some point. That wasn't much to go on, but it was all I had for the moment. Next time Dolores was in The Lounge, I'd try to take a cell phone photo of her without her noticing and shoot it to Lena. I could pretend to be on a call.

I added this to the other information I had on Dolores, which amounted to very little, and emailed it to Lena. Linking Dolores with Olivier might help her turn up more information. Now, I'd just have to wait and see.

If I could get Sully on his own, and make it seem subtle, I'd ask him more about Dolores. I'd have to make it more of a conversation than an interrogation. That might be hard to do without getting his antennae twitching. Subtle was another one of those things I didn't do very well.

After I sent my email, I reserved a table for two at a romantic new restaurant in Tribeca. Pete had mentioned wanting to try it and that was good enough for me.

By the time Eric returned home, I was almost done primping for our evening out. I decided to go all-in with the Pierre Cardin mini dress I'd originally chosen for Shivani's party, along with the accessories and the sleek Twiggy look.

I thought I looked pretty good. So did Eric if his expression was anything to go by. "Wow!" he said as he dropped his suitcase on the living room floor and rushed over to give me a kiss. "You look fantastic." He could have been a businessman returning home to his gussied-up-for-him wife.

I batted my mascaraed out-to-there eyelashes at him. "Thanks," I said. Glad you like it." I gave him one more peck on his cheek, then told him to go get ready for dinner.

While he went to change, I was tempted to peek into The Lounge to see how busy we were, but I knew if I did, I get caught up in conversation with one or two of my customers. Maybe, we'd stop in later after dinner.

I gazed out the window as I listened to Eric humming as he shaved. It was a show tune, one of the rap numbers from "Hamilton," which he sang in his off-key, shaky tenor voice. Lin-Manuel Miranda had nothing to worry about. Me neither, at least for the moment. Eric could sing the worst rendition of the Star-Spangled Banner and it would still make me happy to listen.

I hoped he'd like the restaurant, which offered a modern fusion of French and Asian cooking. The menu I'd looked at online sounded delicious, especially the tasting menu that could be perfect for sampling many of their signature dishes. I'd let Eric take the lead on that.

I was still standing by the window staring out at the night, a few minutes later when Eric came out. He walked over and put his arms around me.

"Happy?" he asked.

"I am. Really," I replied, smiling up at him and surprising myself that I believed it. *I just hope it will last.*

The restaurant was fabulous. A beautiful setting with amazing food. We both chose the ten omnivore tasting menu designed for people who eat everything. I'd never eaten such delicious food, which I would definitely not mention to Pete. From the caviar in fried wontons to caramelized foie gras in a ginger sauce, and venison dusted with herbs over red cabbage, to a pear vanilla cream crumble—and everything in between, it was a feast for the eyes as well as the taste buds.

Sitting back and sipping an espresso, I looked at Eric with a loopy grin on my face, probably from all the wine I'd drunk. "Can you believe they're charging extra for the coffee?" I whispered. "Especially after what dinner cost?" He'd be spending serious bank tonight.

"You're worth every penny. Even if I can't pay my rent this month." He lifted his hands to the ceiling. "I've never had a meal like this."

"Me neither," I agreed.

"Maybe Pete should do a tasting menu for The Lounge."

I started to laugh. "I don't think our customers would go for the two-hundred-dollar-a-person tab."

"You're probably right. Not to mention the wine bill." He picked up his glass of wine and tipped the remaining sip into his mouth.

"Don't lick the glass," I said, leaning in close.

As Eric paid the bill, I realized it would be nice to have a tasting menu at The Lounge, maybe nothing as ambitious, or expensive as this one. Unfortunately, that reminded me that I'd have to find a new chef to create it.

I sighed quietly and kept the smile on my face. I didn't want Eric to see that my mood had shifted and spoil our perfect evening, so I buried that thought. *Just enjoy tonight with the man you love,* I told myself. *Somehow, everything else will fall into place.*

We took an Uber home and decided to stop in at The Lounge. Like a junkie jonesing for crack, I had to have my fix. Well, I wanted to see if Sully was in.

He was. Along with the formidable Dolores. They were sitting at a table in the cocktail lounge, talking quietly.

I squeezed Eric's hand as we moved into the bar and greeted some customers. "Well, you're in for a treat. Look who's here." I nodded toward their table.

Sully must have felt me looking at him. He turned and waved, then said something to Dolores as he stood up, and walked toward us.

"Eric." Sully grabbed his hand and shook it like he was priming a pump to get the water flowing. "It's so good to see you."

I didn't miss the thank-god-you're-back-to-keep-her-under-control look, he shot at Eric. Those bright blue eyes sure could say a lot.

I gave Sully a look of my own that said "We'll be talking about this later."

Ignoring me, he kept speaking to Eric. "Hope you can join us. I'd like you to meet your new neighbor and my friend, Dolores Castel."

He didn't wait for a reply. Just started walking back to where Dolores was staring into a glass of wine as if she were a million miles away. I only wished.

"Think I'm invited, too?" I whispered to Eric as we followed Sully.

"Behave yourself, Jude." Eric pinched me and whispered.

I pasted a serene smile on my face and took a seat as Sully made the introductions. Dolores was dressed in a deep red sheath that was almost purple. Instead of clashing with her auburn hair, it accentuated it.

"You look lovely, Dolores," I said, without meaning it.

"And, you look…very Sixties, Jude." She took in my outfit.

Well, now that we'd gotten that out of the way, Sully took over. He explained that Eric owned an accounting firm and helped me with the books for The Lounge. Then, he gave Eric a brief history of how Dolores wound up on the Lower East Side.

While he was speaking, I took my cell phone out and pretended I had to answer a message. "Excuse me," I mouthed and walked a few feet away, opened the cell's camera as I turned. When I turned back toward the table, I pretended to text and snapped a few shots of Dolores.

I didn't think she'd notice as I could see her attention was elsewhere. She was obviously more than pleased to meet Eric. Had she learned her moves from living among actresses in LA, and using all the tricks she'd picked up? Her body language was sending a message, as she leaned in, stared into Eric's eyes, and seemed to hang onto his every word. If Sully noticed her attention had shifted, he didn't let on. But I could see Eric was becoming uncomfortable.

When I sat back down, I nudged Eric under the table. It was time to go. I said I had to open early for brunch tomorrow and had a million things to take care of. Eric mentioned he had some client work, as well.

Dolores didn't miss a beat. "Eric, I've been looking for an accountant to help straighten out my finances." She paused and put a hand over his on the table in a gesture meant to be sincere, but failing miserably. "Moving from California has left me in a bit of tailspin. Perhaps you could help me?"

This time I gave Eric a kick under the table.

"Let me look at my schedule, and I'll let you know." We both stood up. "Nice to meet you, Dolores."

"Oh, the pleasure was all mine," she replied, and tilted her head to the side, auburn hair cascading over one eye. Bet she practiced that one a lot.

Eric didn't speak until we were out of The Lounge. "Whoo! You were right, Jude. She's a barracuda. Poor Sully."

"He's so smitten, he didn't even notice her blatant flirting." I made a face. "She wanted me to notice it, that's for sure."

I turned to look at Eric. "You didn't like her, did you?" I knew I must have sounded horrified that he might have.

He started to laugh. "Are you kidding? I think she's everything you said she was, and worse." Then he sobered. "What are we going to do about Sully?"

I thought of an expression my Grandma Ree used to say: "There's no fool like an old fool." Sully wasn't that old, but he was surely behaving like a fool. We'd just have to figure out how to save him from himself.

Chapter Thirty-Four

I slipped out of bed and emailed my shots of Dolores to Lena first thing the next morning. Eric was still sleeping, which was fine by me.

We talked about Dolores Castel before we went to bed, and decided we'd have to keep a watchful eye on Sully until we could figure out what game she was playing.

Eric also reminded me to be careful. He was worried that Art Bevins would try to contact me again, or worse. I agreed to watch out for any weird or strange people, and I reminded him that I would have two F.B.I. agents as guards at The Lounge until Bevins was caught.

I showered and dressed and left Eric a note that I'd be downstairs setting up, and whenever he was ready, there'd be a large pot of Cubano café waiting for him.

Eltee was already inside when I got there. His plan was to stick to me like glue. I truly appreciated it but told him to go into the kitchen and grab some breakfast. When he balked about leaving me alone behind the bar, I reminded him that brunch was usually very busy, and he needed to fuel up. I didn't have to tell him twice.

Finally, I was alone—if I didn't count the two Fibbies standing guard at the door—getting in the grove for my shift. This was my favorite time. Time when I could stand behind my beautiful bar and get it ready for my customers. No distractions or interruptions. That is until Sully walked in.

He sat in his usual seat and waited until I walked over and joined him. "

"You're here early," I said.

"Yeah, I know you're not open yet. I just wanted to talk." He took a deep breath. "So, what did Eric think of Dolores?" His voice was hopeful, and his eyes as big as a puppy dog's waiting for a treat.

I'm sure I stood there for a minute gaping like a caught fish. I finally got hold of myself and replied. "He thought she was…nice." This wasn't as easy as I was trying to make it look. "Smart, attractive, a well-rounded woman."

Did I actually just say that? Not that Sully noticed. "Good. Good." He nodded for emphasis. "I knew he'd like her. Do you think he'd help her with her financial stuff?"

Oh, brother! This was worse than I expected. I had to cut this conversation short. I even forgot that I was still annoyed at Sully for calling Eric about my problems.

"You know, Eric will be in later. You could probably ask him then." I smiled and put down the glass I'd been polishing. "I have to go speak to Pete before we open. You know, the restaurant broker is coming in tomorrow, and there are a few things we have to discuss."

"Sure. Go. I'll come in later for brunch when Eric is here. See you then."

I nodded as he left the bar. I'd have to warn Eric Sully might corner him, and ask his opinion of Dolores. I was sure he'd be better than me at deflecting Sully's questions. As if Art Bevins wasn't enough to worry about, now I had to deal with Sully's new mad love. I could share Eric's true feelings about Dolores, that, like me, he thought she was out for something, but would Sully believe me? Probably not.

Then, I had a thought. Maybe Eric could take over my fact-finding mission on Dolores. He could use the pretext of helping her with straightening out her finances. It might just work. Sully would be way less suspicious of Eric than of me.

In the meantime, I did have to speak with Pete. As soon as Dean came in, I asked him to finish setting up while I went into the kitchen.

Pete was in his office checking the weekly brunch menu we printed, chair tilted back against the wall. He gave me a big smile, and for a second it was like old times.

"All set for brunch?" I asked. "Have enough Challah for your world-famous, Bourbon-infused French toast?" I tapped the menu on his desk. It had become our most popular brunch item, and Pete had gotten tired of making it.

"Very funny," he said and tossed a paper clip at me. He peeked around me and looked into the kitchen's workspace. It was buzzing with activity. "Got to get back out there soon. Alain looks a little frazzled." He set his chair back down on all four legs. "Anything important going on?"

I knew he was asking about Bevins, not The Lounge. "No new news," I replied. "But I wanted to remind you that the restaurant broker was coming in tomorrow morning at ten. I'll take him through the bar, dining room, liquor, and wine storage room, go over the books, all that stuff. Then, I'll turn him over to you for the kitchen info." Pete nodded while I was speaking.

"It might take a couple of hours, so maybe I'll bring him back here around noon."

"I'll be here," he said. "Jude, I—"

I cut him off with a wave of my hand. "I got to get back out front before the natives break down the doors." I put a smile on my face, but it only lasted until the door to the kitchen swung shut behind me.

Eric came in a few minutes later and sat at the bar with a big cup of coffee in front of him. We'd have something to eat after brunch was over.

"I need to warn you about Sully," I said.

Eric looked up at me startled. "Warn me? Why?"

"He wants to know your opinion of Dolores."

"Jeez, what am I going to tell him?" Eric looked like he wanted to be anywhere but here. "I don't want to be involved, and now I feel like I'm being pushed into the middle."

"Just say you thought she was nice. Then tell him you might be able to help with her finances."

"This is a bad idea." Eric shook his head. "I'm not sure I can do this."

"You can. Try and find out whatever you can about her from him. Her background. Where she lived." I paused. "He won't mind talking about her. And, he's so happy that you're back to 'take care of me,' he'll tell you whatever you want to know."

Eric's eyes were glazing over. "Jude, I...lying to Sully? It doesn't sound right."

I could see this was not going over very well. "You'll be helping to protect him. It's for his own good."

Where had I heard that before? Oh yeah, I remembered. From my mother.

Chapter Thirty-Five

Elaine Garlinger came into The Lounge a little while later and took a seat at the bar. I could feel a knot working its way up from my stomach to my throat as I walked over to greet her.

"Any news?" I asked, as calmly as possible. Although I knew if there had been, she would have already told me.

I'd turned over the package Sully and I found in the trash at the Fourteenth-street station. Maguire took it to the lab, although he hadn't been happy about it.

A slight smile crossed her face. "There is one thing. As soon as we got the knife and Deems's cap we added them to the jacket from the alleyway. One of the lab techs ran everything through our GC machine to see if any microscopic substances might be on them."

"A what?" I asked. I didn't remember seeing that on *CSI.*

I could sense Elaine thinking of how to explain it so I'd understand. "A gas chromatography machine. It separates microscopic chemical components to determine what elements are present and how much is present."

"And, that's important, why?" I still wasn't sure what we were talking about.

"It helps pick up trace evidence, or residue, like from a wine glass, or oil from fibers," she added.

"So did the tech find anything you could identify?" I asked

"Yes. Traces of light-colored limestone on the jacket and cap, probably quarried from the city's bedrock during the Gilded Age of the early Eighteenth-century plus marble, as well, and residue of calcium carbonate, or blackboard chalk."

Chalk? It'd been around for a long time. I thought of the boarded-up Blackthorne Collier building—once a school—and once again, the feeling I'd had that someone was watching me. Was Bevins using the building as a hideout? "I…" I started to say, then stopped. "How will knowing this help you find Bevins? Why didn't you tell me about it before?"

"I'd put it aside until we could investigate further."

"And, now, you can?" *She was up to something and playing it close to the vest.*

"Sorry." She looked down at her hands clenched together, then up at me. "We're still checking all the CCTV feeds from the stations. He may have gone back down to the subway."

"You're wasting your time." *Time I didn't have.* "The subway was just a ruse. I'm sure he didn't go back there."

"How's Sully?" She asked, changing the subject. "Is he still angry with me?" I could hear a touch of regret in her voice. Though they wouldn't be a couple again, I believed she thought they could stay friends. Of course, it seemed the manhunt for Art Bevins was making that impossible.

What could I say? "I think he's just preoccupied with building stuff."

She gave me a sort of 'hmmm,' then picked up the menu. "I'm starving. What do you recommend?" she asked.

"The eggs benedict with smoked salmon is one of my favorites," I replied.

"Sounds yummy. With a Virgin Mary, please." She slid off the barstool and moved toward the front of the restaurant. "Let me check in with my guys first."

When Elaine came back to the bar, Eric was there. He'd taken the seat next to her, and they began to chat. I watched her with a sideways look now and then, as I served the rest of my customers. She looked pale, her face strained, and her eyes clouded. Chasing a serial killer could do that to you. Not capturing him could do even worse.

Sully came in just after Elaine left The Lounge. He said a quick hello to Oscar and some of his pals at the bar, then made straight for Eric. I made myself scarce as they began to chat. There was no way I wanted to be involved in that conversation.

Sully was doing a lot of gesturing with his hands and Eric was nodding sagely. After about fifteen minutes, while Sully was making a note on a bar napkin, Eric gave me a wild-eyed help signal. It was time to rescue him.

"Hey, Sully," I said. "Oscar wants to know if you're ready to eat?"

"Yeah, sure." He got up and patted Eric on the shoulder. "Thanks. We'll talk soon." He left Eric's side and walked over to Oscar.

"Don't ask." Eric flashed the bar napkin in front of me. I could see it had a phone number written on it. "I'll tell you after we eat, or you might lose your appetite."

"It must be serious, since you know I never lose my appetite." I leaned over the bar and kissed him on the cheek. "I guess it can keep until then."

Eric and I never did get to talk over what Sully had told him about Dolores. We fell into bed, and were both so tired after Saturday night and Sunday's busy schedule.

Chapter Thirty-Six

Saturday night had struck just the right note. Dolores met Sully at The Lounge for drinks. After two shots of Jameson for him and a vodka martini for her, they were enjoying a lovely chat.

Sully had on a light blue collared shirt with a sports jacket and looked rather handsome. *I could have done worse,* she thought, smiling up at him, *remembering some of the bloated, egotistical men she'd met in her younger days in the city.*

She felt the admiring glances Sully was sending her way. As usual, Dolores had taken pains with her appearance. When Jude had complimented her, she knew her deep red sheath had been a perfect choice. She left her auburn hair loose and falling over her shoulders. She tossed it from time to time to let the light catch its shimmering highlights.

Dolores had thought about the best way to bring up her plan of starting a small design business in New York, an extension of what she'd been doing in California. Low key was the way to go, telling Sully she'd get to it when the timing was right and her finances were in order.

Instinctively, he knew it was more about the money. She brushed off his concerns about her finances with an "I'll manage," then changed the subject before he could ask too many more questions. There hadn't been any design business at all and she didn't want to run the risk of getting caught in a lie by making up too many stories.

They discussed art and the possibility of attending another gallery opening next week. Sully was very enthusiastic. She smiled to herself. It seemed like he'd do almost anything to please her.

They were in the midst of this conversation when Jude came into The Lounge, with whom Dolores imagined, was 'the boyfriend,' Eric Ramirez. He was very good-looking and from what Sully had told her, very bright. Time would tell, she thought as Sully went over to greet the couple and invite them to the table.

Now, this could get interesting She'd smiled as she greeted Eric and Jude warmly.

After the couple left, she felt quite satisfied. She had flirted shamelessly with Eric. Sully didn't seem to realize what she was doing, but Jude did. She'd done it mostly to annoy the young woman.

"Dolores, would you like another drink?" Sully motioned to her empty martini glass.

She gave him a big smile. "I have a better idea. Why don't we have a nightcap in my apartment? Just give me a minute, would you?"

She rose and walked to the back of the restaurant as if she were going to the restroom. Once inside, she pulled out her cell and punched in Diego's cell number.

"Hello," he answered in an upbeat tone.

"Diego, darling, are you at home?" Dolores didn't want any surprises this evening.

"No, Dolores. I'm out with friends for dinner. We might stop at The Lounge, after. Will we see you and Sully there?" Now his voice was taunting.

"Probably not," she replied. Have a good time, and Diego, stay out as late as you like. He was getting a little too sure of himself. She'd have to remind him of why they were here.

She walked back to the table where Sully was waiting. She could see the anticipation in his eyes. Unfortunately, he was going to be a little disappointed. Oh, they'd have some fun, but he'd have to wait for the main event. It would make the chase all that much sweeter.

Upstairs, Dolores glanced around the apartment. With its soft lighting and the simple pieces she'd chosen, it looked comfortable, yet elegant. She had always admired Yoko Ono for buying up those apartments at the Dakota to create the home she'd always wanted. Dolores had owned several homes, but not two buildings on prime real estate in Manhattan.

Chapter Thirty-Seven

The next morning, Eric was up before me and off to work at his office in the Bronx. *See you for dinner,* his note on the pillow said in his neat accountant's script. *Love you, E.*

Love you, too. I thought, as I got up and prepared to face the day, Judgement Day, as I'd been secretly calling it. The restaurant broker was coming at ten and it was important for me to be ready.

I was downstairs by nine-thirty, giving my bar an extra polish to make sure it looked its best. The coffee was brewed and everything else was in order. I was ready. Sort of.

At ten on the dot, Mark Brandon walked in with a smile on his face. A tall man with bright blue eyes, he extended his hand and introduced himself in a way that made me feel comfortable. He mentioned that he and Carol Batista had worked together in the past on assignments like this one and he was sure we'd find the right solution.

His professionalism put me at ease and I offered him coffee, which he accepted.

We sat at the bar and Mark took out a notebook and several pages with headings and columns under each. He tapped the pages with his pen. "We'll go over things one at a time. That okay with you?"

"Sure." I nodded.

"But first, why don't we just sit and talk a bit. Tell me about The Corner Lounge." He took a sip of his coffee, then put the mug down and waited for me to begin.

Surprisingly, the story just flowed out of me. I told him how Pete and I had known each other from various places where we'd both worked, and how we decided to put our talents together and open The Lounge.

"Pete is a fantastic chef and our customers love his food. I run the bar and the front of the house." I paused. "Of course, none of this would ever have happened without our great landlord, Thomas Sullivan, who owns the building." I could feel my throat filling up and took a deep breath. "He believed in us and has helped us every step of the way."

Mark was nodding his head as if he'd known this, which he probably already had, from Carol.

"Not everyone is fortunate enough to have that kind of support behind them," he said.

I dipped my head. I knew how lucky we'd been.

"Now, I think we should take a look at evaluating The Lounge. We'll start here, with the bar."

A minute later, we were reviewing every item that was part of the bar—the bar itself, the back bar, the bottles of alcohol, the glasses, fruit, mats, bar naps, stirrers, coasters, refrigeration, sink, etc. I'd never realized there were so many moving parts. If I'd ever stopped to think about it, I might have gone crazy.

After that, we moved on to the cocktail lounge and dining room. Mark listed all the furniture, dishware, cutlery, napkins, workstations, coffee station, artwork on the walls. No detail was left unaccounted for. It was exhausting and going over every detail was making my head spin.

"Okay," he said, putting one list into his briefcase and removing another. "Let's hit the office and storage space next." Mark picked up his paperwork and, coffee and followed me down the stairs. I'd told him I'd turn him over to Pete so they could discuss the kitchen when we were done with my part.

Thankfully, the storage space was tidy. Our night porter kept it mopped and dusted. Metal shelves held our wine inventory, and cartons containing bottles of alcohol were stacked neatly with their contents written on the sides. Canned and boxed goods were stored on separate shelves for easy access. Mark measured the size of the space and made notes.

Next, we moved into my office which was not quite as pristine. I offered him the guest chair across from my desk and computer, and he spread out his papers. "Are your books up to date?" he asked.

"Yes." I smiled. Thankfully, Eric had made sure of that. He looked over our purveyor bills, wine and spirit bills, miscellaneous costs, and payroll with the attendant taxes, social security, and workman's comp deductions.

"I can see you're very thorough." He looked up from the books to me.

"Hmmm," I replied, silently thanking Eric once again.

He gathered up his papers and rose from the chair. Anything else I should see down here?"

I shrugged. "Not really. There's a big, open space just down the corridor past the office. Technically, it's not ours."

"Let's take a look."

"It's not really part of The Lounge," I said quickly. "It shouldn't figure into the evaluation, since no one uses it." I was afraid that would make my share even more expensive.

"Don't worry about that right now. Let's see what's there and we'll figure it out later."

I gulped and followed him into the space. It was pretty large and went past the width of my office and under the first floor of the building.

"I think Mr. Sullivan was planning to use this for something to do with the building." That just popped out of my mouth and I hoped he couldn't tell I was making it up as I was going along.

"You know, Jude, with just a little work, this could be a great room for a music venue or comedy club. It looks to be about thirty by forty feet, maybe bigger, with nice high ceilings. We can measure it later."

"Look Mark...Mr. Brandon...I'm going to have to come up with half of whatever The Corner Lounge is valued at. Adding things to the tab is not helpful." I gestured to the empty space and hoped my message was getting through.

"I think I might have a solution." He gave me a positive glance. "I know some people who would love to have a comedy club in this neighborhood. Comedy is getting bigger than ever. The group already owns a few clubs around the city and wants to expand." His head was going up and down.

"They have a great talent pool with more comics coming up all the time. They wouldn't be interested in running the kitchen or in your upstairs bar business. Just in the club angle."

He let this sink in. "Their investment, plus some cash from you, could let you buy out your partner and keep The Lounge, which Carol suggested you were hoping to do. Or, we could always look for a regular investor to pick up your partner's share or, someone interested in a total buyout."

"No…" I started to say, then stopped. It made me realize just how much I didn't want to lose The Lounge.

"Why don't we leave these options open for the moment and I'll go up and speak with your partner, Pete, and do the kitchen evaluation. When I have all the numbers together, we can all talk again, and get Carol involved." He gestured toward the stairs. "Sound okay to you?"

I nodded and led him back up to the restaurant. Pete was waiting in the kitchen. I introduced the two men. They shook hands as I left for the dining room. I could hear Pete speaking as he began to show Mark Brandon around, and started answering his questions.

I left them to it and went back behind the bar. I had even more to think about than I'd originally imagined. I'd have to talk all this over with Eric and get his take on having a comedy club downstairs, especially the financial ramifications. I had no idea if it made sense. And, I'd have to get Sully on board, too.

I didn't want to become too hopeful about keeping The Lounge, even though my heart was bursting at the thought that it might be possible.

Chapter Thirty-Eight

I grabbed my jacket and told my F.B.I. minders I needed some air and was going for a walk.

The taller one nodded. "Okay, ma'am. I'm with you. Agent Bojack will remain at The Lounge." He gestured toward his partner.

Ma'am? Who did he think I was, the Queen of England? Not to mention we were probably almost the same age. I gave him a look he could interpret however he wanted. Of course, left behind Agent Bojack would probably call Agent Garlinger as soon as I stepped out the door to update her on my unplanned sortie.

How lucky was I? It was like having my own Praetorian Guard marching behind me through the streets of Rome.

"How've you been, Maguire?" I asked my escort.

"Okay," he replied, surprised, I think, that I remembered him from our last adventure.

As we started walking, I looked over at the tall, handsome agent. " Just keep back and don't cramp my style. Behave yourself, and I might buy you, lunch," I added.

"Where? At The Lounge?"

I detected a note of sarcasm in his voice. I might have to tell Garlinger he needed a little more witness protection respect training.

With my Fibbie following, I headed up Avenue B and turned west on Eleventh street. I wanted to check out the Blackthorn Collier building again for myself before I mentioned my suspicions to Agent Garlinger. I'd gotten such weird vibes the last time I passed it. But that may have been from seeing Diego out front watching me.

All looked quiet today. No protestors. Just a few of the squatters sitting on the steps smoking and talking quietly. No lone eye peeked out from behind a boarded-up window to track my movements. I continued on my way and made a loop down to the river.

On the promenade, the wind was whipping around, causing the water to ripple and swirl in ever-changing patterns. Not too many boats were out and the river seemed as if it had been abandoned. It felt good to be there anyway, away from The Lounge and the problems facing me. Even if just for a few minutes. I watched a few gulls soaring above then turned and headed back home.

Time to check in with Pete, get his take on Mark Brandon, and get the bar ready to open. My minder, Maguire, was right behind. I hoped he wouldn't be too disappointed with one of Pete's special sandwiches, instead of a Nobu Bento box. We all had to make sacrifices sometimes, didn't we?

By five-thirty p.m., the bar was crowded and the dining room was filling up.

Everyone was hustling to get the drinks and orders out.

I was always happy when we were this busy. It made me feel successful, especially now that money was an issue.

I was chatting with two of my regular customers when Eric walked into the bar, I made my excuses to the two women who were enjoying Pomatinis and jutted my head toward downstairs. Eric looked confused but loped behind me to the office.

"A comedy club?" Eric said when I told him about Mark Brandon's suggestion. "Maybe I could try out a new career. You know, a boring accountant by day becomes a laugh-a-minute-comedian by night."

I threw a pen at him. "Yeah, the new Marvelous Mr. Maisel," I said.

"Well, what do you think? Good idea? Bad idea?" he asked.

I shrugged. "It could be a good thing. The neighborhood is really on an upswing. More buildings are being rehabbed, and new people are moving in. A club could bring more business to The Lounge for dinner, as well as for the comedy."

I stopped suddenly, a thought rushing through my mind. "But what about Sully? Do you think he'd be okay with it? It's his building after all, and his space." I paused. "He might need to invest money to fix up the room. He might not mind though, now that all the apartments are rented."

"If he has any money left," Eric replied solemnly.

"Wait? What are you talking about? Money? Sully has money. And the buildings, which some developer would scoop up for big bucks," I said. I knew he'd already been approached by a few of them.

Eric just stared at me and suddenly it clicked, like one of those Rubik's Cubes that finally twisted into place.

"What exactly did he tell you about Dolores?" I remembered how intense Sully seemed when he was speaking with Eric at the bar, and how he pressed Dolores' number on him.

"He said she wanted to continue the small design business she'd started in California, but was concerned about her finances."

"Oh, my God! Did she ask him for money?" I was livid. I could feel my face turning red.

"No." Eric grimaced. "She's too smart for that. She told Sully it was more of a long range-plan, something she'd put together when her finances were in better shape."

I thought about what Buster Dunlap had said about the discrepancy of the value of her California property. I'd bet she had no intention of sorting it out. I jumped up from my chair, nearly tipping it over. "That bi—"

Eric reached over and put his finger on my lips to stop me. "Whoa, take it easy, We're not going to let her get her hands on his money."

My head was bobbing up and down like a bobble doll in the back window of a muscle car. Knowing Sully, he probably already offered to help her out. And, of course, she'd refused, conniver that she was. I stopped moving and looked Eric in the eye. "You're right, we're not. You're going to do it," I said.

"Do what?" He asked, total confusion clouding his eyes.

I put a smile in my voice. "What Sully asked you to do. Help Dolores straighten out her finances. You'll be a pal and you'll find out what she's planning. Once we have what we need, we'll take her down."

Eric was the most upstanding man I knew. I could see from the way he was staring I'd hit an ethics nerve. He was torn between the need for justice and his responsibility of confidentiality to a client. He would never betray a trust.

"Jude…I…if she becomes a client—"

"Client?" I waved the word away like I was swatting a fly. You don't have to take her on as a client. I would never ask you to do that. Just keep it informal. Tell her it's a favor for a friend." *She'll love that,* I thought. "All free of charge." *And that even better.*

Chapter Thirty-Nine

We'd agreed to table the discussion about Dolores until I was done for the night. Eric went into the dining room to chat with some customers he knew.

A few minutes later my cell phone beeped and Agent Garlinger's number popped up.

I could feel the excitement in her voice over the phone. "Jude, I have some news." She took a deep breath before continuing. "We found Bevins."

Questions were flying out of my mouth and I felt as though my heart was beating double time. "How did you get him? Where was he hiding? Is he dead?"

As I spoke to her, I was frantically gesturing to Eric who was still hanging out in the dining room. He finally noticed and came running to the bar. I slipped out from under the service port and motioned Eric to a quiet corner.

"Elaine, Eric is with me. We're on speaker. Oh my God, I can't believe it. Eric, they got him. The nightmare is over."

"Jude, hold on a second." The excitement dropped from her voice, replaced by a more cautious tone. "I said we found Bevins. We haven't captured him yet. A team is on the way now to bring him in"

"What are you saying? If you found him, where is he?" My voice was rising by the second and a lot of people at the bar were starting to notice.

Eric turned me toward him and pulled the phone closer as Elaine continued. "We're close. We're going to get him tonight. I promise."

"How," I spat out, "after you let him get away?" I couldn't remember ever being this angry. It made my body shake all over.

"We know where he's going be tonight," she said. We decided to do another review of all the train cams to see if he was on the move again. One of the young techs got lucky and tracked him getting on the number six train on the Pelham line. We caught him getting off at the last stop." She paused. "But we lost him for a while."

"How long a while?" I asked.

Garlinger hesitated. "About fifteen minutes. He's changed his appearance again. He must have shaved his head before he came into The Lounge and has been wearing a wig. He's bald now, may have been for a while.

"The tech going through the footage recognized him from a traffic cam under the elevated station. He was standing at a bus stop, but he was antsy, kept looking around." She paused. "The tech got a good look at his profile, ran it through facial recognition while he was boarding the bus, and confirmed it was Bevins. We're on our way."

I didn't think my body could shake any harder than it already was. My voice came out in jerks. "What bus?" I asked dread creeping up my spine.

"He took the BX24. The team checked the stops through the bus's CCTV and we got him getting off at the corner of Campbell and Stadium Avenues in Country Club. Some minor politician used to live there, and there was another live cam on the corner."

I went completely still at her words. Eric looked at me, wondering I bet, if I was going to faint. It was another sensation entirely—I felt numb.

Elaine continued, her voice was cautious, as if she was not sure of how I would react. "We've got a clear image of him and have the neighborhood surrounded. He won't get away this time."

Eric held onto me as I started laughing uncontrollably. I could hear Garlinger calling my name as my laughter turned shrill.

"Jude? Jude? What is it?"

I gulped in a few breaths before I spoke. "He won't be there when you get there. He's long gone." I couldn't hide my disdain.

"How could you know that. He's—"

I cut Garlinger off in mid-sentence. "I grew up on that block. That's why he went there—to my old house." I grabbed Eric again, clutching him as though he were a lifeline. "Oh my God. The people who live there now… they're in danger…did he…?"

Garlinger's voice changed again into command mode. "I'll get back to you, Jude," she said, then clicked off.

How could he have so much information about me? Only a few people knew about my family and what had happened to them. It felt like someone was feeding him information, but I couldn't imagine anyone who would do that.

I swayed against Eric, feeling everything that was churning inside me. Shuddering in his arms, I came to a realization: this would never be over until either Art Bevins or I was dead.

Chapter Forty

I left Dean in charge and Eric and I went up to the apartment. He made me tea with a good dollop of brandy and I settled on the couch to drink it. Every time he tried to talk to me about what happened, I shut him down.

My thoughts were all over the place, mostly centered on the fact that it was down to me to get Bevins. It was obvious I couldn't count on the F.B.I.

About an hour and a half later, there was a knock at the door. It was Elaine and one of her agents.

Eric opened the door. "Alright if I come in?" She asked, staring past Eric at me.

I nodded my okay, and she walked toward me and sat on the chair facing the couch, head down.

She finally looked up. "You were right. He was gone when we got there."

"The people in the house?" I asked. "Were they…?"

She reached over to take my hand, but I pulled it back. "They were fine. Scared, but not hurt. They're in their forties and have been living there for about five years. Never had a problem before tonight. The EMS people looked them over, and a counselor from the unit is with them now."

She dipped her head again, then look up as she handed me a note enclosed in a plastic envelope. "He asked them to make sure you got this."

Jude,

What a lovely home you grew up in. It's too bad about all the tragedy that still hangs over it like a cloud. The folks who live here now didn't

seem to know a thing about it. But don't worry I filled them in. They had such sympathy for you. I told them not to worry. That soon you and your family would be reunited.
　　AB

I took the note and crumpled it into a ball. "Screw him and his notes. I want answers. And, I'm going to get them."

Chapter Forty-One

Sully knocked on my door at about ten the next morning. I was sure he'd heard what had happened last night.

"It's me. Open up. We're going to breakfast." He issued his pronouncement as though he were marshaling the troops. I was surprised he didn't add 'and stop feeling sorry for yourself.'

I unlocked the door, let him in, and saluted. I don't know why but seeing his scowling face put me in a better mood. "I could eat," I replied and pretended not to hear his muttered, "What else is new?"

"Let me grab my coat. Where are we going?"

"Eggateria."

We left and headed out to the diner on Eighth Street and Avenue A. It was Sully's favorite neighborhood breakfast place. He'd been going there for ages and they started cooking his eggs over easy, bacon, and flapjacks the minute he walked in the door. We took a small booth at the back of the room and I told the waitress I'd have the same, along with a very large mug of coffee.

"Jude," he began, "they'll get the bastard, you know they will."

I put up my hand to stop him. "I don't think so. He practically tweeted where he'd be, and Garlinger's team still couldn't get him."

I shook my head. "I'm going to have to do this myself."

"What are you talking about? Are you nuts?" Sully had stopped eating and his voice was rising. "What makes you think you could go after Bevins and bring him down? That's stupid Jude, and you're not stupid."

"I don't want to talk about this anymore," I said, slapping my hand on the table signaling the subject was closed. I'd had enough advice from everyone.

"There's something else I need to discuss with you."

Sully's expression went from puzzled to guarded, and for a moment I thought he might be thinking I wanted to talk about Dolores.

"You know…" I began drawing circles with my finger around my mug, "Mark Brandon, the restaurant broker Carol recommended, was in The Lounge the other day. He looked at everything, including the big, empty space behind my office."

Sully was nodding. "Yeah, I know what you're talking about. It's been empty since I bought the building."

I looked down at my plate and moved the eggs around, stalling for time. "He thought it might be a perfect spot for a comedy club." I looked up to see if I could read Sully's expression, which was neutral.

"Well," I stammered on, "it's your property and not really part of The Lounge…" I let my voice trail off.

"Continue," he said like he was assessing the situation as he leaned forward on the Formica table.

"Mark, Mr. Brandon, said he was working with experienced people who owned several comedy clubs and wanted to open another spot on the Lower East Side." I paused. "He thought our location was exactly what they were looking for. He believed they'd make a sizable investment, and not interfere with the bar or restaurant business.

"Did you think he was being straight?"

I was a little surprised at the question. "Sure. I mean Carol's worked with him before and it is his business.

"Of course, the space would need some fixing up, and…" I was running out of steam.

"Is he going to discuss this with Carol?" Sully asked.

"Yes. And, find out exactly what those people would want from us…me, and how much they'd be willing to invest."

He reached over the table and took my hand. "It is 'us' we're in this together. Let's see what Carol thinks and we'll take it from there."

I could feel a tear about to slide down my cheek. I hadn't cried from happiness in a long time and surprised myself with the emotion.

Chapter Forty-Two

I'd just finished mixing eight margaritas for a big party in the dining room and was handing them off to the waiter when a familiar voice said, "That looks good. I'll have one, too."

"Mital? What are you doing here?" I looked around for Shivani or any of her friends from the party. "Are you on your own?" I could see from his expression my surprised reaction wasn't the reception he was hoping for. "I mean it's nice to see you. What a surprise." That didn't sound much better.

He smiled, masking whatever he was feeling at my unwelcoming behavior. "I was in the neighborhood and thought I'd say hello. I thought maybe we could make a plan to have a drink together."

"Oh, umm. Sure, sometime soon. It's been kind of busy here…" My voice trailed off and I hoped I wasn't making this worse than it already was.

"Great," he replied in a flat tone. "But, I would love one of those margaritas you were making."

"Coming right up." *Shit, shit, shit,* I thought, hoping Eric wouldn't stop in, which would have been better than what happened next. Instead, Tony strode in and plopped himself right next to Mital.

"Hey," he said with too much good humor in his voice. "You're Shivani's friend, right? We met at her party." He put out his hand to shake. "I'm Tony Napoli."

I wasn't sure if Mital remembered who Tony was, but he made a pretty good show of it. "Yes, right. How have you been?"

"Good enough," Tony replied before turning to me. "Jude, I'll have a Johnnie Walker Black on the rocks." I knew what he wanted to drink, and

129

I'd started to pour it the minute he sat down. I placed his drink in front of him and tossed him a 'what the hell' look.

"So," Tony asked Mital, "are you staying in the city for a while?"

"Yes. I am enjoying myself here. It's been nice to meet Shivani's friends." He gave me a sideways look, which I pretended not to see.

"How about your other friends from home? Are they staying as well?"

Why was Tony asking all these questions? They might sound casual to a stranger, but it seemed like he was fishing for information. I was concentrating on my other customers but leaning toward them trying to listen in on their conversation.

"The Corner Lounge is nice, isn't it?" Tony continued. "Jude runs it pretty much on her own with her partner, Pete, the chef, and her financial wizard of a boyfriend, Eric."

Mital was looking at Tony with a very strange expression on his face. *What was he up to?* I wondered. I was going to kill him when I got him alone.

Mital finished his drink and got up to pay his tab. "Oh no," I said, "it's on me."

"Thank you, Jude. I will see you again sometime soon." He nodded at Tony and headed for the door.

I turned to Tony and asked, "What was that all about?"

Tony shook the cubes in his glass and downed the last sip of his Scotch. He tossed some money on the bar and got up to leave. "Something is going on with that group." He jutted his chin to the spot Mital had just vacated.

"You should be thanking me for getting rid of him. If I were you, I'd stay away from that bunch," were his parting words.

Was it drugs, or something else Tony was fishing for? I stood there staring at him until he was gone, shaking my head in wonder.

The rest of the evening went smoothly. The dining room was crowded, the bar busy. No sightings or messages from Art Bevins. No more conversation with Sully. No more weirdness from Tony.

"Hey, babe, how was your night?" Eric asked when he came into The Lounge at closing time.

"Perfect," I replied, "now that you're here." I gave him a big wet kiss.

131

Chapter Forty-Three

I was expecting to hear from Carol Batista regarding Mark Brandon's report on The Lounge. I was worried that even if the comedy club people made an offer, and Sully contributed to fixing up the empty space, there would still be a shortfall.

Where would I get the rest of the money? A knot grew in my stomach as I paced the apartment, checking my watch, knowing I was going to be late for my shift.

I needed to put this aside for now and get downstairs.

Of course, I couldn't find my keys. I looked everywhere and finally opened my desk drawer on the off chance that I'd put them there without thinking. That's when I saw the envelope sticking out from under a few other pieces of mail, I'd set aside.

It was a letter I'd received from a law firm that had arrived a few months ago.

It landed in my mailbox among the bills and junk mail that filled it every day. A heavy, buff-colored envelope, it had my name and address embossed in fancy script and the return address of a Park Avenue law firm.

Somehow its weight and formality had made it feel threatening, and I didn't think it would contain good news. There was so much going on then, I didn't have the energy to deal with it, so I tossed it in my desk, thinking I'd read it later. Of course, I forgot about it.

I pulled it out and opened it. The pages inside were heavyweight, as well, and the message stunned me.

Dear Ms. Dillane,

Please contact our office at your earliest convenience regarding a trust in your name initiated by Mrs. Marie LaFalce. The proceeds come due on or about February 5th, 2019. I would appreciate the opportunity to discuss the disbursement of the funds with you, as the sole beneficiary.

It went on for several more paragraphs and was signed, Roger P. Heywood, Founding Partner, Heywood, Moran, and Bethune, LLC.

I'd had no idea Grandma Ree had any money, or that she left it for me.

My maternal grandmother, Marie LaFalce, was loving and kind. I thought back to one day when I was probably about six, Grandma Ree and I were baking cookies. We were in the back room of the bakery she owned on Middletown Road in the Bronx. She often minded me after school until my mom could pick me up on her way home from work. Of course, I loved being in the bakery surrounded by treats, and being with her.

She stopped for a minute and stared down at me. "I remember the day you were born. It was one of the happiest days of my life. And, when I held you for the first time, it was as though my heart burst open and all this amazing love poured in."

Then she smiled and dusted the tip of my nose with flour.

She had loved me, and I her. She was my rock when the rest of my family was gone. I thought her unconditional support was my legacy, which would have been more than enough.

I was about to close the desk drawer when I noticed a small red velvet jewelry box tucked in the back. My hand started to shake as I reached for it and lifted the lid. Inside was the silver St. Jude medal my grandmother had given me for my Confirmation. I held it in my hand and could feel it warming from my touch. When had it stopped meaning something to me? I unclasped the fastening and placed it around my neck, looking for the comfort I hoped it would bring.

Then, I sat down and read the letter again. When I finished I was in shock. Grandma Ree had left me quite a bit of money, two-hundred-fifty thousand dollars, which was life-changing. I'd need Eric to help me figure it out, as soon as my heart stopped pounding.

I sat there for a while thinking about life and fortune. This was overwhelming. I finally calmed down and, my pulse got back to normal, I put the letter aside and went downstairs to The Lounge. Maryann, one of our bartenders, was setting up this afternoon. Everything was exactly where it should be. She had a done a good job. I gave her a warm smile and told her I'd be in my office if anyone needed me.

While I waited for Eric to get home, I'd work on the special cocktail for Restaurant Week. It would keep me from thinking about the trust fund money. The term 'trust fund baby' floated to the top of my brain and I laughed out loud.

I had a few ideas about our drink but wanted it to be really special. Something that would become The Lounge's signature cocktail.

Over the last few years, cocktails had become big business in the numerous bars that dotted the Lower East Side. Drinks like the Alphabet City with Absolut Vodka, Brandy and a dash of Casoni Aperitivo, and a Yakuza Fizz, with Saki replacing gin and a spritz of lemon soda, all topped with a cherry blossom, were becoming very popular. I had tried them both and they were delicious.

I wanted our drink to be equally unique, to convey the spirit of The Lounge. I'd come up with a name I loved, The Spring Solace. The main ingredient would be French vanilla vodka, which is warm and inviting, mixed with prosecco, and topped with a float of blueberry liquor.

It sounded luscious. But I'd have to taste it to be sure. I'd make a batch later and try it on the staff. Although, that might not exactly be a fair test, since they all liked to have a drink or two, especially a free one.

When Eric arrived home, I greeted him by waving the letter from Heyward, Moran, and Bethune in front of him.

He sat down on our couch and it didn't take him long to read it, but he must have looked up at me ten times while he did.

"You've had this how long?" he asked.

"A few months." I could see him shaking his head from the corner of my eye. "Why didn't you call them?"

What could I say? That I thought it was bad news I didn't want to deal with? "I was going to read it eventually, but I tucked it away and forgot about it."

I was sure they could hear his sigh of frustration all the way down in The Lounge.

"Here's what you're going to do, Jude. Tomorrow, first thing, you're going to call Mr. Heyward and set up an appointment. You can tell him you misplaced the letter and just found it."

Well, I thought. *It was sort of true.*

"Tell him you'd like your accountant to be present when you meet."

I leaned over and kissed him. "Thank you."

"Now," he handed me my cell, "it's time to call Sully."

Sully knocked on my apartment in under a minute. "What the hell is going on," he asked. "You. A trust fund?" he said with mock sarcasm. "It's better you didn't know about it, or you probably would have spent it all on vintage clothes." He made the word 'vintage' sound like a terrible, life-threatening disease.

I threw a pillow at him and just missed. "C'mon, Jude. I'm just kidding." He turned toward Eric. "Now might be a good time to propose, although two hundred and fifty grand isn't that much these days."

"Could be enough to let me buy back my half of The Lounge," I shot back. Then I smiled at him. "With a little help from my friends," I added.

Chapter Forty-Four

Dolores could tell Eric was nervous from the moment he entered the apartment. She waited a few beats after he pushed the bell, smoothing down the front of the slim Chanel sheath she wore, before opening the door with a flourish.

"Eric! Come in. How nice that you could make time to see me." She beckoned him into the apartment and gestured to a sitting area with two armchairs tilted to face each other and a coffee table between them, which held several files. He followed, her high red-soled Louboutin heels clicking on the shiny parquet floor.

"Please sit. Can I get you anything to drink? Coffee, tea, water?"

"No thanks, I'm fine." He looked at his watch, hoping to indicate this wasn't a social call. "I think we should get started. I have another appointment uptown in a little while."

"Of course," she replied sweetly. "Why don't I tell you where things stand and then you can look over my files."

"Um, before we begin, I have to tell you that I can't take you on as a client. My firm only does corporate work, nothing for individuals." He paused and gave her a big wide smile. "I can take a look, on an informal basis, as a friend, and recommend someone who could help you further.

"Of course, I understand," she replied. *That miserable shrew told him not to take me as a client, I'd bet on it.* "Let me tell you what I've been thinking about," she said as she handed him the files.

A half hour later, Eric had finished. "Well, Your finances look solid. If you want to start a design business though without spending all your own cash, you'll need to raise capital, and that may mean investors." His expression became more serious. "How much you need, and how much someone will be willing to invest will depend on a number of things, like how big you want the business at start up, and your growth projections, plus what percentage they'd want for their seed money. You probably know most of that from your business in California."

When she didn't react, he continued. "Let me give you the number of a friend of mine, an accountant who specializes in capital investments. I know he be happy to take you on as a client and help you with your plans." He stood to leave and Dolores did, as well.

I bet he will, Dolores smiled to herself, *if I ever call him.* "Oh, Eric, I can't thank you enough." She hesitated a moment. "You won't discuss this with anyone else, will you?"

Eric took a step back. "Of course not. Even though you're not a client, I would never discuss your private business."

She walked him to the door and waited until she heard the chime of the elevator.

Dolores leaned against the door and smiled. Of course, she hadn't shown him her real financials. Her wealth far exceeded what Eric had looked at. She actually believed he wouldn't tell Jude…he was that honest. But somehow, she knew Sully would get some of the information from him. In fact, she was counting on it.

Chapter Forty-Five

I was dying to know what kind of double talk Dolores had fed Eric about her financial status. Something to make him sympathetic to her cause for when she finally 'accepted' Sully's proposal to help. I knew she'd never ask him outright, but he'd keep offering until she was 'forced' to say yes.

Well, Eric had said we weren't going to let that happen, but I was sure Dolores had some line she'd toss out to Sully to suck him in.

Waiting for Eric to get home was weighing on my nerves. He had other meetings after the one with the lovely Dolores, but as I've mentioned, patience wasn't my long suit.

When he finally arrived, I'd rearranged all the bottles and cleaned all the shelves on the back bar. The chore kept me grounded, and the waitstaff who were setting up for dinner seemed thankful I wasn't hawking them. Even Pete noticed my unusual vigorous activity and stayed safely in the kitchen.

When Eric walked in the door, I flung myself from under the service bar's portal and grabbed both his arms. "So, what happened? What did she say?"

He gently released my arms and set me down at one of the banquets in the cocktail area.

A heavy sigh preceded his speech. "Well, you might be right about her not belonging on the Lower East Side. She was dressed like she was going to a fashion show, even had on those fancy red-soled shoes.

"Eric, I'm not interested in her clothing choices." I shook my head at him.

"You know I can't tell you about her financials—" He held up a hand as I began to protest. "—even though she's not a client, she still has a right to privacy. I explained that to you already."

I looked down at the gray marble table in front of us. "Okay, why don't we do it this way?" I pasted a big smile on my face. "I'll ask you a question and you can just nod yes if I'm right, or shake your head no if I'm not. That way you won't actually be telling me anything and, not violating any ethical standards." I'd watched enough movies to know this could work, at least on the screen.

He rolled his eyes at me. "Jude, I don't—"

I ignored him and continued. "So, do you think she was telling you the truth about her money?"

He hesitated for a moment, then shook his head from side to side.

I could feel my eyes widening at the news. Although I shouldn't have been surprised. "Do you think she has less than she indicated?"

No reaction.

"Or more?" I made my voice sound incredulous. I got up and started pacing. "If it's more, why is she after Sully?"

Eric pulled me back down onto the banquette. "Stop. This is not getting us anywhere. I can't discuss it."

I was bummed. I'd made him speak with her so I could glean some information, and he wouldn't even toss me a crumb.

"What about Sully?" I asked. "You know he's going to want to know what you two discussed."

"I'll tell him to speak with her himself." Eric sat back and crossed his arms over his middle as if the matter were closed.

Good luck with that, I thought. Then I uncrossed his arms and took his hand. "I'm sorry I got you into this mess." I gave him a real smile this time. "C'mon. Let's go sit at the bar and have a glass of wine."

I knew this wasn't over. It was just the beginning. And, now both men I cared about were in a dangerous position because of me.

Chapter Forty-Six

Eric and I were sitting in the reception area of Heywood, Moran, and Bethune, LLC, waiting to see Roger P. Heywood, the firm's Founding Partner.

It was pretty posh digs, and you could almost smell the waft of old money embedded in its wood-paneled walls, well-worn Persian carpets, and deep leather chairs.

The only thing modern about the space was the sleek iMac computer on the reception desk, and the equally sleek, well-dressed young woman who was typing on its keyboard.

She gave us a big, bright smile, offered us beverages, and directed us to the chairs where we would wait until Mr. Heywood could see us.

Eric and I nodded politely, asked for coffee, and took our seats. We kept tossing sideways glances at each other, both afraid we'd get giddy with laughter over the circumstances.

We'd been there for around ten minutes when Mr. Haywood's assistant came out to escort us to his office. Her appearance was more in keeping with the office décor. A small, trim woman in her fifties with a short bob haircut and a conservative black suit, she moved efficiently as she led us down to the end of the carpeted hallway and knocked on the door before opening it.

Mr. Heywood stood and came around his desk to greet us. After I introduced myself and Eric as my accountant and friend, we shook hands. He invited us to sit at a round table next to the tall windows that filled his office with light.

He wasn't the ancient attorney that I expected. A tall, youthful-looking man in his early seventies with silver-gray hair and pale blue eyes. Dressed as befitting the head of a well-known law firm, his pristine white cuffs snuck out just an inch from the jacket of his navy blue pinstripe suit. My Grandma Ree had been a little older than him and I wondered how she'd come to know him.

"Ms. Dillane, you look rather puzzled. I assure you, this is a very straightforward matter. The trust has come due and the money is yours." He lifted his hands toward the ceiling.

"Well…" I stammered, "I was wondering how my grandmother, Marie LaFalce, found you and set this all up." It was my turn to gesture to the papers on the table.

Mr. Heywood smiled. "Your grandmother and I knew each other for a long time. We both grew up in the Bronx and I knew your grandfather, as well. We played Pinochle together." He leaned back in his chair. "In fact, my winnings helped pay for college and law school."

So not old money after all. Maybe they piped in the smell.

"I hope not all of it from Grandpa Louie."

He laughed then continued. "When your grandfather passed away, he left your grandmother a life insurance policy. She still had her bakery." He paused and a wistful expression came over his face. Probably thinking about her honey buns. "Well, she didn't need the money, so she put it in the bank for safe-keeping." He looked at Eric who nodded that he understood. Banks were paying a pretty decent interest rate at the time.

"Then, when the rest of your family was gone, she asked me to help her put the money to better use and set up a trust for you. She never mentioned that she'd done this?"

I shook my head. "I had no idea."

"Well, I believe your grandmother wanted to wait until you were older and make sure you would be responsible after receiving a large amount of money."

"Umm," was all I could manage. I gripped Eric's hand under the table. *If Grandma Ree knew what's been going on lately, she'd probably take it all back.*

"I was wondering, however, why you hadn't contacted us," Mr. Hayward continued.

"I misplaced your letter and just recently found it and read it." That sounded lame, even to me.

Heywood gave me a quizzical look.

I know, I know. Who forgets about a trust fund?

Eric squeezed my hand and spoke. "That's not a problem, is it?" he asked.

My stomach did a slow flip-flop. I was counting on this money. I didn't want to lose it because of a technical glitch, like responding to the firm's letter three months too late.

"Not at all," Mr. Heywood replied. "Let's review the trust and have you sign the papers. Then, I'll turn over your proceeds."

Twenty minutes later, Eric and I thanked Mr. Hayward and were out on ParkAvenue, my check safely tucked into my handbag.

We were on our way to my bank to set up a money market account so I could have access to the money when and as I needed it.

"Thank you. Thank you." I reached up and gave Eric a long, passionate kiss that made the passersby stop and stare. I thought I heard a muttered "get a room" at one point.

I didn't care. This was a turning point for me and I was going to make the most of it.

"C'mon, Jude. Let's go deposit that baby and get things moving. This money, combined with the deal from ComedyClub Ltd means you're going to be able to keep The Lounge now. You know that, right?"

I smiled up at this amazing man. I was sure my luck had changed and that things, including capturing Art Bevins, might turn around.

Suddenly, a chill ran down my spine interrupting my happy moment. I remembered what John Lennon had said: "Life is what happens when you're busy making other plans."

Well, I wasn't going to give up my plan of capturing Bevins. Not in this lifetime.

Chapter Forty-Seven

I walked over to the table where Pete was already seated going over the menu for Restaurant Week.

"Tada," I said, as I produced two flutes with the cocktail I'd created for the event and handed one to Pete. "I've named it The Spring Solace."

"Looks impressive." He smiled as he held up the glass filled with a pale, shimmering liquid and topped with a swirl of blueberry liquor.

"Let's taste it and see if it's any good." I clinked the rim of my flute against his.

He gave me a wry smile. "You mean you haven't tasted it yet?"

"Well, not the finished drink. I was saving that for us." I'd played with the proportions until I had it down exactly right. Dean and the other bartenders had tried it in various stages, but Pete would be my final taste-tester. We lifted our flutes and clinked a toast. "Cheers," we said at the same time.

"It's really good," he said. "Not my usual—"

"I know, bourbon is better."

"But I think the paying customers are really going to like it."

"Me too." I nodded toward the paper in his hand. "Are we all set?"

"The menu worked out and our special cocktail tastes great. Fingers crossed, we're ready."

"So…" I took a deep breath, "…I have a few things I need to discuss with you."

Pete leaned back in this chair and folded his arms across his middle. He kept his expression neutral probably thinking I was going to tell him something else about Art Bevins. I wasn't. Pete did not need to know about

Bevins' trip to my ancestral home in the Bronx. I suppressed a shudder and smiled at him.

As I told him about my legacy from my grandmother and Mark Brandon's suggestion of adding a comedy club downstairs, his face lightened up in relief.

"You mean that letter was in your apartment the whole time?" He shook his head. "Maybe it's better you didn't know, you might—"

I held up my hand. "Thanks very much, but Sully already covered that territory."

I switched topics to the restaurant broker, Mark Brandon. We hadn't had a chance to discuss it yet. "What do you think about what he had to say."

"I thought the guy was a straight-shooter. He'd been around a kitchen before." His eyes crinkled in a smile. "Really looked at everything and was very open and forthcoming about our place." He glanced around. "You know I'll miss it…and you."

"Me, too," was all I could say.

"A comedy club, huh? I wouldn't ever have thought about that. And, the people Brandon mentioned, they're pros at running this type of venture?"

"Apparently." At least I hoped so.

"I'm sure your lawyer told you he was going to meet with Sully and me, and Mark Brandon at Carol Batista's office next week." I took another sip of my cocktail and realized I was nervous. "Once we find out what the restaurant is worth and what the kings of comedy can add, if your attorney and Carol are okay with the numbers, I'll meet with them afterwards."

"Is Sully okay with the idea of a comedy club downstairs?" Pete asked.

"Surprisingly, he's fine with it. I have a small suspicion, he'd like to perform if anyone will let him."

We both burst out laughing. "My God, I hope not," Pete said. "That would be the kiss of death."

And just like that my good mood vanished. Pete's mentioning death brought Art Bevins's image front and center. Somehow this had to come to an end. And soon.

Chapter Forty-Eight

I made my way downstairs to my office and plopped down in front of my computer. With images of Art Bevins now firmly in my mind, I realized I didn't know him as well as I thought. Well, other than the fact that he was a deranged serial killer who was stalking me, and had hidden behind his profession as a crime writer. I had looked up some of his earlier murders, but now I wanted to focus on the man.

As I'd discussed with Elaine Garlinger, no one knew what made a serial killer into a twisted monster. Art Bevins was certainly no exception; he was as twisted as they came. According to Garlinger, there were more than thirty serial killers operating in the United States. They're not all insane evil geniuses. They tend to kill in their comfort zone, like Bevins. And, believe it or not, some are women.

What had happened to make him turn to killing? I wondered as I powered up my laptop and typed his name into the search engine. I'd read that most serials evolved and became more skilled as they learned from their mistakes. It seemed to be true of Art Bevins. Would finding out more about him help me catch him? Find his true motivation. Or, was it just as crazy as going to a palm reader to learn the future? Eric would probably tell me it was the latter and he might be right.

There were hundreds of hits that came up. Most of which dealt with his recent crimes, which I already knew about first-hand. They were the garnish on the plate. Now, I needed to dig into the meat. A tie to who he'd been before he started killing. Something that would shed some insight on the horrible crimes he committed.

I scrolled and scrolled until I came to a link for the now-defunct New York Theater and Film Academy. I'd already known that he'd studied acting and playwriting there when he'd moved to New York. It was long before he became a successful screenwriter

I clicked on the link and was surprised to see it was still working. It opened to the Home Page, with a photo of the exterior of an old tenement building. A drop-down menu offered several headings and I picked the one titled Performances. This brought me to a description of the types of plays students put on plus several photos.

The third one down interested me the most. In it, the photographer had caught a much younger Art as he was approaching an unsuspecting character with a knife held high in his hand, ready to plunge it into his back. It figured.

I enlarged the photo to get a better look. There were several other actors on the stage, women, and men dressed in the period costumes of ancient Rome. The photo was old and grainy and I couldn't see anyone else's face clearly. The caption below had been cut off after the first line, which listed the academy's director, Emil Straussman, and two other actors. I wondered if Mr. Straussman was still directing and might be able to give me information on Art.

I went back to the Home Page and chose the About Us option. It gave the studio's philosophy and was signed by Emil Straussman, Founder and Director. On the Contact Us page, there was an address and phone number to call.

Don't get too excited, I told myself as I punched in the number but the beep, beep beep, and the 'no longer in service' message told me it was a dead end.

There had to be another way. What were the chances that Emil Straussman was still alive and living on the Lower East Side? I called directory assistance and said his name. If he only had a cell phone, there'd be no listing and I'd be out of luck.

A disembodied, mechanical voice surprised me with a two-one-two number and I asked to be connected.

After three rings, a man answered. "Hello," he said in a soft, cultured voice with just the trace of a British accent.

"Mr. Straussman," I replied, "my name is Jude Dillane. I own The Corner Lounge on Tenth Street."

"Oh, I've passed by it." His voice grew stronger and brightened a bit. "What can I do for you?"

"I'm interested in finding out about your acting studio and one of your former students."

The silence lasted so long, I thought he'd hung up. A sigh escaped his lips. "I imagined someone would call me about him eventually."

It hadn't taken him long to figure it out. "Would you mind speaking with me?" I asked.

Again there was hesitation. "Fine," he eventually said. "When would you like to meet?"

There was reluctance in his voice but he hadn't turned me down. He gave me his address and we settled on coffee the next afternoon, which seemed like years away but would have to do. I couldn't wait to hear what he'd have to say about Art Bevins.

In the meantime, I had to go upstairs and open the bar. A few minutes after five my regulars started streaming in. For a while, I was busy enough that things almost seemed normal.

Chapter Forty-Nine

Dolores had a lot to think about. There were so many moving parts to her plan, as well as several obstacles to overcome.

She sighed and looked out the window, tapping a red fingernail on her chin. The day was bright and sunny. The trees in the park across the street were starting to turn green as spring unfolded. She loved this time of year. The season had such promise attached to it. She might as well take advantage of it and exchange the stuffy apartment for some air down by the river.

Dolores considered calling Diego and asking him to join her but dismissed the thought almost as soon as it occurred. He was always busy with his new friends and was neglecting his responsibilities. He'd been disappearing with Michaela, Roberto, and Celine—wealthy Europeans she hadn't met yet. Worst of all, he avoided telling her where he'd been. That would have to stop. Personal assistants were supposed to be available when you needed them.

She slipped on her short, Max Mara wool jacket, which would keep her warm if the promenade was windy, and left the apartment quietly and quickly, hoping not to run into Sully or Jude.

Walking east, and over the Tenth Street pedestrian bridge, Dolores could see the East River was fairly calm today, with occasional flashes of silver glinting off the small whitecaps that dotted the surface.

She paused and leaned on the railing that separated the path from the river. It had been refurbished but was almost as she remembered it, minus the giant luxury towers that soared overhead. It wasn't like her to be nostalgic, but she realized she had missed the energy and vibrance of the city.

Well, I'm here now, she thought and smiled. Dolores pulled a pack of cigarettes from her coat pocket and tapped one out. It was a guilty pleasure she rarely indulged in. She patted her pocket again, looking for her lighter, but she must have left it at home.

Just as she was about to return the cigarette to the pack, someone spoke from behind her. "Please, let me get that for you, Dolores, or should I say, Maria?"

For a moment, she stood completely still, feeling as though her heart had skipped a beat. No one had called her Maria for years and years. She'd recognized the deep, baritone voice, but not the man it emerged from as she turned to face him.

The rumors she'd heard were true. Art 'Turo' Bevins was still here in the neighborhood and looking for revenge. So was she. And, it seemed she might have it.

She'd loved him once and had felt abandoned by him even though she was the one who'd left the city. Why hadn't he come after her? She didn't understand then but she did now.

He was taking a chance on showing himself to her. She could scream and bring the police running. She considered it but it would not be in her best interest. Not yet.

Hoping he couldn't hear the thundering of her heart, Dolores leaned in and gave him a light kiss on his cheek. If she miscalculated his intentions, he could still kill her in an instant. She brought a slight smile to her lips and raised her eyes to meet his.

Turo looked entirely different from how she remembered him. But then, given the circumstances, he would.

Short grayish-blond hair, horn-rimmed glasses, and a worn tweed jacket gave him the appearance of an academic fallen on hard times. He'd always been a wizard of disguises, using his talent to bring out the essence of whatever character he was playing. Today it was the role of a man who was slightly down and out, low key and not particularly notable, the serial killer well hidden beneath.

Dolores leaned in and tipped her cigarette to the lighter's flame. "Thank you so much, Turo," she said and forced herself to remain calm and keep her hand steady. "I've been hearing quite a bit about you these days." She blew a puff of smoke toward the sky. "I didn't think our paths would ever cross again."

A wicked grin split his face as he put his hand lightly on her arm. "Oh Dolores, we're so much alike. It was inevitable."

She knew that was true—in fact, she'd counted on it—but it seemed as though he was accusing her of something. She'd have to be very careful not to let him see her true intent.

She cleared her throat and tilted her head up toward him. What did he know?

They'd been lovers when they were at the academy when she was still Maria and had stayed in touch after she was with Mark and had become Dolores. He'd teased her about her transformation but had kept her secret. After a while, she had to break off their relationship. It would have been disastrous if Mark had ever found out. Now, she wondered, did Art suspect her of having a hand in Mark's death? Had he tracked her transformation to her new persona, and more importantly, her motivations?

"Don't look so shocked, Dolores. I still know everything that's going on in this neighborhood, including where you're living. A little below your usual standards, isn't it?"

"Oh, Turo you shouldn't be surprised." She shook her head when she saw the confusion in his eyes. "I have big plans. As always."

"I don't doubt that and don't worry, I won't tell a soul about your past life here in Manhattan. In fact, I think we could really make the most of this fortunate reunion." He pointed toward the end of the promenade. "Why don't we walk a bit. I'm sure we have a lot of catching up to do. I'd love to hear all about your life in California and the unfortunate death of your husband. If I'm not mistaken, I think we have some plans to make, as well."

His eyes were like two bright beacons of what hellfire must look like as he took her arm and led her away.

Dolores went willingly. It was a game of cat and mouse they were playing.

She knew what she had to do. After all, she was the one in charge, Wasn't she?

Chapter Fifty

It had been an uneventful night and for once, I really appreciated the calm. All this drama was making me jump at every little sound. Eltee had kept a close watch on me as had Dean.

My bodyguards, I thought and smiled inwardly at the men who were determined to keep me safe. Between them, Eric, and my F.B.I. minders, I should be as safe as England's Crown Jewels. Of course, I knew that wasn't necessarily true when a cunning serial killer was stalking you.

I must have been making a face that Eric caught as he walked in. "What's wrong, Jude?" he asked. as he leaned over the bar to give me a kiss.

I shook my head. "Nothing actually. It's been an easy night. Want a nightcap before I give last call?"

"Sure. Whatever you're having."

I poured two measures of bourbon into cocktail glasses and clinked mine against Eric's. "To us," I said and smiled.

Eric leaned over and kissed me again. "I'll drink to that." He relaxed into his seat and watched as I got ready to close the bar.

"Anything new happening today?" he asked.

I knew he was thinking about the search for Bevins. "Well, there is something but promise you won't get angry," I said, watching for his reaction as the words left my mouth. "I didn't do anything dangerous."

Eric was rolling his eyes. "Then, you'd better tell me, what you did do."

"I was looking up Art Bevins online. You know, just trying to figure out how all this…his killing…started. Most of the information I discovered was about the recent murders, things I already knew, but as I scrolled through the links, I found a reference to the New York Theater and Film Academy he attended here in the neighborhood. You know, where he perfected his craft, as he so often told us." I let the sarcasm seep out in my voice. "Of course the school is closed." I paused. "But, you're not going to believe it, the Director, Emil Straussman, is still living on the Lower East Side. He's going to see me tomorrow."

I could see Eric was not as thrilled at my news as I had been hoping. "Jude you should leave this to Elaine. If he can shed any light on Bevins she needs to be involved."

I nodded. "I get that and I will let her know I'm meeting with Straussman. "It's perfectly safe and my Fibbie minders will be with me. We're going to get together for coffee and hopefully, he'll have something he can share about Art."

"Yeah, his star pupil." Eric sighed. "This is not a good idea. It could be dangerous."

"How?" I shrugged. "Straussman must be about eighty years old. I don't think he's going to jump out of his apartment and stab me to death."

"He's not the one I'm worried about." Eric's voice deepened and his face set in a serious frown. "What if Bevins finds out about your visit? You could be putting both you and the director at risk."

"I haven't told anyone but you," I replied. "I haven't even told Sully, so how would Art find out?"

He couldn't possibly find out, I told myself. *Could he?*

Chapter Fifty-One

The next morning I called Elaine Garlinger and told her about my plan to meet with Emil Straussman. Needless to say, Eric was right and she wasn't overjoyed.

"Jude you need to leave the investigating to us." Her anger came through loud and clear and I could sense the underlying stress in her voice.

"We know Bevins was Straussman's student. Stay home. I'll send an agent to meet with him and see if there's anything he can tell us." She paused. "We staked out the building and Bevins hasn't been there."

"You knew? And you didn't think to tell me? I will not stay home," I said in the calmest voice I could muster, tamping down my anger. "I am not changing my mind. I am going to see him." I'd found him no thanks to the F.B.I. and there was no way I wasn't going to see it through.

"Jude—"

"I'll take Samuelson and Maguire with me. Tell them to be here by twelve-thirty. They can come with me, but I'll be asking the questions." I didn't wait for an answer and clicked off the phone. I'd been gripping it so hard, I couldn't let go.

Eric chose that moment to emerge from the bedroom. He took one look at me and moved to my side, gently sliding my cell from my hand.

"What happened? Are you okay?"

I nodded. "Just aggravated. Elaine was giving me a hard time about speaking with Emil Straussman. They were already aware Bevin's had studied at the academy."

I sat at our kitchen counter and picked up the coffee I'd poured and took a sip. "I know the F.B.I. is working round the clock to find Bevins but the lack of progress is frustrating. I feel like they're going around in circles and he keeps eluding them. It's up to me to do something, make something happen before—"

"No, it's not." Eric interrupted and sat down next to me. "They are going to capture him and put him away forever. I'm sure of it."

"You're right," I said, knowing it was useless to argue. My words sounded hollow, even to me, but I wasn't abandoning my plan.

The agents were waiting downstairs and I handed each of them a go-cup of coffee. "Thanks for coming with me," I said.

Maguire gave me a 'yeah, sure look,' rolled his eyes, and took a slug of the hot coffee.

"I mean it, guys. Let's get going."

It only took a few minutes to walk over to Sixth Street and Avenue C where Straussman lived.

I walked up the short flight of stairs and rang the bell. He answered the door immediately. "Jude Dillane, I presume," he said with that faint touch of a British accent I'd noticed on the phone.

I extended my hand, "Nice to meet you Mr. Straussman."

"Please, call me Emil, I prefer it," he replied as we shook. "Come in." He studied the two agents standing behind me and grinned. "F.B.I., I imagine. Right out of central casting."

I introduced Samuelson and Maguire, who were both dressed in dark blue suits and white shirts. Male or female, it was a look that screamed law enforcement. The gold shields at their waists gave it away, as well.

"We'll just take a look around inside, sir. Then we'll wait here for Ms. Dillane," Samuelson said, "and finish our coffee." She held up her cup.

"Of course," he said and stepped aside as he gestured for Samuelson to enter his home.

Straussman didn't seem surprised that the agents had accompanied me. I was certain he'd known about my involvement with the New Year's Eve Serial Killer case and the search for Art Bevins.

The academy director was tall and slim, with a full head of gray hair and a well-groomed brush mustache. His light blue eyes sparkled with life and made him look much younger than the eighty or so years I thought he must be. He held himself perfectly erect as he led the way into his living room and I remembered my mom telling me to 'stop slouching' as I stood up as straight as I could. A small table was set with a coffee pot, milk and sugar, and cups and saucers.

"Ms. Dillane," he said as he gestured for me to take a seat, "how can I help you?"

"It's Jude," I replied, "and as I mentioned, I found the Academy's website on the internet and through it, you."

"Yes," he said, a former student has been kind enough to keep it going." He lifted his hand in a theatrical gesture and smiled. "Glory days, you know."

"Mr. Straussman… Emil, I would appreciate it if you could tell me anything you can remember about Art Bevins. Any detail could help us… the F.B.I. find him."

"Certainly." He shook his head and a sad expression clouded his face. "I've read about all the murders he's committed and I find it truly horrible. He was so gifted. Turo was a talented actor as well as an insightful writer. I knew he'd be a tremendous success one day. Become famous, but certainly not in this manner."

"I'm sorry," I said. "Turo? Who's Turo." I was confused and didn't know who he was talking about.

"My dear, forgive me. I thought you knew his nickname was Turo, short for Arturo. That's what everyone here called him. Turo Bevacqua was his stage name. "

"I had no idea," I replied. At The Lounge, he was always Art. No one ever called him anything else. Not Arthur or Arturo and never Turo. This was new information. At least, to me. Was it something else Agent Garlinger was keeping to herself? It was possible he might be using the name as an alias.

I tried to hide my puzzled expression and got back to my questions. "What was he like when he studied with you?"

"He was a quick study." He nodded solemnly. "Very smart, as I'm sure you know. And as I said, talented. He had that gift for making whatever character he played his own. When you watched him, you forgot he was acting. It was uncanny.

"And, he was popular with the men as well as the women. No one seemed to resent his ability. To the contrary, they appreciated it."

I was sure my face showed what I was thinking. *How did everyone miss his true nature?*

"If you're wondering if he exhibited any homicidal tendencies while he was here, they only came out when he was on stage." A wry smile flitted across Straussman's face. "Here, let me show you." He reached for an album sitting on the couch next to him and opened it.

I leaned in close as he flipped through the photos. There were several of a much younger Art, or Turo, as he was known, in various roles. Even in these old photos, you could see his star power coming through.

"He was quite the ladies' man," Straussman continued. There was one young woman in particular who seemed to hang onto his every word. Maria." He paused for a moment, then said her last name, "Martime. Of course, that was her stage name." His right eyebrow lifted slightly. "Rather obvious. In any event, she was quite taken with him." He gestured to a group of women on stage off to Art's side and pointed to one in the middle. "Maria was quite attractive. Long brown hair, big green eyes."

I could only see the side of her head. A wistful note had crept into his voice and it sounded like Straussman might have been harboring a crush of his own. I smiled to myself as he continued.

"Ah, well. I thought it might lead to something serious, but I guess it wasn't to be. Lucky for her. She left after a few months. I believe she had a new job and was moving. That probably saved her life."

He held a long finger up to his lips. "Now that I think of it, I do recall that she did return once more about a year after that. I saw her with Turo and it seemed as though they were having a very intense and heated discussion. I'm sure that was the last time I saw her." He picked up his coffee and took a sip, casting his eyes downward.

His last statement sounded slightly off to me. I wondered if he had seen Maria again after the incident with Turo, or approached her and was rebuffed.

"Do you have any records of the students from that time?" I asked. "Maybe Maria's real last name and address?" If he had that information, maybe Garlinger could track her down. It was possible she'd stayed in touch with her Turo.

He hesitated a beat before answering me. "I'm sorry to say, most likely not. When I closed the academy, I got rid of almost everything. There are a few bits and pieces in my study and I will be happy to look through them. These photo albums are really all the mementos I have from that time." He glanced down at the page he'd left open and I could see his eyes linger on Maria's image.

I didn't want to tell him that his Maria would have been safe. As far as we still knew, Art Bevins hadn't slaughtered any women. Neither did I tell him, I was slated to be the first. Lucky me.

I'd taken this as far as I could but my intuition told me he knew more about Maria than he was sharing.

"Thank you for your time, Emil. It was very generous of you to share your memories with me." I stood and extended my hand.

He took it and brought it toward his lips. "I can only hope it helps you capture that murderer, even if just a little."

Outside, Maguire and Samuelson were talking quietly.

"How did it go?" asked Maguire.

"Good," I replied as I pulled out my phone. "I need to speak with Agent Garlinger right now. I think I have a lead she can follow. Actually two."

At least, I hoped I did.

Chapter Fifty-Two

Elaine showed up at The Lounge half an hour later. Like her agents, she was dressed in a dark suit and white shirt. Only her suit was custom-tailored Armani and her shirt the softest silk. Beauty, style, and brains I thought then got back to business.

I relayed my entire conversation with Emil Straussman.

"Turo Bevacqua." We knew that was his stage name but it hasn't turned up in any of our searches.

I was right. She had known about this. "I imagine he changed his name when he came to New York to study acting and not only for his career on the stage."

Elaine grasped exactly where I was going. "You're probably right. It would have been good for him to have an easy alias to slip into if anyone started looking for Art Bevins, wanted in connection with several brutal murders in Pennsylvania and beyond."

My hmmm came out as a sardonic chuckle. "But once he started to get real work and fame was in sight, he changed it back to Art. His ego insisting that people know it was him gathering all the praise and not some student named Turo."

Elaine and I were sitting at a cocktail table in the lounge area. She picked up the coffee I'd handed her when she arrived and took a long swallow.

"What about this Maria Martime?" she asked. "You think Straussman was so smitten, he'd want to protect her true identity even after all this time?"

"I'm not sure. It seemed like he was telling me almost everything he remembered, but he had this strange look on his face when he mentioned the last time he saw her. It didn't ring true. Maybe she didn't actually move, or he kept his eye on her from afar.

"He did say he'd look at any of the old papers he could find from that time and let me know if there was anything of interest. Why don't I give him a day and then visit him again? Tell him there was something else I wanted to ask him."

"Okay." Elaine was making a note on her tablet. "But you have to be extremely careful. I want an agent with you. In the meantime, we'll check all the databases for the name Maria Martime, social security number, and any work records. I'll run it through NCIC, the National Crime Information Center, to see if she's ever been arrested. We'll track her down, whoever she may be now."

"I'd guess that if the students were college-age then, she'd be somewhere in her early to mid-fifties."

"About the same age as Bevins," I agreed.

Elaine gathered up her things and prepared to leave. "You know I didn't approve of you seeing Straussman, but you may have opened up a few new possibilities. Thank you, but please be careful and don't go running off on your own." She glanced over at Samuelson and Maguire. "You know, you're not alone."

With that, she was gone.

I sat there for a few more minutes replaying the morning in my head. Could we actually be onto something that could lead to Bevins? I was hoping but not entirely hopeful.

I spent the rest of the afternoon in my office reviewing our food and beverage orders for Restaurant Week. It was just two weeks away and everything needed to be perfect. I felt I owed it to Pete. He'd been such a good partner and I didn't want to let him down. This was going to be his special moment for the restaurant he had helped create. A premier event to showcase his amazing cooking, even if he was taking his skills somewhere else.

I looked over the list one more time, then emailed it to him. I told him to make any changes he wanted and I'd take care of it.

The next two weeks were going to be very busy and Restaurant Week was just a part of it. I was scheduled to meet with Carol Batista in two days to go over the finance options for The Lounge. Then, a meeting with the comedy club owners to discuss what they had to offer. Not to mention, getting in touch with Lena to see what she'd dug up on Dolores Castel.

My head was spinning as I went upstairs to get the bar ready for business. A little after four-thirty, Sully walked in. His expression, as they say, was as serious as a heart attack.

He took his usual seat and I hustled over. "Sully, are you okay? What's wrong?"

"Wrong? Nothing." He scowled at me. "In fact, things couldn't be better."

It sure didn't look like it to me. I poured him a Jameson and placed it in front of him. "Okay." I pasted a smile on my face. "What's going on?"

He took a long sip of the drink, then a deep breath. "I have something to tell you, but hear me out before you say anything. Alright?"

I nodded dumbly. *Oh no, he's got cancer or some other fatal disease. He just doesn't know how to tell me,* flashed through my mind as I waited for him to continue.

He reached into his pocket and pulled out his cell phone. He opened its photos app and turned it to face me. It looked like he was showing me a diamond ring. It *was* a ring with a diamond, a very large one. Even in the photograph it gleamed and glittered, a beautiful emerald cut solitaire. I could only imagine what it must be like in person.

Why was Sully showing me this? Oh no. It hit me like a bag of bricks thrown from the top of a skyscraper: it was for Dolores. I knew I had to say something but my voice was stuck somewhere around my stomach.

Sully was looking at me. "What is...?" was all I could finally croak out.

"It's for Dolores. Or it will be." He held up his hand to forestall the protest that he knew I'd make. "Look, Jude, I know you don't like her all that much. It's hard to explain but...I feel like she's the one I've been waiting for. She's really a wonderful woman."

Didn't like her didn't begin to cover it. I disliked her with an intensity that bordered on loathing. From the minute I met her, I thought she would do harm to Sully; at the very least break his heart, at the worst ruin his life completely.

He'd thought his last crush, Miriam Birkman, had been wonderful, too and she turned out to be a murderer. Had he forgotten his taste in women wasn't so great?

Of course, I couldn't say any of that and took a deep breath before I spoke. "That's not it at all." I smiled at him. I knew he wanted my approval but how could I convince him this would be a really big mistake. Like his affair with Miriam, a peek into my own past would show I wasn't the best at relationships either.

"Sully, you hardly know each other. It's only been, what a few weeks, since she moved in? Take some time to find out who she is, what you have in common. Getting engaged can wait a little bit longer. If you really love each other, it will happen." So could her getting her hands on all his assets as the future Mrs. Sullivan. A chill crept down my spine.

"I'd like to get to know her better, too, become friends, but that will take time." Did I sound sincere? Maybe my ploy would work to slow things down.

"I don't know. I'm not getting any younger and I know she cares for me." He toyed with his phone and looked at the photo of the ring again.

"It's beautiful," I said as I put my hand on his, "and it will still be beautiful a few months from now. You've waited so long for someone like Dolores, you can wait a little longer and be sure." I was making myself ill with my platitudes.

"Maybe. I guess there's no rush. Dolores is happy here. She isn't going anywhere."

"Right." I was nodding my head so fast, I thought it might separate from my body. "You know, they say diamonds are forever and that one will still be here when you're ready. Just think about it, okay?" Were there any other cliches I could toss out?

I reached for the bottle of Jameson and poured Sully another drink. I left him to it as I moved down to the service end of the bar and finished my opening prep work.

Oh God, this could be bad. I knew I had to do something before Dolores got her hooks into him for good. But what that was, I had no idea.

Chapter Fifty-Three

I'd been making cocktails for one of the waitresses when I heard someone calling my name. Tony Napoli was sitting a few stools down. Great. Just what I needed. I pasted a smile on my face and walked over. I was still annoyed with him from the last time he was in.

"What can I get you, Tony?"

"Make it my usual, Johnny Walker Black, on the rocks, thanks."

I plunked down the drink a little too vigorously and startled him. "Whoa. What's up with you?" he asked.

"Nothing, " I snapped, then dialed down the attitude. "It's been a tough day."

Tony was nodding as he sipped his Scotch. "Listen, Jude, I don't want to pile on to your problems, but I need your help."

I took a step back and gave him my serious face. "With what?" He looked so intense, I dreaded the answer. "I'm a little worried about Shivani." He glanced down at the bar and toyed with his glass.

Shiv was not someone who people generally worried about. Capable, self-sufficient, and super smart, she was an independent woman who held her own in any situation.

I ignored the throb that started pulsing in my head and asked, "Worried about what?"

Tony took a deep breath. "Her friends from home. Mital," he spat out the name like it was poison, "and his buddies. I don't have the proof I need yet, but I think they're smuggling drugs into the country and they're using Shivani's business to do it."

I was shaking my head before he even finished speaking. "Do you have any evidence to back this up?" I asked.

"I'm working on it," he replied.

"Shivani would never be a part of something like that. You know that, right?"

His eyes said he wasn't sure. Tony finished his drink and held up his glass for a refill. I poured it and he downed it in one gulp.

"Could you talk to her? Feel her out about these 'friends from home'? See if she thinks there's anything suspicious going on with them?"

His behavior toward Mital from his last time at the bar made sense now. He'd warned me in his own inimitable style. Now he was staring at me, waiting for my answer. Could I say no to the man who had literally saved my life? Probably not.

"Okay." I agreed. "I'll invite her to lunch somewhere nice and have a chat. Will that do?"

Tony nodded and lifted his glass for another but I snatched it away. He got up and left without another word.

I gave last call, said goodnight to my minders, and Eric picked me up and we went upstairs. I had quite a lot to tell him, starting with my visit to Emil Straussman, my conversation with Elaine, and my possible leads. I decided not to mention Tony's visit. He wouldn't like me prying into a possible drug business, even from afar.

Instead, I left the best, or worst, for last. I told him about Sully's intention to become engaged to Dolores and marry her.

I was overcome by emotion when I got to that part and Eric held me close. "We can't let him do that," I said hugging Eric closer. Sully usually thought things through. He was tough and courageous. A real ohh-rah Marine. Traits I was sure wouldn't help with the wily Dolores.

"Sully's the bait fish and Dolores the shark in this relationship. She'll swallow him whole and spit up his bones."

Eric didn't remind me how dramatic I was being, or that sharks didn't spit up any leftovers. He just hugged me tighter. "I agree with you, Jude. Do you think Sully will take your advice and wait?" Eric pulled me closer. "He didn't buy the ring yet. That's something."

The corners of my mouth turned up just a little. "True. I know he wants my approval and I held out the possibility of me becoming friends with her, but in the end, it may not matter."

"You and Dolores friends? In what universe?"

"Now that would be something, wouldn't it?"

Chapter Fifty-Four

The next morning, I decided to check in with Lena Larsson. I hoped she'd been able to find out something—something bad—about Dolores Castel.

Lena answered on the first ring. "Larsson." Brisk and efficient like the woman herself.

"It's Jude. I was wondering if—"

She cut me off before I could ask my question. "Jude, I can't talk now. Come by the office in an hour and we'll speak then."

"Okay" was all I managed to get out before she was gone and the line went dead.

I was dressed and was ready to go when Agent Maguire showed up. His face registered surprise when he saw me. It was probably the loose cream silk shirt with cuffed balloon sleeves tucked into high-waisted Hepburn-style pants that had startled him. Quite a change from my usual all-over black.

"What?" I asked, tilting my head and putting him on the spot.

"Ah, um, nothing. You look nice." At least he didn't add 'for a change.'

"I have an appointment with Lena Larsson at her office on Twelfth Street. If you're coming with me, you're going to have to wait outside. This is personal business."

I must have sounded like I meant it because he held up his hand in surrender. "Okay. I got it."

Lena's assistant showed me into her office and I took a seat opposite her.

She nodded and held up a finger to indicate she'd be finishing the call she was on in a minute.

After she hung up, she sat back in her chair and stared at me, nodding her head slightly.

She placed a folder in front of herself and continued. "I made you a printout of what I've uncovered on Dolores Castel." She placed a hand on it indicating that I shouldn't open it yet. "Let's talk about it before you take a look." Her voice was calm, but I could see the excitement in her eyes. She'd definitely found something. "This woman. She's someone to watch out for."

"Okay," I said, forcing out the word around the lump that had suddenly formed in my throat. "So what did you discover about her?"

"Well, that's not her real name. At least not the one she was born with.

"Our Dolores was born Maria Dolores Martinez in Queens in Nineteen Sixty-eight, where she lived until she was eighteen."

Queens. So much for her not ever living in the city. "How did you find this out?" I asked.

Lena gave me a *Really, this is what you want to know?* look before she continued. "I worked backward from her California driver's license. When she married Olivier Castel and moved to Los Angeles, she turned in her New York license and applied for a new one.

"The name on the New York license was Dolores Martinez. She'd already changed her name from Maria. I don't know if it was legal or not." Lena raised an eyebrow.

Not too far off from Martime, I thought. I made a strangled noise and Lena looked up. "Jude are you okay?"

"Just something in my throat," I said, hoping she wouldn't call me on it.

"I went back further using her license photo and address and tapped into her info from the Motor Vehicles Bureau and then I...um...found her Social Security number and statements."

Hacked was more likely, but I kept that to myself.

"Did the statements show a record of her jobs?"

Lena nodded. "She lived down here on Eighth Street and First Avenue. Worked as a waitress and salesperson in the local shops. Then after about two years, she left the LES and moved uptown and got a job at a very fancy men's boutique on Madison Avenue. Not too surprising, since she was very attractive."

Lena turned the computer slightly so I could see the images of Dolores she'd captured from those years. "Anyway, that's when her true talents came out. She met a very wealthy man at the boutique who fell madly in love with her. His name was Mark Lowell. He divorced his wife, bought Dolores a townhouse, set up a trust, and changed his will in her favor—right before he asked her to marry him."

There's one born every minute was the look she tossed me as she shook her head.

"Unfortunately, he died of a coronary just days before the wedding."

I was sure my mouth was hanging open.

"His family was certain she murdered Mark, although they couldn't prove anything. They sued her but had to give up the case. There was no real evidence linking her to his death—he had a long-term heart condition and had been on meds for years. It was a big scandal at the time but eventually, the high society crowd got bored and moved on to other things.

"She doesn't surface again until about a year later when she moved to California and married Olivier Castel after knowing him for just two weeks."

I was shaking my head from side to side.

"What is it, Jude?" Lena asked.

"Probably nothing. Sorry. Keep going." *Dolores was careful to introduce Diego as her assistant, and he uses the name Lowell. Why? What was going on?*

Lena tapped the tip of her pen on her bottom lip before she continued. "In quite the coincidence, Castel also died of a coronary while he and Dolores were hiking in the hills outside of LA.

"She disappeared soon after he was cremated." Her tone was skeptical.

Cremation was a good way to get rid of any pesky evidence. "Did the police out there know about Mark Lowell?" I asked.

"Not at first. They found out later. When I called the LAPD and spoke with the detective who investigated Castel's death, John Mackelvoy, he was surprisingly forthcoming. Initially, they were going to let it go as a normal death but they became suspicious after the medical examiner thought Castel's death might have been hours earlier than Dolores told them. By the time they got the ME's report, he'd been cremated and there was no body to autopsy. They began to look into her life and uncovered her connection to Lowell and his death in New York

"In any event, she left California before the police finished their inquiries into the case." She sat back and stared at me. "I'm sure Detective Mackelvoy would be interested in speaking with her if he knew where to find her."

I didn't miss her meaning.

She handed me a piece of paper. "Here's his name and number if you want to contact him." Lena gave me a wicked smile.

"Thanks," I said and tucked the paper in my pocket."

I wanted to say more, but my thoughts were a jumble and no words would come. Finally, I asked, "Did you find anything about her taking acting classes at the New York Theater and Film Academy on Sixth Street. It's closed now but was open when Dolores lived here."

"Sorry. There was no mention of that. Here, Jude," she said as she handed me the folder. "Take this and look it over."

Her eyes told me she could see how upset I was by what she revealed. Although, she just nodded as I thanked her again and said goodbye.

"Don't worry. You'll be thanking me with dinner for the next year."

Outside, I stood in front of Lena's office and clutched the folder to my chest. Dolores had murdered two men. I was sure of it. She was a Black Widow, like the poisonous female spider who mated and then killed its partner. What did she have in mind for Sully? Get everything she could, then murder him, too?

I shuddered and started toward Agent Maguire who was waiting, passing the time texting on his cell.

"Call Agent Garlinger and see if she can meet with me now. It's urgent." My voice was strident and it startled Maguire.

"Sure." He punched in her number, said a few words, and nodded. "Okay, let's go.

Chapter Fifty-Five

"Want to tell me what's going on?" Maguire asked as we Ubered down to Federal Plaza.

I shook my head and clutched the file Lena had given me to my chest, afraid if I opened it I'd find a nest of hissing vipers all named Dolores waiting to strike.

Agent Garlinger was waiting in her office when Maguire and I entered. My words came tumbling out as I filled her in on what Lena had uncovered, then handed her the file.

Maguire and I sat across from her and she gave him a look that pinned him to his seat. "Why didn't you inform me of where you and Ms. Dillane were going?" she asked.

"It's not your agent's fault. I told him it was personal," I replied defiantly. I had believed it was. "Blame me."

"Don't worry, I will." She picked up the file. "Ari, give us a minute will you?"

He nodded and left, chastised and embarrassed.

It was obvious she was not thrilled that I'd gone off on my own again but opened the folder and read through Lena's notes.

When she was finished, she closed it and placed her hands on top. Her mouth was drawn into a straight line and worry was evident in her eyes. I knew this was not easy for her. She had emotional ties to Sully, the same as I did.

"We have to let him know who she is," I said. "He's thinking of asking her to marry him. We can't let that happen."

As soon as the words left my mouth, I realized I shouldn't have blurted it out like that. Elaine still had feelings for him. *Nice goin', Jude.* I watched as she fought to keep her emotions in check. I knew from personal experience how hard that could be.

Containing my feelings was not part of my DNA. I felt terrible about what I'd said, but it was something she needed to know.

After a moment, she took a breath and shook her head. "There's no real proof that she killed either of these men. If we tell Sully now, he won't believe us. And, we'll tip our hand to Dolores.

"Let me talk to Detective Mackelvoy in LA and see what, if any evidence they have of foul play in Castel's death. I'll also look back into the death of Mark Lowell."

"Do you think you can make a case?"

"It was a long time ago, Jude. There might not even be any useful files. Let me find out if his ex-wife is still in New York and listen to what she has to say."

She sat back in her chair and folded her arms across her middle. "Why did she turn up now? And on the Lower East Side? Who's her contact here?"

"Do you think it could be Bevins," I asked, "from their time at the academy?"

"I think that's a stretch. Why would she associate herself with someone on the run? There's no benefit to that. I think Emil Straussman is more likely."

I thought back to what Straussman had said about Maria, aka Dolores. The way he'd looked away when I asked if she'd been in touch. I was pretty certain she had been.

Dolores was tricky though. She may have hedged her bets and contacted Bevins, as well, not knowing, or caring, he was a serial killer.

"I think I should visit Straussman again as we planned." I checked my watch. "I have some time before I need to be back at The Lounge. Maybe Agent Maguire can come with me."

Elaine shook her head, raised her eyes to the ceiling and pointed to the door. "Just get Ari and go."

Chapter Fifty-Six

aguire and I made it back to Straussman's apartment in record time. As soon as we exited the car, he told me to wait until he checked out the building.

I shook my head. "No way. We're doing this together."

He let out an exasperated sigh that spoke volumes about how stubborn I was and then we headed up the stairs.

I could see into Straussman's parlor through the large windows at the top of the staircase. "It's dark inside," I said. "Maybe he's out."

"Let's see." Maguire rang the bell. We could hear its echo as it chimed inside. He waited a minute, then knocked on the door.

I stepped back in surprise as it swung open. An older man like Straussman wouldn't leave his door unlocked. I started to enter, but Maguire grabbed hold of my arm and held me back.

"Wait here," he whispered, his tone more serious than I'd ever heard, and for once I didn't argue. "Let me go in and check it out."

I nodded okay knowing in my gut that something was wrong. I didn't have to wait long to find out what.

A few minutes later Agent Maguire came out of the building. His face told me all I needed to know.

"Emil Straussman is dead," he said. "It looks like he was stabbed through the heart."

Maguire held on to me as I started to slide down the railing I'd been leaning against. My head was spinning and I felt faint.

"Jude I've got to call this in." He grabbed his phone and a moment later was speaking to Agent Garlinger.

I half-listened to his side of the conversation as I clenched my fists at the thought that Art Bevins had struck again. What would it take to make it end, I wondered as the sound of sirens got closer and closer. I knew the answer, as well. My death.

I was back at The Lounge. Garlinger had joined me and was trying to get me to calm down. It wasn't working. I couldn't stop pacing up and down in my tiny office.

"Why haven't you arrested him yet?" I spat out the words. "How many more people will you let him kill?" I moved up close to her and tossed the words in her face.

She took a step back. I knew I'd shocked her.

"Jude, we're—"

"Stop!" I held up my hand. "No more excuses. You know he's hiding nearby, somewhere you haven't looked. You have to find him. Now. Today."

I took a breath but not a cleansing one and started ranting again. "He's following me. I can feel him all over me like lice making my skin crawl. He wants to kill…"

My words petered out. I sunk down into my chair and held my head in my hands. I'd never felt such rage and hated and I couldn't control it. I took a few more deep breaths and this time it worked and I finally released my face from the prison of my fingers. "Sorry," I said. "I just…"

Elaine nodded and spoke softly as though I were a child in need of comfort. "Let's go over your conversation with Emil Straussman again. Okay?"

Agent Maguire and the NYPD were processing the scene for evidence. Elaine had decided to keep the murder as quiet as possible. No press, and no publicity about Bevins to put the public on edge with news of another murder. And, by the way, the perp was a serial killer the F.B.I. hadn't been able to catch.

"Are you sure you don't remember anything else from your visit? Did he indicate that Dolores might have been in touch with him?" She asked.

"The answer is still no, Elaine." I know I was still being curt and unhelpful, but I was fed up and exhausted. "It was just the feeling I got when he was looking at the old photos of the acting class."

She'd been leaning forward as she spoke but settled back in her chair. "Okay, Okay. Do you suspect Dolores had anything to do with the murder?"

"Not unless she's been in contact with Bevins and told him she and Straussman were still pals." I shook my head as though it was filled with pebbles I wanted to drop into a pond.

Her eyes lit up, "Maybe Bevins found *her*." She gestured toward the ceiling. "If he's hanging around the neighborhood, I bet he spotted her and recognized her."

She was warming to her theory. "Bevins would know how to find out all about Dolores, just the way your private investigator did. He'd use that information to threaten her and ensure she'd help him."

I let that sink in. Elaine was right. Bevins wouldn't hesitate to ensnare Dolores, especially if it meant getting to me.

"I'm going to put some agents on her. We'll watch her and see if she and Bevins meet up. She's a tricky one but if she'd had anything to do with this murder, we'll get her."

"You mean you'll get them both, right?" I could see my last jab hit home as she picked up her things and left.

I opened the bar as usual. Thankfully, Sully was a no-show. I wouldn't even be able to begin to explain the day to him. I knew I couldn't tell him what Lena had discovered about Dolores, never mind our theory about her connection to Art Bevins and possibly Straussman's murder.

It was a quiet night and I left the bar in Dean's capable hands. I went up to my apartment where Eric was waiting. I'd told him everything earlier. He wasn't happy about today but he wasn't angry, either. I'd done the right thing by going to Elaine but it didn't make me any less sad that Emil Straussman had died.

Was his death my fault? The odds were that Bevins had followed me to his apartment. If I had stayed away, would he still be alive? These were my thoughts as I tossed and turned trying to find the peace of sleep that just wouldn't come.

Chapter Fifty-Seven

Dolores was sneaking out of the apartment again, desperate not to run into Sully, or worse, Jude. Her hands were shaking and she slipped them into the pockets of her jacket as she walked down the six flights of stairs being as quiet as possible.

Art Bevins had 'arranged' for them to meet in the back garden of St. Mark's Church-In-The Bowery on Tenth Street, just a few blocks west. She was used to being the one in control, not the one following orders.

She'd tried to convince him it was a terrible idea; that he was putting himself at risk. He'd laughed at her transparent subterfuge and told her to be there at exactly three p.m.

The old stone church with its soaring spire and gardens was a beautiful setting even Dolores could appreciate. She entered the tree-filled space through an old iron gate and didn't see anyone but a doddering bag lady dressed in tatters and surrounded by her belongings.

Dolores took a seat on the bench Art had told her to choose. She'd give it five minutes, then leave.

A moment later she recoiled at the shrill mutterings of a woman's voice and assumed the bag lady a few benches down on the other side of the path was talking to herself.

"Oh, Dolores, you should see your face. Still a snob, aren't you? It's me, Art," he said as he waddled closer to her. The disdain he felt for her was like a slap in the face.

She sucked in her breath and started to rise. "Don't," Art barked in that same voice. "Don't look at me. Just listen. I've left an envelope at the left side of the gate at the entrance to the garden. It contains detailed instructions of exactly what you have to do to help me get rid of that bitch, Jude."

He'd figured out how much she hated Sully's favorite tenant. Well, it wasn't that hard to do.

"Listen carefully, Dolores. It's extremely important. If you don't do exactly what I tell you to, not only will I expose your past, but you will be my next victim. Do you understand?"

Dolores sat perfectly still, hardly daring to breathe as cold dread slid down her spine like a snake ready to strike.

"Nod, if you do."

She tipped her chin down toward her chest.

"Excellent. I'll be going now but I suggest you remain here for a few minutes and enjoy the lovely afternoon." With that, the bag lady heaved herself off her bench with a grunt, gathered her packages, and lumbered to the other end of the path, muttering under her breath until she was outside.

How had this happened? She was supposed to be the one in charge; the one getting revenge. What did Bevins know about her life in California? Had he found out the truth? Dolores wanted to run screaming out of the garden, and leave the city for somewhere safe. But she knew if she did that, no matter where she ran, Art would find her and kill her. She couldn't go to the police. Art would make sure everything she'd done would be exposed. She had no choice but to do what he asked.

She sat quietly for a few minutes longer, calming herself before leaving. Where, she wondered, was Art's bolt hole. He seemed able to appear and disappear at will, always as some other character that no one recognized. She was certain he was hiding somewhere nearby.

Dolores checked to make sure no one was watching as she stopped at the exit and picked up the envelope waiting there, and stuffed it in her pocket.

Sully had told her that Art had enjoyed leaving threatening notes for Jude. She was sure this one was no exception. Only this time, both she and Jude could be marked for death…unless she could turn this to her advantage. She had to stay calm and think clearly. And, maybe, just maybe, she'd find a way to survive.

Chapter Fifty-Eight

My bed was covered with piles of clothes I'd pulled out of the closet and was systematically discarding. *I don't have a thing to wear,* I thought.

Okay, I had plenty to choose from but I was meeting Shivani for lunch and I wanted to look great, maybe wear something newer than a vintage outfit from the Sixties.

I finally settled on a slim gray skirt, orange sweater, and the new orange buckled cape from Michael Kors that Eric had given me as a gift. He was such a good boyfriend, wasn't he? Or, maybe he thought I just needed a new look.

Of course, Shiv breezed in, looking like a million dollars, which was probably almost the cost of the clothes on her back. I had instant shoe-woo envy for her over-the-thigh black suede red-soled Louboutin stiletto boots. Maybe in another lifetime.

We double air-kissed and were seated opposite each other at a small table near the front. A prime table. Of course, Shiv knew the bistro's owner who was fawning over her just a bit too much.

He offered us menus, clapped his hands, and left. Shiv rolled her eyes and whispered, "He has a little crush on me."

"No. Really? I'd never have imagined."

"It's good to see you, Jude." She looked over my shoulder toward the plate glass window in the front of the restaurant. "Any creepy guys following you today?"

I laughed, brushing off the question. *How about a serial killer who's been stalking me for weeks? You know, that guy who killed all those people.* Of course, I kept that to myself. Shiv hadn't noticed Maguire who was sitting at the tiny bar upfront. Better not to mention my Fibbie minder.

By the time our entreés arrived—a friseé salad for her and moules marinière with extra French bread on the side for me—we'd pretty much exhausted our small talk about the neighborhood and our mutual friends.

I'd spent the morning, aside from choosing my outfit, trying to think of a way to bring up Mital without arousing any suspicion that I was prying.

Shiv did it for me. "Did you have fun at my party? My friends from home seemed to enjoy your company very much." A wicked grin crossed her face.

I knew she meant Mital. I looked down at the pristine white table cloth and nodded. "I did. It was fabulous, as usual. I enjoyed talking to Mital." I looked up and smiled. "He stopped in at The Lounge last week."

"And?" She leaned forward expectantly.

I shook my head. "He didn't ask me out. Even if he did, I would have had to say no because of Eric. We're back together."

Shiv looked disappointed. I think matchmaking ran in her blood.

"We chatted for a little while. He had a drink, then left." I hoped I sounded matter of fact. *Thanks to Tony Napoli,* I wanted to add.

"How is Mital doing? Is he planning to stay in the city?" These were questions you might ask about someone's friend, right? At least I hoped so.

"He's going to be here for a while. He just started a new import/export business."

"Wow. That sounds exciting. What kinds of products will they be shipping? Beautiful things from India, I hope. I wouldn't mind ordering a gorgeous silk sari. At a friends and family discount, of course."

Shiv shook her head. "No clothing or art, I'm afraid. Actually, they'll be selling different kinds of spices and sauces. I'm going to be working with Mital on the company's PR efforts. It will be a change from my usual clients. I think it will be fun."

Don't do it, I wanted to scream, Tony's talk of drug trafficking running through my head.

"Is Tony Napoli setting up their IT systems?"

A tiny frown appeared between her brows. "I think they have a friend who's going to do that for them. Why do you ask?" Her voice changed as well, her tone clipped.

I could see Shiv was beginning to wonder why I was asking so many questions. I had to cut this off. "I thought since Tony worked for your company, you might have recommended him."

The frown deepened. "You seem more interested in Mital and his business than you let on, despite Eric." Then, she must have realized how sharp she sounded and smiled. "You can have Mital, but forget about Tony. I'm not sharing him with anyone. His IT skills are all mine."

We paid our bill and said our goodbyes. I really didn't have much to show for lunch. Except that somehow I'd annoyed Shiv along with the nagging feeling that Tony would ask me to spy for him again.

Chapter Fifty-Nine

Sully came into The Lounge around four-thirty to keep me company while I set up the bar. He'd done it every day like clockwork after getting home from The Big City Food Coop where he volunteered. Until Dolores showed up. Today, he took his regular seat at the bar and I poured his usual shot of Jameson, praying he wouldn't bring up Dolores or the photo of the ring burning a hole in his pocket.

"I haven't seen you for a while," he said, giving me a wary glance. "What have you been up to?"

I gulped before I answered. Did my guilt for spying on his girlfriend show? Did he know what I'd actually been doing? I went on the defensive. "What are you talking about? You were just here two nights ago."

"Yeah, well." He sighed like a miser having to drop some money into the collection plate. Dispirited and desolate. "I haven't seen Dolores for a few days. I hope she's not getting tired of me."

Fat chance, I almost blurted out. She's making her plans to trap you and finish you off. I hoped these thoughts didn't show on my face.

"C'mon, Sully, maybe she's been busy." After all, it takes skill and cunning to get away with murder.

I had to stop my brain from going in that direction, or Sully was sure to notice something was going on with me, like a parent who knows you've been lying. He'd probably think it had to do with Dolores since lately, he thought everything had to do with her. I couldn't let that happen. Not until I figured out how to stop her.

"How is her project to start a design business going? That's a big endeavor.

It's going to take a lot of her time to set up."

"You're probably right." He nodded.

Thank god, he was buying what I was selling.

"I think I'll call her and see if she's free for dinner so we can talk about her plans." He finished his drink, performed his usual routine, signaling that he was done.

"Good idea," I said, forcing a smile.

I couldn't keep lying to him like this. Okay, I wasn't exactly lying, but I was avoiding the truth. We, Elaine and I, would have to figure out something soon. Before Dolores acted.

I had to put this out of my mind. At least for a little while. My bar needed tending before we opened.

I blasted some Bowie as I washed out the bar spill mats, restocked the well bottles, and grabbed a fresh batch of bar wipes. Unfortunately, that took all of fifteen minutes, and I was back to dwelling on the problem of our Black Widow.

I had another ten minutes before I opened officially, and decided to check in with Agent Garlinger.

"Sully was just here," I said, the moment she answered. "I don't know what to do. I...we...can't tell him. Can we?" By we, I meant her.

"Not yet," Garlinger replied. "I just got the go-ahead to put people on her. We'll be watching her twenty-four-seven."

"Will Sully be safe?" The idea of that brave, strong Marine being felled by that murderous witch, made me dizzy.

"We'll do everything to keep him that way," Garlinger replied.

Not exactly the answer I was hoping for. But one I'd have to take for now.

"And you," she continued, "don't do anything stupid, like confronting Dolores. And, under no circumstances, do not go anywhere without Maguire." Her voice was clipped and strident. "Understand?"

"Is something going on I should know about, aside from Dolores?"

She took too long to answer. "No. Nothing to share. But Bevins is still out there, so be careful."

After she hung up, I stared at my cell. Garlinger was up to something and she was shutting me out. Well, we'd see about that.

I opened The Lounge for business. The crew and Maguire, my babysitter, who was now officially one of them, had finished family dinner. I called him over and told him I wanted to speak with him later. His expression told me he wondered why. I'd let him stew about that for a while.

In the meantime, the bar started to fill up and I was finally able to concentrate on serving drinks.

Maguire kept glancing over at me, most likely wondering what it was I wanted to talk about. He texted a few times, probably to Garlinger asking what was happening. Good. When I finally did get to speak with him, he might let something spill. My strategy seemed to be working. Well, that was nice, for a change.

A few hours later, Maguire was still sending me glances every few minutes. I guess I had let him stew long enough and I nodded toward the bar for him to come over.

"How about a glass of wine, Ari?" I asked, adding to his confusion. I usually called him Maguire.

"I…well…" He glanced at his watch. "Sure, why not. My shift's officially over."

"Oh, so you're going to abandon me then?"

"No. No. I didn't mean that. I'll be here until you close and the other team takes over."

I'd poured him a glass of a ruby red Montepulciano d'Abruzzo while he'd been speaking and put it in front of him.

He took a tentative sip, then made a satisfied murmur of contentment.

"Delicious, right?" I asked.

He diverted my question with one of his own. "So, what did you want to speak about?"

"What's Agent Garlinger holding back from me? Does she have new information on Bevins?"

"You know I can't tell you anything without her approval." He raised his hands in a what can I do manner.

"You'd better. Or, I'll tell her you were drinking on the job. That should go over big." I pinned him with a stare to underscore my words.

His mouth opened in a big 'O' and I knew he couldn't tell if I meant it or not. There, I'd ruined another relationship.

"You wouldn't do that, would you? She'd be…really upset."

What he meant was that she'd probably move him to a branch office in Staten Island.

"Possibly. But we can avoid all that, don't you think?" I gave him a few seconds to mull it over. "Just tell me what's going on and she never has to know."

"I…umm…" He couldn't decide whether to trust me or not. He finally caved. "She got an anonymous tip that Bevins is living somewhere on Tenth Street between First and Second Avenues."

"Where? What building?" I'd figured he was hiding somewhere in the neighborhood, but it finally hit me, he was close, way too close.

Maguire shook his head. "We don't know. We got a tip on the hotline and it seemed credible."

"Was it a woman?" I asked. Dolores was the first person I'd thought of.

"No. It was a guy."

"Are you sure it wasn't a woman?" I knew how devious Dolores could be.

"No, A guy. Wouldn't leave a name and disguised his voice. But he had details that Garlinger thought were worth looking into."

"What kind of details?" I was pacing back and forth in front of him, like a lawyer in front of a jury.

"I don't know. " He shook his head. "She didn't share that with me. All I know is that teams are going door to door, checking every apartment and building on that block as well as Ninth and Eleventh Streets. And, we're supposed to keep an extra careful watch on you."

He looked crestfallen over the fact that he'd broken Garlinger's trust and told me but he understood my reason for wanting to know. "We won't let you down. We'll get him, Jude. And soon."

And, I felt like a shit for forcing it out of him. It was a mean trick to get him to talk. "You know I didn't mean it about letting Garlinger think you were drinking, don't you?"

"Yeah, I do," he said. But something in his tone made me think he didn't quite believe me. And he might never believe me again.

Chapter Sixty

Sully had been so preoccupied with thoughts of Dolores, he forgot to remind me the usual five times about our meeting with Carol Batista and the ComedyClub Ltd. people. Mark Brandon, the restaurant broker, would also be there to answer any questions either side had.

Sully picked me up at ten with a curt "Ready to go?"

I got the idea that things hadn't gone that well with Dolores last evening but this time I kept my thoughts to myself.

Once again, I dressed for a professional business meeting in soft black wool pants a gray button-down shirt, and a darker gray cardigan.

Sully didn't speak the whole time it took us to get uptown to Carol's office. His silence reminded me of the military's former policy of 'Don't ask. Don't tell.' and right now that seemed like a really good idea.

The Upper East Side couldn't have been more different from where I lived and worked. The buildings were much fancier and the people I noticed seemed to be exceptionally well-dressed. No wonder Dolores had gravitated to this part of town all those years ago. It was where the money was and still is.

Inside Carol's office, the same lovely young receptionist greeted us with a smile and let Carol know we had arrived. Two minutes later, Carol came out and escorted us to a conference room with a large, round glass table, comfortable chairs, and a modern sideboard.

"Well, Jude, are you ready for this?" she asked after we had taken our seats around the table.

"Yeah, I am, but I have to admit I'm kind of nervous." Sully leaned over and patted my shoulder like someone trying to calm their favorite pet. I shook him off, still a little annoyed that he'd shut me out this morning.

Carol nodded. "That's understandable. It's a big change for your business, especially with Pete Angel leaving."

I didn't want to think about Pete now, or I might go to pieces. "Yes, it is," I replied, keeping my voice matter of fact.

"Well, the good news is that Nancy Carrol and Bill Blair, the owners of the ComedyClub Ltd. are very enthused about being part of The Corner Lounge. "And," she paused as she handed me a folder, "their business is very reputable and profitable. I think their offer is fair and with the money you inherited, you'll have enough to buy out Pete and even have some left over."

Just then, the receptionist buzzed to let her know everyone else had arrived. When she went out to get them, I looked over at Sully.

"Sully…" I started.

"It's good, Jude. It's going to work."

Carol came back into the conference room and made the introductions. Nancy, a tall, pretty blond, and Bill, an even taller dark-haired man, were both immediately open, friendly, and enthusiastic. We discussed their offer and what it would entail over coffee and pastries from the fancy bakery I'd noticed on the corner.

It was obvious that Bill had been a comedian before stepping up to a management role. Nancy rolled her eyes at some of his jokes, but you could tell they were a good team. Mark Brandon answered the few questions they had about The Lounge and the space downstairs. He'd described it to them previously and shown them the building's floor plan and it had sounded ideal.

Sully explained that it was an empty space and that he'd work with them to renovate it as a club. They were going to stop by in the next day or two to look it over and share their ideas on a layout and décor.

We all shook hands and the three of them left. I looked at Carol and smiled. "It's going to be okay, isn't it?" I asked.

"Yes, it will." She smiled back. "What do you think Sully?"

"I agree," he replied unemotionally, not meeting her eyes.

Carol shot me a look that asked *what's up with him?*

I shrugged as if I didn't know, even though I did. The disease had a name: Dolores.

She got back to business quickly. "Jude, why don't you look over the papers on ComedyClub Ltd., and in the meantime, I'll work on the agreement for the partnership. I'll also let Pete's attorney know that we are moving forward and set up a meeting. We'll talk soon and go over the agreement together," Carol added. "Okay with both of you?"

"That sounds good," I said while Sully remained silent.

We left Carol and slid into the Uber that was waiting for us. Once we were settled, I turned toward Sully. "What's going on with you?"

"Not now." He shook his head. "We'll discuss it later."

We rode the rest of the way home in silence. When we arrived, I headed for The Lounge and Sully walked toward his apartment with a half-hearted wave tossed over his shoulder.

This was not good. Not good at all.

At the Lounge, I went straight to the kitchen and poked my head inside. Pete and Alain were at the marble prep counter, heads together going over what I presumed was the list for dinner. I cleared my throat letting Pete know I was there.

He looked up and smiled. "Hey. What's up?" he asked.

I felt a twinge in my chest. He seemed much happier now that he'd made the decision to leave.

"Let me know when you have a few minutes to talk," I replied.

"Alain and I are almost done. Give me five."

True to his word, five minutes later he called the house phone at the bar and told me to come on back.

We went into his office and he closed the door for privacy.

"So…" I started, "I just got back from a meeting with my lawyer and the comedy club people," nodding my head quickly as I spoke. "It went well and I'm going to do it." My words had poured out in a rush, the only way I could say what I had to. I paused, taking a deep breath to steady myself. "Carol

Batista will call your attorney and put the paperwork for the sale of The Lounge in motion. It might take a month or so to finalize."

Pete cut me off. "Don't stress about how long it takes, Jude. We'll work it out." He leaned forward and took my hand reassuring me. "Now, how about some lunch while we talk about Restaurant Week."

Pete made us fat roast beef and cheddar sandwiches with horseradish mustard on homemade ciabatta. Delicious, of course. We chatted while we ate, making sure everything was in place for this important milestone for The Lounge.

It was less than a week away and I wanted it to be perfect. It made me remember what my mom used to say to me when I 'wanted' something. "Umm, it's nice to want things, honey, but you have to work for them." The way things had been going lately, what I wanted might not matter.

Chapter Sixty-One

Eric came by after work and I filled him in on that day's meeting. He gave me a big hug and told me I was doing the right thing. Then, I told him how weird Sully had been acting. Eric thought Dolores might be giving him a hard time but we both knew if she was, it was just for show. I had no doubt she'd just keep stringing him along to get what she wanted.

Well, it was working, wasn't it?

I kept my eye on the door all night, but Sully didn't appear. Tony and Oscar showed up around the same time and plopped down next to each other. I served them and moved off down the bar, but I could feel Tony glancing at me every few minutes. I knew he was jonesing to know about my lunch with Shivani.

When Oscar went downstairs to the men's room, I moseyed over to Tony. "So, how's everything going?" I asked, lifting an eyebrow.

"Cut it out." He moved in closer and kept his voice low. "Did you learn anything from Shiv about Mital?"

"Maybe." I shrugged my right shoulder toward my ear.

"Jude." I could hear the impatience in his voice.

"Okay, okay." I held up my hands. "Mital and some of his friends are starting an import/export business marketing spices and sauces from India. He plans to be here for quite a while."

"That's it?" Tony asked.

You're the cop, not me. You find out. I wanted to say.

"Yup. And Tony, I know I owe you but don't ask me to do this again."

Just then Oscar rejoined Tony at the bar. He looked from me to Tony, a frown forming on his face. "What's going on?"

"Tony just mentioned he didn't want to eat alone and he'd like to invite you for dinner," I said. "I'd recommend the steak pomme frites." It was one of the most expensive items on the menu. If looks could kill, Tony would've nailed it.

"I accept," Oscar said in a flash. "Let's get a table."

I laughed silently as the two men went to the hostess station. A little levity in the midst of a disaster was good every once in a while, wasn't it?

Chapter Sixty-Two

I tossed and turned while trying to fall asleep thinking about Bevins being so near to me. What did I expect? He wasn't stalking me from New Jersey. I kept thinking that Dolores had something to do with the 'tip' to the hotline. Not that I could prove it, or ask Garlinger about it without ratting out Maguire.

With a sigh, I slid out of bed and left Eric to sleep peacefully. I walked into the living room and stared out my window onto a moonlit street, quiet in the hours before dawn.

Sister Mary Margaret's threats of burning in hell were nothing compared to this. The here and now felt much scarier than the idea of a searing afterlife.

I watched the sky lighten and the sun come up over the East River. I made coffee and took a mug back to the window and thought about everything that had happened.

I was sort of off in la-la land when I heard the building's front door bang closed. I looked down and noticed a figure emerging from the front of the building and walking along Tenth Street in the direction of the river.

It was Dolores looking over her shoulder every few steps. Where was she going at six a.m., sneaking around like she didn't want to be seen?

I put the mug down on the coffee table and scrambled into my clothes, making it out of the apartment in record time.

On Tenth Street, I could see her walking toward the pedestrian bridge to the river promenade. Could she just be taking an early morning walk? If that were true, why was she being so furtive?

I stayed well back so she wouldn't see me. I was about to walk onto the bridge when I felt a hand grip my arm. I gave a little gasp that was sliding toward a full-scale scream, when a voice said, "It's me, Jude."

"Sully? What…what are you doing here? You practically scared the life out of me."

He stood there, head hanging down, looking sheepish. "I was following you following Dolores. I know, before you say anything, it was a stupid idea."

"But why?" I asked.

"It's hard to…explain. Let's go home and we'll talk."

I nodded in agreement. We definitely had to talk. I looked across the Drive and didn't see Dolores anywhere. She'd disappeared after she crossed the bridge. Hopefully, the team of Feds Garlinger had on her were watching, although I hadn't noticed them.

What the hell was going on, I wondered as Sully and I walked back home.

We went up to his apartment, which looked the same as usual, not a cushion or a magazine out of place. But something felt weird as soon as I stepped inside, like an awful, hovering black cloud was about to descend on us. I sat down on the edge of the couch hunched forward, unable to shake the feeling as I waited for Sully to tell me what was on his mind. Although I had a pretty good idea of what it might be.

Sully fiddled around making coffee and I could tell he was working up the courage to say whatever it was he wanted to say. Eventually, he handed me a mug and sat down opposite me.

"So," I said, "what is it?"

"It's…Dolores."

Well, gee, right again. "What about her?"

"She, umm, thinks I'm spending too much time with you. That it's not healthy for either of us." At least he had the good sense to look embarrassed.

I almost spit out the mouthful of coffee I'd just taken. "Wait. What the hell is that supposed to mean?"

He finally looked me in the eye, his own silvery-blue ones clouded with sadness. "I think she might be a little bit jealous of our relationship."

"Of me? That's ridiculous. We're friends. Good friends. Like family. That's our relationship. Why would she be jealous?" I asked.

But I knew the real reason. She knew Sully was helping me financially, with construction for the comedy club and my legal fees, which I intended to pay back eventually. What a bitch. She was afraid she'd miss out on a big chunk of change that was coming my way before she could get her hands on it.

My anger started hissing out like the steam from the cappuccino machine at the coffee station. I tamped it down and tried to think calmly. Sully had always had my six, marching in protective mode right behind me.

She'd put Sully in a choose-or-lose position without coming out and saying it. She'd set the bait and sprung the trap. Dolores knew how much he cared about her...and me. One of us...me...would have to go. Not if I had anything to say about it.

I couldn't tell him what Garlinger and I had found out about her. Not yet. Not until we had all the information and proof. But I couldn't let him run off and marry her either.

I took a deep, cleansing breath before I spoke. "I know you care very deeply for her and I respect that. I would never want to come between you—*like hell, I wouldn't*—but you know how much I value your friendship. I don't want it to slip away. But if that's how it has to be..." I dipped my head and let my words trail off.

"No, Jude. That's not what I...It's just I feel..." A look of confusion spread across his face. Not something I was used to seeing in this strong, confident former Marine.

I decided to turn the tables on our resident Black Widow. "I know that Dolores really cares for you and she really wouldn't want you to abandon your friends. She's probably just a little confused about your feelings for her. Talk to her and explain to her there's no reason to be jealous. Let her know how much I'm looking forward to being friends. I mean it. I'm sure she'll come around." My voice was dripping with as much sincerity as I could manage and saying the words wasn't easy. The only thing I was sure of was that she'd want to kick my butt from here to the river.

Sully nodded. With that, I got up, put my mug in the sink, and left his apartment without another word. Although it was hard, I'd behaved like a grown-up, albeit a sneaky one, and I hoped my ploy had worked. I was barely inside my apartment before I had my cell out and was speed-dialing Garlinger. The situation was critical and we needed to take command of it very soon.

Chapter Sixty-Three

Dolores kept glancing over her shoulder certain that Bevins would appear from nowhere, strangle her and leave her gasping for air as the life flowed out of her. She'd never lived in fear before and shuddered at what it was doing to her.

The note he'd given her was extremely strange. It directed her to visit an address on Sixth Street on Friday at midnight. Her breath caught in her chest. She recognized the address immediately. It was a building right across from the New York Theater and Film Academy she and Bevins had attended.

Once at the building, Dolores was to ask for a man named Wills and pick up an envelope, which she was to hold until further instructions.

What was Bevins playing at? Wills sounded like a character in one of the plays they'd performed all those years ago.

If she disobeyed Bevins's instructions, there would be consequences. Dire consequences.

She had no doubt he meant every word. *How had he turned the tables on her so easily?* She wondered again.

A new spiral of fear curled up her spine and she felt the hair on the back of her neck stand up. She whipped around but didn't see anyone suspicious on the promenade, certainly no bag ladies today. She was letting her imagination and fear get the best of her again.

Even though it was early, there were a few people rollerblading along the path, some people on benches talking quietly, and a youngish couple walking hand in hand.

Finally, she stopped walking and stared off into the river.

She'd taken an enormous chance when she'd met Art in the garden of St. Mark's Church. She prayed—something she hadn't done since she was a girl—he hadn't spotted a disguised Diego waiting at the other exit who she'd instructed to look for anyone unusual coming out of the garden and follow. For once, he'd paid attention and trailed the odd-looking bag lady to the abandoned Blackthorne Collier building on Tenth Street.

When he reported to Dolores later that afternoon, she was extremely pleased. She had him call the F.B.I. tip line and leave a semi-cryptic message about seeing the wanted serial killer, Art Bevins, somewhere near Tenth or Eleventh Street.

Diego seemed hesitant to do this. "What if they find out who I am? They might arrest me."

Dolores could sense the fear in his voice. "There's nothing to worry about, darling. It's an anonymous call. They won't know who you are."

She knew if Art discovered what she'd done, he wouldn't hesitate to kill her. And, if he delved into Diego's life, he would become a victim, too. She could not let that happen. If the F.B.I. got him quickly, she'd be free to continue with her plans to separate Sully from his 'good friend' Jude and make sure he married 'the love of his life' Dolores.

She looked around the promenade again. The sun had come out and a few more people were walking along the path. She turned her face to the sky, took a deep breath, and decided to return home.

She never noticed the young couple who followed from afar.

Chapter Sixty-Four

As calm as I'd been with Sully was exactly the opposite of how rattled I was speaking with Elaine. She asked me to tell her everything again, slower this time.

I did. "What are we going to do?" I asked. "We can't let her get him." I knew I sounded desperate. I didn't want to lose someone else I cared for. I could do without Sully for a few days, but not if he was gone for good.

I could feel Elaine's dismay as if she were standing next to me. When she replied her voice sounded tired and old. Chasing a serial killer and a crazy black widow were catching up with her.

"Okay, Jude. Let me talk to Detective Mackelvoy one more time and see what's happening in California. Last time we spoke, he said he had one more lead to chase down. Once, I do that, we'll go see Sully together."

We both remained silent for a moment. *It won't be pretty,* I thought.

"Sure," I finally spat out. Then, in the most casual way possible, I segued into the other problem, Art Bevins.

My "So any new leads on Bevins's whereabouts?" was met by another silence.

"What makes you ask that? You know I'd tell you if there was. I thought we were talking about Sully." Suspicion laced her words.

"C'mon, Elaine. I do have an interest in catching him. I'm sick and tired of looking over my shoulder and having minders with me everywhere I go."

"It's for your safety. You know that. And yes, we do have a lead we're following up on. Before you ask, I can't tell you about it just yet." She'd matched my tone with her own.

Instead of answering, she abruptly changed the subject, probably hoping I wouldn't ask any more questions. "Is Maguire with you?"

Damn. Were we busted? Was she going to ask him if he'd told me about the hotline tip? "No," I said. "I'm in the office and he's upstairs in the restaurant. Want me to get him?"

There was another long pause. "No. I'll speak to him later. And, I'll get back to you after I talk with Mackelvoy.

"Behave, Jude. Don't go looking for Bevins and make me put you in protective custody." She waited a beat then said goodbye.

I sat there staring at my cell. Elaine had given me an idea. She'd think it was a bad one, but it seemed pretty good to me, something I could definitely carry off. The only problem was my minders and how I could shake them. Well, I had all night to figure it out.

Dean and I were mixing drinks and pulling beers like there was no tomorrow.

Everyone was in a good mood. Maybe these people knew something I didn't.

Eric was sitting in Sully's usual seat. I filled him in a little at a time, whenever I was down at that end of the bar.

"Close your mouth," I'd told him at one point, his incredulous expression making his face almost comical.

"What are you going to do?" he asked.

"Tell you later," I replied and sped off to the service end where the orders seemed to be non-stop.

To make things even more chaotic, Nancy Carrol and Bill Blair stopped in for a drink. I could see they were impressed by the size of the crowd. *Thank you, God, for small favors.* They took the two stools just becoming vacant next to Eric. I made the introductions, got them some drinks, and left them to chat.

I knew my boyfriend would do me proud and he didn't disappoint. When they left, they told me how much they enjoyed meeting him and that they were looking forward to seeing him again.

When things quieted down, I finished telling Eric about my conversation with Sully and how I'd tried to manage it, including my conversation with Garlinger.

"That Dolores qualifies as a super bitch." He shook his head. "Jeez, how are you going to handle this?"

"Garlinger is going to speak to Mackelvoy in LA and get an update on her status there with the police. After that happens, we'll tackle it together."

"But that could take time. What about right now? Is Sully with her? Will she convince him to drop you…drop all of us?" Eric's voice was filled with tension.

"I don't know." I sighed. "I also feel guilty because I tricked Maguire into sharing information he shouldn't have."

"C'mon. He knows you'd never rat him out. He has to realize you were just phishing for info."

I smiled up at Eric. "Probably. Maybe. We'll see."

I did my closing chores, locked up The Lounge, and Eric and I walked upstairs arms around each other.

I couldn't tell him what I had planned for tomorrow. I wouldn't lie to him but he couldn't know because he'd never approve.

Chapter Sixty-Five

I was out of bed the second Eric tossed me a 'bye, honey,' and left for his office, already planning what I'd need for my morning's excursion. Actually, it was Bevins and his disguises that had given me the idea.

I planned to bring everything down to my office early and have it waiting. I'd tell Maguire I was spending the morning finalizing our Restaurant Week menus and going over all the orders. I was not to be disturbed by anyone, no matter who or what they wanted. I'd set the answering machine to pick up after one ring and I'd return calls when I got back.

Keeping Maguire away would be the tricky part. He was already suspicious of me and I'd have to convince him I was going to stay put. I was still on shaky ground about him trusting me and if he ever found out about what I was doing, he'd never speak to me again. Worse, he could lose his job. *Is this worth it?* I asked myself.

Still not sure, I drank a cup of coffee as I gathered the clothes I'd change into: really old, faded, and ripped jeans from when I was a teenager, now a little short; A ragged hoodie that bagged and sagged; a well-worn jeans jacket; and old, mismatched sneakers.

I put all these clothes into a tote bag along with a ratty, long blonde wig I'd worn for a Halloween party, and the kind of makeup that would transform me into a zonked-out junkie.

I know, maybe not the best disguise. But I could stumble around like I was looking to score while I'd really be searching for Bevins.

I zipped up the bag, showered, and dressed in my regular work clothes. At eight o'clock, I texted Maguire and told him I was starting early.

He got to The Lounge pretty soon after and I explained that I needed total privacy and was not to be disturbed under any circumstances.

"I should be done by one o'clock at the latest and I'll come up then. In the meantime, order breakfast on me and relax."

He gave me a suspicious look, sure I was up to something.

"What? Pete will have my butt if I don't get this done." Maguire'd been around The Lounge long enough now to know that Restaurant Week was a really big deal for us.

"Okay, I won't let anyone bother you." He held up his hands. I hope he was including himself. "Call up if you need help."

"Will do," I replied and headed downstairs, locking the staircase door next to the bar behind me.

The first thing I did was remove my disguise from my tote bag, and lay out the makeup I'd use to make myself over into a strung-out street junkie.

I was pale by nature but added an almost white foundation to my face, so now I looked ghostly. I blended in ashy gray hollows under my eyes and cheekbones to give me a gaunt appearance. Then I applied eyeliner in bold strokes, smearing it under my bottom lids, and finished with layers of mascara so thick they made my lashes stick together.

When I put on the blonde wig and looked in the mirror, I was shocked. I looked bad. Really bad. Good. I was ready.

In all the time I'd owned The Lounge, I'd never thought much about the extra space downstairs. A corridor led to the back of the building, my office on one side and bathrooms and a storeroom on the other. At the very end of the corridor, was the space we'd be transforming for the comedy club and across from it, a door to the back staircase, which opened next to The Lounge's rear exit.

This was how I planned to get out and back in without being seen. I listened for a minute then tiptoed up the backstairs, making sure the door behind me was locked.

At the top of the staircase, I cautiously opened the other door a few inches, again listening for anyone who might be lurking—okay, I was the one lurking. I could hear Maguire on his phone and knew it was a good moment to leave.

I slid out through the small opening and quietly latched the door, then opened the restaurant's back door and scrambled out. No one was around and the alleyway was clear.

I hoped to get this over with sooner than I'd planned, so I could be back at The Lounge well before one o'clock.

I pulled the hoodie up over my blonde hair, dipped my head, and hunched over losing a few of my five-foot-nine inches. I stumbled from side to side as I walked. Once I was out on Avenue B, I headed west to First Avenue.

The few people I passed kept a wide berth. They probably thought I was going to hit them up for money, or even worse, touch them.

When I got to First Avenue and Tenth Street, I zigzagged to the uptown side, so I'd be across from the Blackthorne Collier Building. Then, I sat down on the ground, drew my legs up, and placed my head on my knees bobbing it up and down while I waited and watched.

A few street people went in and out of the building, via a loose board on the side of the main staircase. There was a mother with a baby, a short man wrapped in layers and layers of clothes that made him look like a bowling ball, and two teens furtively looking over their shoulders who had probably just scored some drugs. Not one of them could be Art Bevins, even in disguise. If he was here, he was staying put.

I'd noticed a pile of garbage on the other side of the staircase. Maybe I'd find some evidence that Bevins was inside. I crossed the street and began to sift through the pile of junk, sure no one would notice another junkie digging around. A small cardboard box caught my eye. It had the name of one of our suppliers on the top. I scooped it up and stuck it under my hoodie. Then, I scurried back across the street.

After a few hours, I decided it was futile and I was getting up to leave for home. I took one more look at the building and just as I did, a man stepped. out from the side entrance. I sat back down and caught my breath. It was Diego Lowell. What was *he* doing here? Had Dolores sent him to

Art Bevins? Had Bevins spotted me watching the building? It was time to go. Defending myself against Diego was one thing, but if Bevins saw me it could be deadly.

Before I got to The Lounge, I ducked into an alleyway and tossed my wig. I wiped off as much of the makeup as I could with the tissues I'd tucked into my pocket.

At the restaurant, as I slipped in through the back door I could hear some activity in the kitchen. I unlatched the door at the top of the staircase and scrambled down fast and made it to my office without anyone noticing.

I sat at my desk and got my emotions under control. It had been a dumb idea to look for Bevins. I wanted to get him as much as he wanted to get me. I tried not to imagine what would have happened if he had been there and seen me. I'd risked my life and maybe the investigation on a whim.

I took out the box I'd found. When I lifted the lid, I recoiled as if Bevins was standing in front of me.

The box was filled with photos of me, all with my eyes scratched out. I couldn't help myself from reaching out and touching them. There were a few dozen of these horrible images and I could feel the hate wafting off of them. After a minute, I pulled my hands away, anger and pain coming in waves. Why had he thrown them out? Did he believe his plan to kill me was almost complete?

I shook my head. No more playing detective.

Somehow, I had to let Garlinger know about these photos and that Diego was part of Bevins's plan. Since I couldn't tell her I'd slipped out without Maguire seeing me, I'd have to figure out something else.

I washed off the junkie makeup and changed back into my work clothes. I returned a few calls I'd missed then headed upstairs.

Maguire looked up when I arrived. "Hey, you finished earlier than I thought you would," he said.

"Finished?" I shook my head. "I'm just taking a coffee break, then back to it.

"Hey, Maguire, why don't you come in on Monday for Restaurant Week.

Bring a date and be my guest."

I could see I'd surprised him with the invitation. "Sure. I mean I'll be here already looking out…anyway, yeah, that'd be great."

I left him wondering why I was being so nice and headed back to my office, this time to actually work on the last-minute details for our Restaurant Week event.

Chapter Sixty-Six

Elaine Garlinger called just as I was finishing up. I barely said hello before she interrupted.

"I have some news." She spoke the words softly but I could hear an undertone of excitement in her voice.

"What's going on?" I asked, anxious to know what she'd learned.

"I heard back from Mackelvoy and I think we've got enough to bring her in." There was triumph in Elaine's words.

"Oh my God! Really?" I said.

"She made a mistake and it will be her undoing. Mackelvoy knew that the Castel home had been closed up since Dolores left. She hadn't listed it with any realtors, so no one's been in it. Since he reopened the case as a suspicious death, he was able to obtain a warrant to search the home again and went in with his team.

"One of the forensic techs noticed some bright blue flowers outside next to the porch. He thought they looked familiar and He thinks she used the flowers to murder Castel. He's going to speak with a plant expert to confirm it."

"Tell him not to bother," I blurted out, remembering the photo of Dolores and Olivier in front of their house.

"I know what they are. When we were kids, our next-door neighbor had some planted in front of her porch." I paused, thinking about Mrs. Guido who loved gardening, and warned us never to touch those particular flowers because they were dangerous.

"They're aconite, beautiful but extremely poisonous. I looked them up, thinking Mrs. Guido was just trying to keep us out of her front yard. But she wasn't joking. Just a small amount can cause respiratory failure and cardiac arrest in about two hours."

Had Dolores gotten the poison into Olivier and watched as he was dying for over two hours? That was truly evil and she really was the devil.

"How do you think she did it?" I asked.

"Mackelvoy will have to figure that out. She must have added it to his water bottle."

"How'd the detectives get the water bottle?" I asked.

"They found it on the property."

"She kept it?" I was stunned. It seemed sloppy for someone who was so careful and controlled.

"Mackelvoy said it was a stroke of luck. The patrolman who drove her home from the scene had put her backpack in the patrol car, as well. While they were searching the house again he remembered that she'd run right to her assistant to tell him about Olivier. Dolores asked the patrolman to put the backpack in the garage, which he did. He'd seen her pack up the water bottles but didn't think anything of it at the time. He looked in the garage and the backpack was still there.

"Taking into account the tech's suspicions about the flowers, he thought he might be onto something, and called in Mackelvoy. They knew they had to document the backpack as evidence, so they photographed it before they opened it and found the water bottles were still inside. They took more photos and got the bottles to the lab, tested them for fingerprints, and found both Dolores's and Olivier's on one of the bottles. The tox screens on the water inside that bottle were positive for the poison.

"Now, thanks to you, we know what it is."

"You think she just forgot about the backpack or thought no one would go looking for it?" I was shaking my head as I spoke.

"I think her focus was on getting the body cremated and leaving town as quickly as she could," Garlinger replied.

"Once I send Mackelvoy this information he should have no trouble with extraditing her to California. I'm also planning to contact Mark Lowell's ex-wife and see if she'd be willing to have his body exhumed."

"Do you think you'll be able to find anything on a body that's been buried for almost twenty-five years?"

"Our Head of Forensics, Dennis Amagado, says it's possible. If Mrs. Lowell agrees and a judge signs off, his team can exhume Lowell's body and take bone and DNA samples to see if he was poisoned. There are many poisons that would cause a heart attack, as well as rat or rodent poisons."

The mention of Mark Lowell got me thinking about Diego. Was it a coincidence that his last name was Lowell? I didn't believe in coincidences. But I did believe that Dolores was sick enough to make her assistant use her former lover's name.

Then, I got so quiet, Elaine called out my name several times before I answered. "What about Sully?" I asked, a sadness coming over me. "We need to tell him this right now."

"I'm waiting for Mackelvoy to send us the extradition order, and then we'll pick up Ms. Dolores Castel. We can speak with Sully right after I get her processed and locked up."

I agreed to her plan. Telling Sully about the murdering Dolores was not something I could do on my own. It would break my heart, as well as his.

"Let's do this by tomorrow." I swallowed my emotions as I spoke.

Elaine agreed and then clicked off.

I sat at my desk for a while, holding back the urge to murder Dolores in the most horrible way possible. She was pure evil and Sully had fallen for her. He'd take this hard and there wasn't much I could do to make it better.

I called Eric and filled him in on what Garlinger had told me. He wasn't too surprised. He'd instinctively felt there was something off about her and her creepy assistant, Diego.

I wanted to tell him that I'd seen Diego coming out of the Blackthorne Collier building, where I was now positive Bevins was taking shelter. But, that would only cause a discussion I couldn't deal with on top of everything else.

"See you when you get home," I said instead and left my office. I trudged up the stairs like I was climbing Mount Everest without oxygen and a heavy load on my back.

Evidently, Agent Garlinger had called Maguire and filled him in. No doubt telling him to take extra precautions on my behalf. He looked more serious than I'd ever seen him, grim even.

"Don't worry. We won't let anything happen to you." He placed his hand on my arm. "You know, I mean it. I'm here for the duration."

Great. Now, I felt even worse for sneaking out on him this morning. I went behind my beloved bar and stared out the restaurant's huge glass windows. For a moment, I thought my imagination was playing tricks on me. There, standing on the sidewalk in front of The Lounge, was Diego, grinning at me and shaking his head from side to side like some crazy-ass circus clown. All that was missing was the bulbous nose and pointy hat.

I must have gasped out loud because Maguire was over like a shot. "What is it, Jude?"

"That was…I just saw…Diego…the assistant. He was…I don't know… staring at me in a weird way." I pointed at the window.

"Are you sure?" Maguire asked turning to look out the window, then back to me staring at what I imagined was my stunned expression.

I nodded slowly, looking at the shimmering glass again.

"Okay, let me alert the team outside. One of them can follow him and see where he goes and what he's up to."

He got on his cell and let the agents know.

"Maybe Dolores sent him," I said, "or maybe someone else."

"Who'd you have in mind?" Maguire's words were filled with skepticism.

"Art Bevins." I shuddered as I said his name.

"Bevins? How would he know Diego?"

I wondered how much Elaine had told him about Dolores's connection to Art Bevins, and what she might have told her assistant.

"I'm not sure he does. Seeing him like that…leering just reminded me of Bevins. It gave me the creeps."

Maguire's expression grew more concerned but I wasn't sure he entirely believed me. "You look so stressed. This… everything going on, is a lot."

You think? I almost said but knew he was speaking out of concern for me. "Why don't you take another break. Let's have something to eat."

His suggestion made me relax a bit and I smiled at him. "Starving are you? You're getting too used to Pete's good food." He blushed at my comment. "Just kidding. Let's go raid the kitchen. Pete's been in for a while."

Pete took pity on us. He was used to feeding me and liked Maguire. He stopped his prep work for dinner and made us delicious burgers and fries. We were quiet as we ate, Maguire sneaking worried glances my way when he thought I wouldn't notice. Me, wondering when Bevins would strike again, as I was sure he would.

Chapter Sixty-Seven

olores was becoming more and more concerned about Diego's absences. He was not answering his phone when she called. When she let herself into the apartment it was eerily empty and, in his bedroom, it appeared some of his clothes were missing.

She knew he'd made some friends—the rich Europeans he'd been partying with. What could he be doing?

God forbid, he'd found a girlfriend. He was so good-looking, women were always falling all over him. A girlfriend at this stage would be a disaster. Who knew what he would tell her about Dolores and what horrible consequences it would have.

She shuddered at the thought. Everything was coming to a head. Sully was on the verge of proposing. She managed to cast doubts about his friendship with Jude and was almost sure he'd take her advice, given his options. Having the bartender out of the picture would make fulfilling her plans so much easier.

She'd been avoiding Sully since they'd spoken and she'd leave him in limbo for a few more days to come to the conclusion that he needed her more than Jude.

In the meantime, she'd focus on Diego and find out why he was behaving so mysteriously. She'd have to rein him in; keep him closer than ever.

She picked up her phone and speed-dialed him. Once again, her call went straight to voicemail. She disconnected and threw the phone across the room in anger. This wouldn't do. It just wouldn't do at all.

Chapter Sixty-Eight

I was in the zone, working the bar and chatting with my customers when Tony Napoli slid onto a stool near the service end. I hadn't seen him for a few days and was not sure I liked him showing up now.

He dipped his head and said, hey in greeting.

I nodded back and started to pour his usual Johnnie Walker Black and placed it on a coaster in front of him.

He put his hand on my wrist to stop me from moving away. "Jude, we need to talk."

I snatched my hand back. "I told you, I wouldn't do anymore spying for you. Remember?"

"You don't have to. Mital and his friends are in the clear." He paused and looked down at his drink. "They're not the ones running drugs."

"I knew it," I replied, crossing my arms in front of my chest and giving Tony a smug look.

He raised his eyes to mine before he spoke. "Shivani is. She's using his business, not the other way around."

"What? No. That can't be right." I shook my head in denial. "How can you say that?" I glared at him. "She…she has everything, a successful business, piles of money, and she supports the LES anti-drug coalition. You're wrong. Shiv would never deal drugs."

"I'm not positive yet and I shouldn't even be telling you this, but you helped me and I trust you to keep this to yourself. Not share this with anyone." He arched his eyebrow and I knew he meant Sully and Eric. "I might need your help again," he added.

Stunned, I stumbled against the back bar, almost knocking over the bottles on the glass shelves. "Me? How could I possibly help?"

I was trying to take in what Tony said, the idea of Shiv in the drug business made me want to heave.

"She's clever, Jude. Shiv's made it so she appears to have it all. But her business is failing and bleeding cash. Her clients aren't spending what they used to and some of them are going elsewhere. You've been friends a long time. Maybe there was something she said that…"

I was shaking my head as his words trailed off. "No. There's nothing I can tell you." I felt bewildered and disoriented.

"Please, Jude. Think about it. She's looking for a way to make up her lost revenue and is angling to use Mital's import/export business to do it."

"How do you know this?" I asked, accusation heavy in my voice.

"I'm her IT guy. I have access to all the data, financial and otherwise. Last time I was in her office, I was going through the files as usual when I found a link for one I hadn't seen before. It told the real story. She probably thought she'd hidden it."

He shrugged. "She made some mistakes in dealing with her suppliers in India and I caught them. It was all in the file."

"Have you confronted her?"

"Not yet. I'm still gathering evidence. As soon as we confiscate the drugs that she secreted in Mital's shipment, we'll arrest her."

I just stood there in shock. *Why didn't she find another way,* I wondered. "Did you speak with Mital?"

"Yeah. He didn't believe me at first, but when he checked the first shipment, he found some packets of curry powder that had been tampered with and filled with white powder that turned out to be heroin." Tony paused. "He's a stand-up guy and agreed to cooperate."

"But you—"

Tony held up his hand. "This is just between us, Jude, so remember keep this to yourself."

I nodded at Tony then cradled my head in my hands as he left.

It was one more horrible thing to add to the list I'd been keeping. If Tony could make a case against Shivani, she would spend a very long time in jail.

I thought back to our lunch and wondered if what I'd read as annoyance on her part at too many questions about Mital's business had actually been fear that I'd twig to her plans.

You thought you knew someone, who they were, and what they stood for. But you were wrong. Or as an old friend used to say: "Just when you thought it was safe."

Chapter Sixty-Nine

The next morning a knock on my apartment door surprised me bright and early. Elaine Garlinger was standing there holding two cups of to-go coffee.

I gestured for her to come in. "What are you doing here? Where's Ari?" I asked, looking over her shoulder.

She smiled. "You've gotten used to having him around, haven't you?"

I shrugged, not taking the bait. Even though I liked Maguire, I could do without a Fibbie minder following me everywhere.

"Let's sit, Jude," she said.

"Sure." I gestured to the stools at the kitchen counter.

"I wanted to fill you in on the extradition process for Dolores Castel." Elaine said the words with regret in her voice. "The judge wouldn't sign the order. Said he needed more concrete evidence for us to execute an arrest warrant, then have Mackelvoy extradite her."

"What?" I couldn't hide the anger that filled me. "How about the water bottles? It's proof she murdered Olivier. I thought Mackelvoy had it locked up. That you could get her to LA right away."

"It's a little more complicated than we thought. The judge was questioning the chain of evidence. The backpack and water bottles were in her garage for a while and the thinking is someone else could have put them there."

"But her fingerprints are all over the bottles and the place was locked up. Jeez, you're the F.B.I. Can't the bureau do something?" Elaine reared back and I could see my comment stung, but the longer she was on the loose, the harder it would be to keep Sully out of Dolores's clutches.

"We are," she replied in a voice designed to calm me down. "The California Bureau Chief is aware of the situation and the need to get this done quickly. He's working with the Los Angeles District Attorney's office and will certify the evidence and approach a different judge today."

"This is ridiculous." I could feel my face getting hot and my voice becoming shrill.

"Listen, Jude, I know it's hard to be patient, but we're going to get her… and Bevins." She paused. "We're still following her and so far, she hasn't met with anyone who could be Bevins."

I snorted. "With his talent for disguise, he could be anybody."

She nodded in agreement. "You're right. But we are working around the clock on both Dolores and Bevins. If they've been in contact, we'll find out."

Garlinger put her coffee down, leaned forward, and changed the subject. "Ari reported that you spotted Diego Lowell in front of The Lounge yesterday and that you mentioned he reminded you of Bevins." She tilted her head to the side, waiting for me to reply.

"It was just strange, that's all. Reminded me that Bevins could be watching me." It would have been a good time to tell her about my misgiving about his last name. But something made me hold back.

"You know, he hasn't committed a crime," she said.

Unless you counted living with that horrible woman, I thought.

I knew I should also tell her about Diego's visit to the Blackthorne Collier building and my suspicion Bevins was inside, but I knew she'd go ballistic. I couldn't explain I'd tricked Maguire into telling me about the tip and the canvas of the neighborhood. She'd probably fire Maguire for letting me out of his sight. Besides, I had no real proof Bevins was there.

She shook her head. "Diego is incidental. We're going to concentrate on watching Dolores. Make sure she's not planning to leave the city."

I snorted. "Fat chance while she's still after Sully."

Garlinger's big blue eyes focused on mine and I had to stop myself from turning away. "Are you sure that's all that happened, Jude? He didn't say anything or do anything to make you connect him to Bevins? It was just a strange feeling?"

I shook my head. "No, nothing." Unless you knew about his surreptitious visit to the abandoned Blackthorne Collier building. "Really, that's it."

"Okay." She couldn't hide the doubt in her voice and I knew I hadn't convinced her. She stood up and gathered her purse and notebook. "I'll keep you apprised of the extradition proceedings. It should be settled today. And, don't worry, we'll keep Sully safe until this is done."

What about later, after his heart is broken? I wanted to ask but didn't.

Chapter Seventy

Carol Batista called with good news. She'd received a contract signed by Nancy Carrol and Bill Blair and was messengering it over to me. She explained it covered everything we'd discussed and it was fine with her if I agreed. I told her I'd read it over carefully and share it with Eric and Sully, then sign it. Once we got that out of the way, she'd sit down with Pete's attorney and work out the sale details.

Carol paused, then cleared her throat. When she spoke I could hear the concern in her voice. "How's Sully doing?" she asked. "He seemed so distracted the other day, and kind of down." Her voice lightened a bit. "Not the boisterous guy I'm used to."

"I know what you mean," I replied, thinking of the conversation he and I had had later.

"Carol, can I ask you something?"

"Sure," she replied, curiosity spilling into her voice.

"I know you're helping me pro bono because of Sully. I asked him about it and he said you owed him a favor. But, that's all he'd say." I paused choosing my next words carefully. "I'm not trying to pry, honestly. It just seems like he's done so many favors for so many people, including me."

"He has."

I waited for more but it wasn't coming. Like the excellent lawyer she was, she knew how to avoid questions she didn't want to answer. Those two words were all I was going to get about Sully's favor to her.

She was also good at changing the subject. "Are you sure Sully's okay?" she asked again.

"He's a little preoccupied right now, but you know him. He'll be fine." *As soon as we get Dolores out of his life,* I thought.

I could be just as evasive when I wanted to. "So…I'll read the contract as soon as the messenger delivers it."

"Great," Carol replied. "Let me know when you're done." With that, she was gone.

Of course, now I was bursting to know exactly what it was Sully had done for her. Mr. tight-lipped Marine would never tell me and neither would his lawyer.

I stewed for a moment at not getting the scoop, then thought better of it. In the scheme of things right now, derailing the dreadful Dolores and finding Bevins took top priorities.

I checked in with Elaine Garlinger. She still had no word on the extradition from Mackelvoy but reminded me California was three hours behind us. She'd call me as soon as she heard anything.

My mom used to tell me I was always in a hurry and it drove her and my father crazy. The memory made me smile.

"What's so funny?" Maguire asked just walking into The Lounge and catching my grin.

"The idea of an F.B.I. agent cleaning my bar," I said as I tossed him a bar mop. "Don't skimp on the elbow grease. Put those muscles to good use."

He took off his jacket, rolled up his sleeves, and started at one end as I moved to the other.

I turned on the music as a distraction. Not even Queen could make things better. I don't know what Maguire was thinking about while he worked, but my mind was focused on Dolores. She'd become an obsession as overwhelming as Bevins. Every ten minutes or so, I looked at my watch, hoping Elaine would call with good news.

Finally, a sparkling bar and a few hours later, my phone beeped with the call I'd been waiting for.

"Mackelvoy got the judge to sign the warrant. All he needs to do is run it by the prosecutor's office and then send it to us. It shouldn't be more than a few hours and then we'll pick her up."

"And Sully?" I asked.

"As soon as Dolores Castel is in custody, we'll tell him…together."

I tried to swallow the lump that was forming in my throat. "Okay," I finally eked out. But it wasn't okay. And it might never be.

Chapter Seventy-One

Dolores was starting to feel the slightest frisson of panic. She still hadn't been able to find Diego. It looked like he'd been in the apartment while she was sleeping, but was gone this morning. *He's just punishing me,* she thought, *as payback for dragging him to New York, most likely hiding out with his new friends.*

When she finally did get a hold of him, she'd have to explain everything to him very carefully. There'd been no other choice. She knew he wanted to return to California, which was no longer an option.

Of course, she could never tell him the truth about Olivier's death. She'd made up some excuses about finances and fresh starts to ease her grief as a reason to leave Los Angeles. And, needless to say, she expected him to accompany her.

She'd wanted to see Turo, but it wasn't going the way she expected. If he ever found out the truth about why she'd left New York, he'd kill her for sure.

She slid the letter Bevins had given her out of her purse and read it again. Who was this Wills and what could he possibly have to do with her?

She'd arrive at the destination tonight at the stroke of midnight. She sighed. Turo did always know how to create drama.

That wasn't the only thing pricking her imagination.

For the last few days, she'd had the strangest sensation she was being watched. Every time she left the apartment, she was extremely careful, checking the street and the people around her. No one seemed the least bit interested in her, but still, she found the hair on the back of her neck standing up. Was it a forewarning of unseen danger she couldn't ignore?

And, then there was Sully. He'd left her several messages which she hadn't answered. She believed their discussion about his relationship with Jude had struck just the right note. He was on the fence, now all it would take was the right moment to ease him over to her side.

Well, it would have to wait until tomorrow, until her 'errand' for Bevins was completed.

The apartment was closing in on her. She missed her sprawling, open-plan home in Los Angeles. A walk would do her good. And, while she was out, she'd search for Diego.

Although she felt safe from Art Bevins for the moment, she knew it might not last past midnight. If she didn't do his bidding, who knew what would happen?

Chapter Seventy-Two

I jumped when my cell beeped. I'd been deep in thought about the events of the last few days, my hands resting on the bar, staring down at the patterns in the wood. I was ignoring my customers, a big Friday night crowd, and Dean was tossing me looks left and right. It was ten-thirty and we were busy.

I hardly had time to speak before Elaine did. "Okay, Jude. we're on." I could hear the excitement in her voice. "The LA prosecutor's office okayed the extradition request. We'll get our agents prepped and we'll pick her up before dawn."

"Why wait until then?" I asked, impatient for this to be over. "What's wrong with right now?"

"First of all, I'm still waiting for the paperwork. I should have it within the hour." I could almost see her ticking off the points on her fingers. "Secondly, I have to get my team ready. Go over all the possible entrances and exits to the building.

"But there aren't that many—"

Elaine cut me off. "I don't want any surprises. Last but not least, nabbing her when she least expects it and is sleepy and disheveled, will be very appropriate."

I decided not to mention all those middle-of-the-night F.B.I. raids that had gone very, very wrong. Instead, I asked her to let me know when it was done and when we could speak with Sully.

"We'll go see him first thing in the morning after we get Castel processed and behind bars." Her voice took on a conciliatory tone. "Look, Jude, I know

Sully wouldn't do anything on purpose, but he may not believe the evidence and he could…somehow let her know."

"He wouldn't," I replied. But I hadn't seen Sully for a few days and I wasn't certain about anything at the moment, especially his state of mind. "I guess you're right," I added grudgingly. "I'll be waiting to hear from you."

They're going to get her, kept repeating in my head like a soothing meditation mantra, as I finally snapped back to the present and began working the bar to Dean's relief.

About an hour later, all that changed as a half-dozen fire engines roared up Tenth Street heading west toward First Avenue.

Eric had just come down from our apartment to keep me company until closing. "Any idea what's going on?" I asked him.

"Let me take a look." He pulled out his phone and opened a new app he'd discovered that gave up-to-the-minute information on anything happening in the neighborhood.

"Jeez. It's a five-alarm fire at the Blackthorne Collier building over near First Avenue." He paused. "I bet those developers had something to do with this."

He was so preoccupied with the story, he didn't see me grip the bar like my life depended on it. I could feel the blood draining from my face and my body beginning to shake. When Eric looked up, his eyes registered alarm at my appearance.

"What is it? What's the matter?" He came around through the service port and held onto me.

"I just felt hot and woozy all of a sudden." I took a few deep breathes to steady myself. "I'm better now." I couldn't tell him about my suspicions that Bevins was in that building, and that he was the one responsible for starting the fire.

Before I could say another word, Maguire came running up to the bar. "Jude, I'm going to leave you with Eric. Agent Garlinger called and I'm needed at the…at a scene," he added lamely.

Somehow, the F.B.I. had figured out Bevins had been hiding there. Well, they wouldn't find him or his ashes in the remnants of the building. He was too smart for that.

"Okay, no problem," Eric said, shooting me a worried look. "I think we'll be closing soon."

Dean came over to see what was going on and I explained I didn't feel well—an understatement. The crowd had thinned out and he said he could handle it and close up.

Eric and I said goodnight and left for home.

My head felt like it was wobbling on my shoulders and Eric helped me get ready for bed, where for once I fell into a dreamless, deep sleep. Until the loud pounding on our door woke me to a nightmare that was only beginning.

Chapter Seventy-Three

Dolores got dressed in black pants and a black top. This was not the time to be noticed leaving her apartment or the building. It was eleven-thirty, plenty of time to walk to Sixth Street before meeting with the mysterious Wills.

Sully had mentioned the hole in the fence next to the dumpster Jim Deems, Bevins's serial killer assistant, had used to get back and forth from his garage on the next block. Of course, Sully hadn't had it repaired yet and Dolores would take advantage of that.

As much as she hated the idea of being anywhere near the filthy, germ-filled dumpster, it was the best way to leave unseen.

She knew from Sully that the Deems garage was no longer being watched by the F.B.I. They did not think Bevins would ever return there, so it would be a safe path to the street and her assignation at midnight.

Dolores had been careful when she left the building earlier in the day to be certain no one was following her and had let out a huge sigh of relief when she realized she was alone. The notion of being watched was obviously just the product of her vivid imagination and the horrible circumstance she found herself in.

Still, she was extremely cautious now as she slipped out of her apartment and made her way down the stairs to the building's back door. As she opened it slowly, she heard the loud, shrill sounds of sirens roaring past. The clanging and wailing seemed to go on forever. With all that noise, attention would be diverted to the street and no one would hear or see her slip out.

The dumpster area was poorly lit but neater than she'd imagined. Still, she was careful as she moved around it and to the break in the fence. Just an easy shove of her gloved hands allowed it to open enough for her to squeeze through.

She pulled out a small flashlight she'd tucked into her pocket and flicked it to life. The path along Deems's old garage had been neglected and was strewn with garbage. She didn't dare touch anything on the side of the building or along the path until she arrived at the wooden door on the street side.

Again, moving slowly she pushed it open and stepped out onto Avenue C. Brushing off her clothes to make sure no leaves or dirt had stuck to her, she started to walk downtown to Sixth Street.

Dolores would have more than enough time to get there before midnight and survey the building to make sure it was safe. Whoever this Wills was, she'd take whatever Bevins had left for her and finally get this over with once and for all.

Chapter Seventy-Four

Maguire and Samuelson were standing outside my apartment door, their faces so solemn, I thought someone had just died. "What is it? Why are you here?" I asked as Eric ushered them in. "Has something happened to Sully?"

"No. No," Samuelson said, shaking her head making sure her words were getting through.

I know I must have sounded frantic, but Eric took hold of my shoulders and sat me down on the couch.

"Oh my god!" I exclaimed. "Did you guys get Dolores?" A sense of relief began to replace fear as I waited for an answer.

"No. She's gone," Maguire answered.

"Gone? Gone," I repeated like a parrot in a cage.

"Not gone, exactly," Maguire clarified.

"Not gone? What then?" This back and forth was ridiculous. "Did you check the apartment?"

"Not there," Samuelson replied. "And, neither is her assistant. It looks like he hasn't been there for a while."

I was slowly coming out of my fog. "So they're both missing?" I couldn't keep the snark from my voice. "How did you let this happen? Where's Garlinger?" I demanded to know.

"She's outside the Blackthorne Collier building which just burned to the ground," Maguire replied.

Eric's app had been right. The fire trucks were headed to the building on First Avenue. I thought about seeing Diego leave the Blackthorne Collier building. Had he been staying there with Bevins?

"What has that got to do with me?" I couldn't let on I had any idea of what I was thinking. I reached for Eric's hand and practically squashed it.

"Agent Garlinger will explain. She's going to stop by when she's done at the scene.

Half an hour later Garlinger arrived and I could smell the remnants of the fire clinging to her.

"What are you doing here?" I hoped she could feel my irritation at this middle-of-the-night visit.

Elaine ignored it and spoke. "We think…no we're certain that Art Bevins caused the fire."

She was watching me so closely, I was afraid to breathe, sure I would give away the fact that I'd been right across the street looking for him, and found the box of those disgusting photos.

Eric saved the day. "How can you know that?" he asked.

She ignored his question and focused her eyes on mine. "You need to be careful, Jude. He's close, too close."

Tell me something I don't know, I wanted to say.

"We're going to keep you safe until we find him."

Where had I heard that before?

Chapter Seventy-Five

Dolores rang the bell to the outer door of the old tenement building and was buzzed in. Of course, the apartment she was visiting was on six, the top floor. The old, rickety elevator had an 'out of order' sign on the front, so she was forced to walk up.

The building was falling apart. Peeling plaster was coming off the walls. It was covered in filth, filled with sour cooking smells, and splattered with urine and garbage in the stairwell corners. Many of the apartments she passed had doors swinging loose and showed empty decrepit rooms beyond. She imagined the place would be demolished soon and the remaining tenants would have to find another squalid place to live. As she climbed, she tried to breathe through her mouth but the rank odors seeped in anyway.

Who could live like this, she wondered? In such a disgusting place? Was that a rat that had just darted across the landing? She shivered and drew her jacket closer around her. Best to find Wills get what Bevins left for her and be on her way as soon as possible.

When she stood in front of Apartment 6C, she lifted her hand to knock and was hesitant to touch the greasy, dirt-encrusted door. Gathering her courage, she reached out a gloved fist and rapped softly, then louder.

When the door eased open with a loud squeak of old hinges, she almost fainted. Diego was standing there.

"Hello, Mama," he said. "Surprised to see me? Please come in." He opened the door wider and gestured to the hallway behind him.

Dolores was transfixed. She stared at her son, mouth hanging open. Finally, she was able to speak. "What...what are you doing here?"

Diego took her arm and guided her down the hallway into a small, dark, and dreary living room. "Visiting my father," he replied as Art Bevins stepped out of the shadows.

"You've lied to me my whole life, Mama. Art explained Olivier wasn't my real father, that he is. How could you do that to me? I trusted you. But not anymore."

Art finally spoke. "Dolores, so nice of you to join us." The face Art turned to her was a mask of hatred. "Did you actually think you could keep my son a secret from me? Telling everyone he was your assistant?" He tsked at her. "You never seem to get it quite right. You didn't imagine I'd find out you were back in the city, did you? Or that Diego was my son? Emil Straussman told me everything right before I killed him." He sighed. "Please take a seat." He gestured to a lumpy, worn-out couch.

Dolores was stunned. Emil dead. Her one and only true friend. She stumbled into the couch Art had gestured toward. She sat on the edge and looked around at the meager furnishings, buying time to regain her composure. "Where is Wills?" she finally managed to utter.

Bevins laughed, doffed a pretend cap from his head, and bowed deeply with a flourish of his hand. "Right here, dear lady," he replied and bowed lower.

Dolores understood then. Wills referred to William Shakespeare, the playwright Turo had most admired.

"I don't understand. What do you want with me…and Diego?"

"Don't worry about Diego, dear Dolores. He'll be fine. Won't you, son?" He beamed at the young man. "You, on the other hand…" He let his words trail off as he walked closer to her, extending the gleaming blade of the knife he was holding.

Chapter Seventy-Six

I didn't sleep much and clung to Eric for most of the night. I understood how much Bevins hated me for interrupting his murderous reign on The Lower East Side, but what was his motive for burning down a building? He'd lost his refuge and sent the F.B.I. on another chase.

Maybe he'd noticed my druggie-girl performance the other day and this was his way of showing me he could one-up anything I did.

If that was the reason, it had worked. I was staying put until they caught him…and found Dolores and Diego Castel.

I slipped out of bed quietly so I wouldn't wake Eric, who'd comforted me most of the night.

In the kitchen, I started a pot of coffee, picked up my cell, and called Elaine.

"Look," I started, "I know you're just as frustrated as I am, probably more so." *It was the F.B.I.'s job to catch him after all.* "I know you're doing your best, but…"

"We will get him, Jude. He'll make a mistake and we'll be right there."

"Ummm," I muttered, not wanting to discuss this anymore. "There's something else," I said instead. "Sully. We need to speak with him…now, today. If Dolores is gone, he has to know who she is and what she was planning."

Elaine waited a beat before replying. "Yes. You're right. Let's meet at your apartment in an hour and we'll go see Sully together." She sounded worn out and sad.

I found myself telling her it would be alright. Imagine that.

Elaine and I went upstairs as soon as she arrived and we were standing in front of Sully's apartment. We could hear the radio inside, turned to the news program on NPR.

Elaine looked at me and I knocked lightly. "Sully, it's me, Jude."

"Jeez, I know who you are," he said gruffly as he pulled open the door, noticing Elaine. "What's this?" he asked, pointing his finger from one of us to the other.

"You finally got Bevins?" His question was directed to Elaine.

She shook her head. "Can we come in? We need to speak with you."

"Why not." He turned his back to us and we followed him into the apartment.

"So, if you didn't get Bevins, what's going on?" He raised a coffee pot offering us the dark, aromatic brew.

"Sully, let's sit down." Elaine's voice slid into a soft, caring tone. "We have something we have to tell you."

"Sure. Okay." Elaine and I sat on the couch and Sully took the armchair opposite.

"This is very hard to talk about. I know you'll be upset, but you need to know."

Sully tossed me a look. "Is this something to do with Dolores?" I couldn't meet his eyes and felt my face growing hot. "Just spit it out." His 'and then leave' was implied.

Thankfully, Elaine took over. "It's not that simple."

She began to build the case against Dolores from when she first lived in New York to the present. Her dead lover on the Upper East Side and the husband in LA she was accused of poisoning; her association with Art Bevins, her plan to ensnare Sully, obtain his assets, and get rid of him, as well. Elaine explained there was an order for her extradition to California but she and Diego had disappeared. In short, her career as a Black Widow.

"I'm sorry, Sully. I know you care for her." Elaine reached over to take his hand, but he pulled it back.

This time, when he looked at me, his eyes were dull and his face had turned ashen. He suddenly looked frail and older than his years. He took a deep breath, stood up and glaring, pointed a finger at me. "This is all your doing, Jude, isn't it? You didn't like her from the beginning." He glanced at Elaine, blaming her, as well. "I think you both need to leave. Now." His voice was a roar in my ears.

Elaine and I rose and walked to the door. I made it to the hallway before I burst into tears. I hadn't cried this much since I was a teen and I pressed my hands over my eyes trying to stem the flow. Elaine put her arm around my shoulder and led me back down to my apartment. She went to the stove and put on the kettle for tea.

Eric was already gone for the day and left me a note that he'd try to be back for dinner. It was just as well he wasn't here to see me in this state.

"It's crazy to feel so guilty," I said. "We did the right thing. Didn't we?"

"Of course we did. If we hadn't intervened and told him the truth she'd have gotten him to marry her and then…" Her words trailed off.

I knew she was right. Dolores was a murdering evil criminal who had to be stopped. Eventually, Sully would understand that. At least I hoped so.

Elaine went into my bedroom to make a call as I sat sipping my tea. I rested my head back on the couch and thought about the photo of the beautiful, gleaming engagement ring on Sully's phone, wondering if he'd be able to bring himself to delete it.

When she emerged from my bedroom, Elaine had a slight smile on her face. "We got a lead on Dolores, as well as on Diego. One of the uniforms on patrol saw a guy coming out of a tenement on Sixth and thought he'd seen a poster of him at the morning briefing. He checked the BOLOs and recognized him as Diego Lowell."

"Where ever Diego is, Dolores won't be far behind," I said, remembering her control over her boy toy assistant and praying they'd spot her, too.

"The uni is tailing him and I've got a team going over to the building now. If she's in there, we'll find her."

"Good. I bet she'll have some information to share about Bevins." I was positive they'd been in touch.

"If she knows anything, we'll get her to give it up. She'll do whatever it takes to save herself. I'm sure of it." Elaine paused and looked at her watch. "I've got to get back to the office. I'll call you as soon as I learn anything."

She stopped at the door. "Jude, don't feel guilty about this. It was the right thing to do."

Was it? I wondered. *What would it take for Sully to forgive me, or trust me again?*

Chapter Seventy-Seven

What a day it had been. I called Eric's cell and left a message with a very brief rundown of what had happened. Even though it was Saturday, I knew Eric was in back-to-back meetings all day and had told me he wouldn't be home until very late. I'd have to wait to fill him in completely until then.

Everything that was going on made me think of my Grandma Ree. She always told me to be patient and things would eventually work out. I thought of my family's deaths and knew that hadn't always been the case. But this time, I touched my St. Jude medal and prayed that Grandma Ree was right.

Instead of moping in my apartment I went downstairs to the bar and helped Dean set up for the weekend crowd. He was surprised to see me but welcomed the extra pair of hands.

While we cleaned the bar mats and polished glasses, we discussed Restaurant Week.

"I think it's going to be dope," he said, trying to rattle me by using slang, which he knew I really hated.

"Glad to see you're woke," I tossed right back at him, using a word I'd recently heard, and we both laughed.

"You and Pete did a great job on the menu. Some friends of mine from my acting class booked for Monday night. I know they're going to enjoy it."

"I hope so," I said, praying that nothing would go wrong.

We opened the door a few minutes later and it didn't take long for the bar to fill up. Pete had posted a special on the board for pork chops with apples, pecans, and brown sugar. It sounded so delicious, the dining room filled up quickly, as well.

I kept checking the entrance to see if Sully would make an appearance, although that was totally wishful thinking on my part.

Instead, Tony Napoli sauntered in and took a seat in my station. Oh, joy. Now what?

I poured him his usual Johnnie Walker Black and nodded a hello.

He picked up the drink and knocked it back in one gulp, then held out the glass for a refill.

"Are you drunk?" I asked, hesitant to pour him another.

"Nope. Not yet." He lifted the tumbler toward me and wiggled it in the air. I took it from his hand and filled it.

"She's gone," he told me, "in the wind." He started to lift the drink toward his mouth but I stopped him halfway.

"Who are you talking about?" He couldn't have known about Dolores. Not yet anyway.

"Shivani. Skipped town in the middle of the night. Someone warned her."

I held up my hands. "It wasn't me."

"I know." Tony shook his head.

"Was it Mital?" I asked, knowing how close she was to her best friend from home.

"No. Not him, either." He'd been leaning forward talking in a conspiratorial whisper. Now, he slumped back against the bar stool. "Someone she was partnering with from the Cartel probably got wind of the investigation and warned her to get out before their bosses found out." He shook his head. "I was the inside man on the case. I found the evidence that proved she was stealing from them." His eyes clouded over with sadness as he spoke.

I stared over Tony's head as he sipped his Scotch. I still couldn't believe she was a drug trafficker. It really proved appearances were deceiving. Shiv did seem to have it all. Prestige, money, and all those gorgeous clothes. I wondered if she'd had time to pack them.

Tony broke into my thoughts of silk blouses and leather pants. "Jude. Hey, where'd you go just now?" He was back to his old self, giving me a look like he knew where my mind had wandered.

I felt myself blushing. Leave it to me to be thinking of clothes. Beautiful clothes, but still. "Just wondering why she'd do something like this."

"Money." He rubbed his thumb and first two fingers in the universal sign for cash. "Some people always want more."

He was probably right. I'd never had the desire to want more than I needed and I didn't need more than I had. Although my grandmother's trust fund money had come at just the right time.

"Do you think you can find her?

Tony nodded. "The Drug Enforcement Agency, the F.B.I., and Interpol are looking for her."

"That's a lot of manpower to find one woman." I whistled under my breath.

"Well, she's obviously a very clever woman. Fooled us all." He paused and looked down into his drink.

When he spoke again his words were flat and heavy like ominous gray rain clouds hovering over the city. "If her bosses think she's a threat—that she might talk to save herself—they'll eliminate her." His words were as somber as a dark and dreary winter day.

"You mean kill her?"

"Unless I find her first." Tony finished his drink and fished out some cash to pay.

I waved it away. "On the house." I looked into his eyes and realized Shivani had meant more to him than anyone knew and shivered at the realization.

Chapter Seventy-Eight

Eric and I had stayed up late, rehashing the events of the day. He wasn't too surprised at Sully's reaction to the news about Dolores. He understood how Sully felt about her, but he'd seen up close what a conniver she was with all her talk of starting a business and finding an accountant. "I knew she'd never call the guy I referred her to. Sully will be so much better off without her."

"Not to mention alive," I added.

What really bowled him over was my news about Shiv fleeing the city right before she was going to be arrested. The idea of Shiv as a fugitive seemed as likely as a Martian stopping in the bar for a martini.

And, Tony? I couldn't shake my suspicion that he really had it bad for her.

"Do you think he'll try and find her and make it all go away?"

I shrugged. "I don't know. Tony's a stand-up guy, as my Italian Grandpa Louie would have said. His job means a lot to him. And, he's good at it.

"He might try to help her though," I continued, "but I don't think he'd let her go free. I guess we'll have to see."

Talking about today was exhausting and we finally moved to the couch to cuddle and watch a movie. A comedy, I'd insisted.

We were canoodling and making snarky comments about the movie when there was a sharp knocking on the door. Eric got up to open it and found Elaine and Maguire outside once again. He ushered them in and gave me a searching look. We'd seen Elaine earlier in the day. Why were they here now? I wondered. It was pretty late.

"Jude," Elaine said tipping her chin toward the couch, "let's sit down. I have news about Dolores and Bevins."

"What's going on?" I shut off the movie and gave her my full attention. "Have you arrested both of them?"

She hesitated before she spoke. "Dolores is dead. We found her in an apartment in the building where Diego was spotted. She had a knife through her heart."

I gasped out loud. "My God. Bevins killed her."

"Right now, it appears that way." She seemed to consider her next words.

I gulped. He'd been after Dolores as well as me.

Elaine continued. "We found handprints on the floor in blood next to the body. They don't belong to Bevins."

She took out a photo from her portfolio. In it, I could see the side of Dolores's body and the handprints, fingers splayed out and facing the body, which made it appear that someone had knelt down and looked at Dolores.

"We matched the prints to the ones in her apartment and they belong to Diego," she said.

"Diego?" The name faltered on my tongue. "He watched her die?" The idea was horrifying and brutal.

She sat back and laid out her theory. "There's more. Diego wasn't her assistant. He was her son, and Art Bevins was his father.

"She hid it from everyone, even Diego. Mackelvoy found the birth certificate, listing Arturo Bevacqua, Art's stage name, as the father. Somehow, Bevins found out, and befriended his son."

Emil Straussman, I thought. *Dolores must have confided in him before she left town. Bevins got the information out of him, then killed him.*

"Who knows what Bevins told him about Dolores." She shrugged. "Most of it was probably the truth. Anyway, whatever he said, it was enough to turn Diego into an ally and not stop him from killing her.

"We canvassed the area." She gestured to the building that was a twin to mine, "No one has seen him there today. We think he's hiding out with Bevins."

"But how did Dolores sneak out and get to Sixth Street? Your team was watching her or were supposed to be. How could they let her slip away?" Anger was sliding into my voice again, but I didn't care.

"We think she got out the back way when all those firetrucks were headed to the Blackthorne Collier building. Bevins must have lured her to his hidey-hole some way."

Damn. The hole in the back fence that Sully never fixed. I bet that's how she did it.

"Any idea where Diego and his dad could be?"

"We spotted Diego lurking on Sixth Street by himself. He was just standing on the corner staring at the building where Dolores was murdered." Elaine shook her head. "He's not too bright, so we're hoping he'll slip up and lead us to Bevins."

"Maybe." I knew Diego wasn't all that sharp, but Bevins was another story. He hadn't managed to evade capture by counting on unplanned, rash moves. "Bevins is a master at thinking a step ahead. I bet he told Diego to let your guys follow him for now."

I closed my eyes and shook my head. "When Bevins is ready, he'll either let Diego be picked up or kill him, too."

"That's cold," Eric spoke for the first time.

"Think about who you're dealing with. He's a psychopath with no feelings or empathy. One more life won't mean anything to him, even his own flesh and blood."

Unless that life is mine. I imagined he'd be happy to dance on my grave.

"Maguire is going to stay close by for the next few days." She looked at Eric who nodded. "Samuelson is going to be downstairs with another team."

"Sure," I replied, standing up thinking of the horrible task I had to perform. "Let me go get dressed and get upstairs to Sully. He needs to know about Dolores's death."

"No, Jude. This is my responsibility and I'll tell him. It's better this way."

For once, I didn't argue. I understood she was trying to protect what was left of my relationship with Sully.

"And, please, stay put." She indicated Eric and me. "Okay? Bevins could be anywhere holing up until he's ready to show himself. We have some ideas, but until we check them out, we won't know for sure."

She turned to Maguire and gestured for him to follow. "Ari, a word, please." Then, she looked me straight in the eye. "Don't worry. He'll be right back."

Was Elaine trying to reassure me, or threaten me?

I nodded half-heartedly and watched them leave my apartment. As soon as they closed the door, the pieces snapped into place.

Bevins had a need to make everything personal: his trip to the restaurant, his visit to my former home in the Bronx. I knew where he was. And, if the F.B.I. didn't figure it out very soon, I would have to lead them to his door.

Chapter Seventy-Nine

I tried to go to sleep but I couldn't. My mind was a whirl of everything that had happened interspersed with bloody knives, corpses, and Bevins's jeering face when my cell phone hummed.

I answered right away, keeping my voice low, not wanting to wake Eric.

A voice I recognized instantly whispered into my ear, "Jude, it's me, Tony."

"Tony?" I tried to focus my sleep-deprived brain on the call and moved further away from Eric to the edge of our bed. "What's going on? Has something happened? Did you find Shivani?"

He was quiet for so long, I thought he might have clicked off. Finally, he cleared his throat and replied.

"Yeah, I did."

"Oh my God. Where? Is she okay?" I hissed into my cell. Visions of what drug lords did to the people who betrayed them and stole their drugs filled my head. It was not a pretty picture.

"She's okay…we're okay." He paused. "I'm getting her out of the country, somewhere safe."

"Wait. No, Tony, you can't…your job…you'll be a fugitive. This is crazy."

I was pleading with him. "Bring her in to the task force. That's the best way to help her."

"I can't do that. She won't last a day in jail. The cartel will see to that."

I didn't know what to say. He was probably right.

"I'm sure you'll be hearing things about me, but you know who I am and I think you can understand why I'm doing this.

"I love her, Jude. I don't know when it happened, or why, but I can't let her go. I have to protect her.

"When things settle down, Shiv and I will figure it out and come back. We'll make it right. I wanted you to know that.

"I left something for you in your desk drawer in your office. Use it if you need to, Jude. Take care and be safe."

"Ton…" I started to reply, but he was gone.

What was going on? Could life get any stranger? What could Tony have left for me? He *was* a good man. I had no doubt he meant what he said about making things right, but how?

I hoped he and Shivani could stay safe until they figured it out. Running was beyond risky, and everybody, on both sides of the law would be looking for them.

I slipped back under the covers and eventually nodded off, dreams of Tony and Shiv running through a forest, looking over their shoulders for their pursuers filled my head.

The next morning, I slid out of bed and put on my robe, trying not to wake Eric who was still sleeping like a baby.

How could men do this? Put their heads on their pillows and conk out in a heartbeat like they didn't have a care in the world?

Maguire was in the living room, sitting in my comfy armchair, reading the Sunday paper. He'd already made a pot of coffee, which I made a beeline for. I needed to seem normal—whatever that was—and not give him any indication of the disturbing phone call from Tony. I also needed to get downstairs to my office to see just what it was that Tony had left in my desk drawer. I had to find an excuse to head down so early, a believable one.

Mug in hand, I started to walk over to where he sat then stopped abruptly. "Damn," I said, "I just realized I left the computer on in the office. It's so old and finicky, it needs to be powered down every night or it doesn't always work. I gotta go make sure it's okay. Want to come with me, or is Samuelson in The Lounge?"

He picked up his cell and called her. "She's there. She'll meet you by the elevator and walk you into The Lounge."

"Okay, good. See you in a few," I said and headed for the door.

Samuelson was waiting by the elevator and escorted me around to the back entrance to The Lounge I handed her my keys and she unlocked the door. I shut off the alarm as she proceeded me in and checked that all was as it should be.

"Be right back," I told her as I took the stairs down to my office. The door was unlocked. Tony's doing I imagined, although how he'd gotten into the place, I had no idea.

I didn't have much time before one of the agents would become suspicious. I walked around to my desk and pulled open the drawer. There was a small fabric-wrapped package sitting next to my pens and pencils. I removed and unwrapped it and nearly dropped it when I saw what it was, a compact black metal Glock 42 if the name on the side of the barrel was correct. I hadn't held a gun in a long time. It felt cold and dangerous.

A small slip of paper was nestled underneath. *It's loaded and ready. Point, pull the trigger, and don't stop.*

Succinct and to the point. I re-wrapped the gun and slid it back into the desk, shuddering as I felt its weight. Would I have to use it and could I?

Chapter Eighty

B ack upstairs, Eric was still sleeping and Ari still reading the paper. I put my surprise present out of my mind, at least for the time being. Neither of them needed to know about the weapon in my desk drawer.

"Anything in there about Dolores's death?" The paper was the *New York Post* and I expected to see one of their famous headlines like 'Heartless Bitch Found With Knife Through Heart'.

"Nope. Agent Garlinger's keeping it on a need-to-know basis for now. We're hoping the media doesn't find out about it before she's ready to release the information."

I nodded and thought about Jared Jones, the rumor-monger who'd pursued me after I found the body of Michael Bevins in our dumpster out back on New Year's Day. Sully had booted him out on his butt and Elaine made sure he stayed away.

Thinking of Sully, I turned toward Maguire. "How did it go when Elaine spoke with Sully and told him about Dolores?"

Maguire looked down at the paper, reluctant to speak.

What was I expecting to hear? Not anything good. "C'mon, Ari. You know this is important to me. How did he take it?"

He took a sip of his coffee before answering. "Not well."

"Not well, how?" Maguire shook his head and didn't answer me.

"Oh my God! Did he…he think it was my fault that Bevins killed her?" The thought was so horrific that I doubled over trying not to hyperventilate.

"Whoa." Maguire snatched away the mug that was tipping in my hand

and helped me sit up.

"What did he say?" My eyes were pleading with him to tell me.

"Honestly, I don't know. Agent Garlinger is coming by in a while. She'll fill you in then."

I was sure Sully thought that somehow I had betrayed him; had literally taken away the one person he wanted most. I didn't know how I'd convince him otherwise.

Elaine Garlinger showed up half an hour later. She told Ari to take a break while we talked.

"I called Mackelvoy in Los Angeles and explained what happened. It saves us the hassle of extradition."

"Sure, there's no need to send back her to California now. Instead, we can ship her to Potter's Field."

Eric joined us then in time to hear Elaine relay Sully's reaction.

"At the end of it all, he needs some time to process what happened. With everything we revealed about Dolores and then her death, it was a lot for him to take in. He's not blaming you, or me, for that matter."

Right. That was F.B.I. double-speak for he-hates-my-guts-and-never-wants-to-see-my-face-again.

"Has he seen or heard from Diego?" I wondered if Bevins's son would try to get to Sully.

The agent shook her head. "No, and I warned him not to reach out if Diego calls him. He needs to let us know."

I didn't think Diego would stop by unless his dad told him to. I also didn't believe Bevins would try to get to Sully just yet. He'd bide his time before striking. Maybe make it a two-fer and slice and dice us both at once.

"How is the search coming along? Did you check out everything on your list?"

Elaine gave me a strange look. "How many times do I have to tell you, I'll let you know when we find him." She was exasperated with my questions.

"Of course, I know." *No. I did not know that for sure.* "Just wondering if you found any new clues," I replied snidely.

She shook her head at me. "Stop it, Jude. Whatever you're thinking, put it out of your mind. Concentrate on staying safe."

"Will do," I replied. "That's why I have Eric and Ari to protect me. So, I guess it's safe for me to go take a shower."

Elaine got up and left without another word and Eric just shrugged.

Chapter Eighty-One

Eric had some paperwork to catch up on and I didn't have to be at The Lounge until later. Since I'd helped Dean yesterday, I asked him to work brunch with Maryann until I came in.

Pete and I were going to meet after the brunch rush to go over our Restaurant Week preparations one final time. We both wanted it to be perfect. I had plenty of time to do what I'd planned. And, I wouldn't be alone.

"Hey, Ari. How about a walk? It's such a nice day and I could use some air."

"Sure. Let me know when you're ready."

"Now's good," I replied. Let me get a jacket and tell Eric we're leaving."

"Have fun," was all he said, when I kissed him on the top of his head and told him I'd be out for a walk. The building could collapse but if he was looking at a spreadsheet, he'd never know.

"Where to?" Maguire asked when we were out in front of the building.

I put on my sunglasses and looked around. "Let's go downtown for a bit, then we can walk back up by the river."

I tried to keep the conversation flowing, asking Maguire about his family and friends. "You're still coming to dinner tomorrow night, right?"

"Yeah, I wouldn't miss it."

"Bringing a date?" I asked in a teasing voice.

"Umm…no. I'm coming on my own."

"Oh, okay. You can bring someone if you change your mind." I had a feeling that Maguire had a crush on Mariana and didn't want to jinx anything.

We walked along the east side of Thompkins Square Park and when we got to Sixth Street, I turned and started walking toward the river. This part of The Lower East Side hadn't changed much in the last twenty years. Many of the buildings were old tenements bisected by high-rises, schools, and churches. It was all pretty quiet on this Sunday morning.

As we walked between Avenues B and C, Maguire noticed we were near the New York Theater and Film Academy. A cany look crossed his face. "Any reason you wanted to come this way?" He gestured toward the building which was up the block on the other side of the street opposite of where Dolores was murdered.

"Not really. It is sad though, isn't it, that Straussman had to die because of Bevins, especially since the academy seemed to be the one place where he could show his true self." *Playing a cold-hearted killer. Even if it was just practicing for the role of a lifetime.*

"Yeah." Maguire nodded, giving the gracious brownstone another look. "Sad."

"Let's go back. It feels creepy to walk by it, almost as if evil is lurking inside." I was laying it on thick but I didn't know how else to steer him toward my idea that Bevins was hiding there. What else could I say to move him in this direction?

"I guess Agent Garlinger had this marked as one of his potential hideouts, especially since it's empty." This was as personal as it could get for Art Bevins. The place where he started his career as an actor and a killer.

"She didn't share all of that with me," Maguire replied. "I'll check with her when we get back. I'm sure it was on her list."

Not likely, I thought, as I looked at my watch, or she would have found him by now. "Time to head home and get ready for work." I couldn't say or do anything else without voicing what I was sure of.

As we turned and started walking uptown, my spidey sense kicked in. I could feel danger circling around me. My body was tingling and I knew it was close. I expected Bevins to jump out at me and any moment. I took a quick look over my shoulder and thought I saw a man duck into an alleyway next to the academy. I picked up the pace and headed for home.

Chapter Eighty-Two

"Hey, Mr. CPA, I'm home," I said to Eric who was still hunched over his computer when I returned to the apartment.

He looked up and smiled at me. "I forgot to tell you I read through the contract Carol Batista sent over. It looks fine." He handed me a sheaf of papers. "If you sign it, you can messenger it over to her in the morning."

"Actually, I'll give it to her in person tomorrow night. She's coming in for dinner." I opened the file, signed in the appropriate places, and placed it on top of my dresser. "Make sure I don't forget to bring it downstairs to the office."

"Did you ever get to show it to Sully?" he asked.

"No. Not with everything that's been going on and I know now is not the right time."

Eric must have heard the sadness in my voice and rose to hug me. "Just give him some space. It might take a while, but eventually, he'll come around."

"From your mouth to her ears." I raised my eyes heavenward. "In the meantime, I am needed at the bar."

I changed into my work clothes and told Ari I was ready to go downstairs. Dutiful minder that he was, he followed me without question.

I didn't want to press him about speaking to Garlinger and mentioning checking Straussman's house. So, I let it go for the moment.

Ari took a seat at what I now called 'his table' by the coffee station and started chatting up Mariana. I gave her a pointed look and she moved away to take care of the actual paying customers.

Dean said brunch had been busy and a lot of our customers were looking forward to next week. I looked at our reservations and was happy to see we were fully booked for the next few days.

He told me there'd been a small problem with the lights in the downstairs hallway shorting out. He'd noticed it when he'd gone down to the office and mentioned it to the busboy when he came back. One of the customers having brunch overheard their conversation and had said he was an electrician and could take care of it. He'd gotten it done in about five minutes. Dean had offered to pay for his time, but the guy had waved it off with an "on the house."

Good to know that some people could be nice, I thought before turning my thoughts back to Bevins. It was a gorgeous day and lots of people were out and walking around. I kept looking out the window to see if Bevins was one of them. Just like at Straussman's building, I knew Bevins was near. I couldn't shake the feeling that something bad was about to happen.

If I mentioned this to Elaine, I knew she'd just reassure me that I was totally protected by her team. No one would get past them. Right.

The bus people had cleared away the brunch detritus and The Lounge was fairly quiet. Pete and I sat down and did a final review of our list for the next two weeks.

We were ready and I was sure it was going to be great for both Pete and the restaurant. I mentioned the contract my lawyer had sent me from ComedyClub Ltd and that everything looked good.

"Damn," I said. "I signed it but forgot to bring it down to the office. I'll go get it later. and give it to Carol when she's in tomorrow. We can celebrate that the deal is done. Six Feet Under At The Lounge, New York's newest comedy club, will be opening in a few months.

"So you're good, right?" Pete smiled.

"Yeah. Good." I leaned in close and whispered. "Don't tell Eric, but I'll really miss you."

"I'll miss you, too."

"Any luck with finding someone to replace yourself?" I smiled. "I know you're irreplaceable, but…"

"There are a few chefs that were recommended by friends. I'll try them all out."

He tilted his chair back and continued. "One of the guys, Derrick Marable, is coming in tomorrow to help out. It will give me a chance to see how he works under pressure."

"What's his background?" I asked. After all, whoever Pete chose, I'd have to be sure we could work together.

"He's been cooking uptown at Lumen. Their menu is good, a lot like ours but with some Asian twists, and he seems to have some interesting ideas."

"Interesting, huh?" I rolled my eyes. "We'll see. In the meantime, please get back to your stove and make me something delicious. I'm starving."

"Aren't you always?" Pete asked as he sauntered toward the kitchen.

I called Eric and told him to join me. While we ate, we talked about everything but Sully.

Eric glanced over at Maguire who was on his cell. "Anything new?" he asked me.

"Not that I've heard."

I hadn't mentioned my idea that Art Bevins was hiding out at Emil Straussman's house. I know he'd give me the stink eye and tell me to let the F.B.I. do their job. I was but all this waiting for them to catch on, was nerve-wracking.

The action at the bar heated up a little while later and I didn't have too much time to dwell on my nemesis. Samuelson had joined Maguire. They had their heads together and were looking at their phones.

Somehow, I didn't think they were scrolling a hook-up site. "What's going on?" I asked as I walked over to their table.

"Nothing," both of them said at the same time. A second later Samuelson jumped up and hurried out.

Sure. "Okay," I said and stopped at the coffee machine before returning to the bar. I could feel Maguire's eyes tracking me the whole way. Something was definitely happening.

I gave last call at ten o'clock and I remembered I hadn't brought the signed contract down to the bar with me.

"I'm running upstairs to get the contract for Carol. If I don't do it now, I'll totally forget it."

"I'm coming with you," Eric said.

"But I'll be right back."

"No buts."

I held up my hands in surrender. Eric walked in front of me holding his arm out across my body until he scanned the street and the entrance to our building. "Okay, let's go," he said like he was a bodyguard in an action movie.

Inside my apartment, I grabbed up the papers and was ready to leave. "Eric, why don't you just stay here. Ari is downstairs. After I close up, he'll walk me back home."

"Not a chance. I'm a round-trip, full-service kind of guy. C'mon."

I headed out the door with Eric close behind.

Back in The Lounge, I asked Eric to lock the front door. Maguire was texting, as usual, a frown on his face.

"All good?" I asked. When he nodded, I gathered up tonight's receipts to stash in the safe along with the contract. "I'm going to put all this away, then we can go home."

Eric rose to follow me. "Stay here," I said. "It will only take me a minute." I walked down the stairs and into my office, where I completed my task.

I tried hard to resist thinking about the Glock resting in my desk drawer. I'd looked it over carefully before I put it away. Now, I gave in to temptation, slid it out, unwrapped it, and held it in my hand. It was lighter than I expected but still deadly.

I was just about to head back upstairs when I heard a creaking noise outside in the hallway. It sounded like it was coming from the back room where the comedy club would be.

Just your imagination, I told myself, turning off the desk lamp.

When I opened the door to the hallway, the overhead lights flickered a few times then went out plunging everything into blackness. I thought Dean had said the brunch customer had fixed them. He probably wasn't even an electrician.

As I stepped out into the dark passageway, I heard the noise again. A slow, repetitive creak. "Ari? Eric is that you?" I asked. The noise stopped for a few seconds, then started up again.

"Guys?" I started walking toward the back, feeling my way by putting a hand against the wall. I reached for my cellphone. It was sitting on the back bar where I'd left it and its flashlight. I couldn't see a thing and I was getting spooked. "Someone turn the lights back on, please. This is scaring me."

When I reached the door to the unfinished room it was slightly ajar and gently swaying on creaky hinges. There was a small safety light on at the very back end of the room that cast deep shadows into the empty space. Not enough light to see by, but reassuring.

I let out a sigh of relief at that tiny beacon. I hated when I let my imagination get the best of me, especially with Art Bevins still out there. I reached to pull the door shut.

That's when I heard the maniacal laugh and stopped dead.

A familiar voice whispered from behind. "I wish I could see your face, Jude. Surprised, are you? How stupid are you people, especially Dean, to let a strange electrician tamper with the lighting system? I gave some guy who was a studio tech a fifty and told him I was playing a joke on the manager. He thought I was another guy he used to work with. So easy to fool people isn't it?"

I started to turn toward him. As I did, his hand snaked around my neck and he began to drag me into the darkened room. "Jude, you never give up, do you? This is all your fault. You do know that don't you?"

I couldn't let him see that I was terrified. "Don't blame me for your killing sprees. You're sick, a demented sociopath. No feelings, no remorse, nothing inside."

He pulled me tighter. "You don't know anything. You're an ignorant woman without any power. I'll show you who's smart, who's going to win."

He pulled me further into the room, away from the door. "Don't struggle.

It will all be over soon." With his other hand, he removed a long-bladed knife from his pocket—the knife he planned to use to kill me. It picked up the scant light and twinkled with a wicked glint.

"Be a good girl and I'll be swift. You won't have to suffer. You always were a fighter," he said with pride in his voice as he raised the knife about to plunge it into me.

I thought of Dolores then and how stunned and uncomprehending she must have felt as the knife plunged toward her heart.

That's when my self-defense training kicked in. I dipped my chin so I could get a breath and I stepped to the side. I grabbed the wrist that was around my neck with my right hand and lifted my left elbow up and into his side.

He loosened his grip just enough for me to spin around and I pulled out the Glock I had unconsciously tucked into my jeans and pointed it at him. We were a breath away from each other when I shot him.

Art Bevins was stunned, his face a mask of hatred that lasted as long as it took him to fall dead at my feet a bright red blood stain blooming on his chest.

Point, pull the trigger, and don't stop, Tony's note had said. And, that's exactly what I did.

Then I screamed.

Chapter Eighty-Three

I was sitting in the back of the ambulance, wrapped in a blanket. My shirt and jeans had been covered with Bevins's blood and it was soaking through to my skin. It smelled and felt disgusting, like death and all I wanted to do was wash it off.

The ambulance lights were still flashing their red beams striping the buildings all around me. My body had stopped shaking. The attack by Bevins that seemed like it lasted forever, had been over in a few minutes.

The paramedics had checked me over and said I was okay. "You might have a sore throat for a few days," one of them told me.

Eric was holding my hand. He hadn't moved from my side since he found me staring at Bevins's lifeless body. Elaine and Maguire were in the alleyway with Samuelson and her team reviewing the events that had just transpired. We were all waiting for the Medical Examiner to take Bevins's body away.

It seemed that when I went down to my office, Ari got another text from Rita Samuelson telling him that Bevins was in the alley behind The Lounge and sneaking toward the entrance.

Elaine filled us in on what happened. "You know," she said, speaking to me, "Straussman's house was on our list. Maguire noticed how interested in it you were when you went for your walk."

"I should have known you'd figure it out." The F.B.I. was unrelenting after all.

"We had it under surveillance since your walk and saw Bevins as he left." She paused. "Surprisingly, he wasn't in a disguise."

"Guess he wanted to make sure I knew it was him when he killed me."

Elaine gave me a wry smile and continued. "The team tailed him and realized he was coming here. Rita and our other agents moved to the alley and waited. He got in through the hole in the back fence."

That damned hole again. "Why didn't you pick him up then?" I asked, my body hunched and shivering at how close I'd come to dying.

"We wanted to get him in a contained environment, make sure he couldn't escape. Ari was waiting inside and we believed you were with him and Eric, safe.

"We didn't know you'd gone down to the office until Ari alerted the team. In the meantime, Bevins moved in through the back door and used the back staircase. When he lured you to the empty room, we were in position to get him." She shook her head at me. "We just didn't expect you to go all commando and take him out."

Neither did I. I hadn't fired a gun since my dad and I went target shooting at the gun range near Pelham Bay in the Bronx when I was a teenager. After he died, I never went back. But there are some things you never forget.

After she left us to talk with her people, I leaned into Eric. "Maybe I should sell The Lounge instead of buying out Pete. Try something new, you know."

"Like that would work," a voice boomed out. I turned to see Sully glaring at me and shook my head. *Now what?*

"You can't go," he continued. "Everyone would miss you...I would miss you. This is your home."

My Sully was back. He came over and gave me a hug. "I'm so sorry about... everything," I said into his shoulder.

"Me, too." He stepped back, his steel-blue eyes focused on me. "I know that now."

Chapter Eighty-Four

I was sitting at a table with Eric, Elaine, Sully, Maguire, and Samuelson. We all raised our flutes of The Spring Solace and made a toast to life.

I was grateful to be alive and to be here with these amazing people. It had taken a while, but the nightmare was over and a gruesome serial killer was gone for good.

I'd asked Elaine about Diego. By the time they got to Straussman's home, Diego was no longer there.

"There's an interstate manhunt out for him. He may be heading back to California and if by some miracle he gets there, the police will be waiting for him."

She noticed the frown on my face. "I don't think he'll come after you, Jude. I don't think he has it in him."

Well, he was his mother's son, not to mention his father's. I certainly hoped she was right. Just then, our dinners were served. The food was as delicious as I knew it would be. Pete and his staff had done an excellent job. Everyone seemed to savor every mouthful, especially Sully.

Friends again, and for always, I hoped. A lot had happened over the last year but we'd made it through. Sully seemed to be doing okay, He'd accepted the truth about Dolores but it would take a while for him to get over her.

I expected to see him tomorrow at his usual seat at the corner of the bar, a Jameson on a coaster in front of him keeping me company while I got ready to open.

The Lounge wouldn't be the same without me, he'd said. But I knew I wouldn't have been the same without him.

Acknowledgements

I would like to thank my editor and publisher at Level Best Books, Shawn Reilly Simmons, for her dedication and hard work. Her suggestions helped make this novel the best it could be. I'd like to thank all my friends and fellow authors who have supported my writing over the course of my career, especially Lori Robbins who is always there when I call. I'd also like to thank my sibs at Sisters In Crime New York Tri-State for their support. And, of course, my amazing family, Lauren, Mike and Madison, and my husband Paul, who always has my back.

About the Author

Cathi Stoler is an Amazon best-selling author. Her Murder On The Rocks Series features The Corner Lounge owner, Jude Dillane, and includes *Bar None, Last Call, and Straight Up,* published by Level Best Books. She's also written the suspense novels *Nick of Time* and *Out of Time,* and the Laurel and Helen New York Mysteries. She is a three-time finalist and winner of the Derringer Award for Best Short Story. Cathi is a member of Sisters in Crime New York/Tri-State, Mystery Writers of America, and International Thriller Writers. She lives in New York City with her husband Paul. You can reach her at www.cathistoler.com.

https://www.cathistoler.com

https://twitter.com/cathistoler

https://www.facebook.com/CathiStolerAuthor

https://www.cathistoler.com/contact

Instagram @cathistolerauthor

Also by Cathi Stoler

Praise for *Last Call*: A Murder On The Rocks Mystery

"A tangled web of murder present and murder past leads to a heart pounding conclusion." — Terrie Farley Moran, Multi-award winning and national best-selling author

"Cathi Stoler's *Last Call* opens with a bang, on New Year's Eve, and in this clever, twisty mystery the fireworks don't quit until the very last page. Fans of the award-winning author's first novel in this series, *Bar None*, are in for another suspenseful read." — Lori Robbins, award-winning author of *Lesson Plan for Murder* and *Murder in First Position*

"How about a serial killer for the holiday season? It's New Year in New York and the corpses are dropping. Jude does her best to keep scandal away from her beloved bar (and save her relationship too) but the trail leads straight to her door. With Cathi Stoler's trademark inside scoop on the city and the bar business, *Last Call* is as satisfying as could be."— Catriona McPherson, multi-award-winning author of the Last Ditch Mysteries

"A taut and twisted thriller, Cathi Stoler's *Last Call* will have you feeling a serial killer's breath on the back of your neck. Start a tab because you'll want another round with Jude and friends at The Lounge." — Gabriel Valjan, Agatha and Anthony-nominated author of *The Naming Game*.

Bar None

Bar None, set in the heart of New York City, is an edge-of-your-seat mystery that features Jude Dillane, owner of The Corner Lounge on 10th Street and Avenue B. When Jude finds her friend and landlord Thomas "Sully" Sullivan's work pal, Ed Molina, dead in a pool of blood in Sully's apartment, she's sure it wasn't suicide as the police suspect. Jude investigates and adds murder to her plate as she delves into a case of major fraud at the Big City Food Bank.

Last Call

It's New Year's Day and Jude Dillane, owner of The Corner Lounge, is cleaning up after last night's celebration when she discovers the body of a man with a knife through his heart in the dumpster out back. She recognizes the victim immediately—it's Michael Bevins, younger brother of her customer and neighbor, Art Bevins. Devastated, Jude becomes even more horrified when she learns that Michael is the latest victim of the New Year's Eve Serial Killer whose horrible crimes stretch back more than twenty years. Determined to find this monster, Jude risks her life as she gathers evidence that leads her closer and closer to the killer and the staggering truth that he may be someone very close to home.